MEMORIES AND SCENES

Shtetl, Childhood, Writers

For Ellen and Bob —
with all best wishes,

Scott Nelson

MEMORIES AND SCENES
Shtetl, Childhood, Writers

Jewish Short Stories by
Jacob Dinezon

Translated from the Yiddish by
Tina Lunson

Edited and with an Introduction by
Scott Hilton Davis

Published by
Jewish Storyteller Press
2014

Jacob Dinezon photograph courtesy of
Archive of the YIVO Institute for Jewish Research, New York

Shtetl photograph courtesy of
Library of Congress Prints & Photographs Division

Translated from
Zikhroynes un bilder:
Shtetl, kinder yorn, shraybers
Originally printed by "Akhiseyfer" through the
"Tsentral" Society, Nowolipki 7, Warsaw
No date (circa 1928)
(Note: chapter order has been changed from the original.)

Published by
Jewish Storyteller Press
Raleigh, North Carolina
www.jewishstorytellerpress.com
books@jewishstorytellerpress.com

Printed in the United States

ISBN 978-0-9798156-1-4

Library of Congress Control Number: 2013923802

For Mike and Doris Davis, of blessed memory,
for sharing their love of *yiddishkayt* and Jewish culture
with their children and grandchildren.

Jacob Dinezon, 1913

CONTENTS

DISCOVERING JACOB DINEZON

There is somewhere in the city of Warsaw, a tiny, spare, graying, little man with tiny but spotlessly clean little hands, with a little graying beard—it once was reddish—and with kindly eyes forever smiling, even when moist with tears. . . . He smokes little cigarettes rolled with his own little fingers; he drinks his own tea, made in his own little teapot; and he always sits on the same chair at the table, where he keeps hidden in a most unusually well-organized fashion, other people's secrets, other people's troubles, and other people's anguish, which he holds so close to his uncommonly big heart. And this good uncle is called Uncle Dinezon.[1]

— Sholem Aleichem

In 1909, when Sholem Aleichem, author of the "Tevye" stories, wrote these words to "Uncle Dinezon," Jacob Dinezon was one of the best-known and beloved Yiddish writers in Eastern Europe. Not only was he a successful novelist in his own right, he also befriended, advised, and mentored almost every major Jewish writer of his day. He championed Yiddish as a literary language and wrote books in Yiddish that became bestsellers. Yet by the end of the twentieth century, Jacob Dinezon's role in the development of modern Yiddish literature was all but forgotten.

My introduction to Jacob Dinezon came quite by accident while I spent a year teaching a ninth grade religious school class at my local synagogue in Raleigh, North Carolina. I have jokingly referred to my students as the class from *gehenna*, the class from hell (may no shame befall them). When they weren't sleeping, they were laughing, teasing, and punching each other.

One day, while trying to figure out a way to keep them engaged, I ran across an old book that I had been carrying around with me since my own days as a teenager: *The Magician and Other Stories*, a book of translated Yiddish tales by Sholem Aleichem, Isaac Leybush Peretz, Mendele Moykher Sforim, and others.

"Why not?" I thought. I had loved these stories as a teenager; perhaps my students would enjoy them, too. So I brought in the book and began to read aloud I. L. Peretz's "The Little Chanukah Lamp." Suddenly I noticed the room had become very quiet. "How could they fall asleep so quickly?" I wondered. But when I looked up, I couldn't believe my eyes. Everyone was wide-awake, totally attentive, staring back at me. A few weeks later, I tried it again with a story by Sholem Aleichem and obtained the same effect.

Although these stories were written nearly a century before my young students were born, they still had the power to hold the attention of an audience—even an audience of ninth graders! Suddenly I wanted to know more about these Yiddish writers.

So I began collecting anthologies of Jewish short stories, author biographies, and histories of Yiddish literature. I spent hours locating and purchasing out-of-print books on the Internet. I devoured everything I could find in English translation, because, like most American Jews of my generation, I don't read Yiddish.

The search became an amazing adventure filled with exciting discoveries. I learned that in the mid-1800s there was a hierarchy between Hebrew and Yiddish, the two primary Eastern European Jewish languages. Hebrew was the *loshn-koydesh,* the holy language, the language of the synagogue, the scholar, and the enlightened intellectual. Yiddish, on the other hand, was the *mame-loshn,* the mother tongue, the language of the home, the street, and the less educated Jewish masses. It was often disparagingly called *"der zhargon,"* the jargon. Supporters of the Haskalah, the Jewish Enlightenment, believed that serious literature should be written in Hebrew and looked down their noses at books written in Yiddish.

Then in the late 1860s, Yiddish took a giant step forward as a literary language when the successful Hebrew writer Sholem Abramovitsh created the character of Mendele Moykher Sforim, Mendele the Book Peddler, and began to write stories in Yiddish to instruct and improve the lives of *dos yidishe folk,* the Jewish people. Other writers soon followed, including Solomon Rabinovitz (writing under the pen name Sholem Aleichem) and I. L. Peretz. In only a few years, these three writers achieved great fame as Yiddish storytellers, and readership soared as more and more Jewish writers jumped onto the Yiddish bandwagon. By the first decade of the twentieth century, Yiddish had become a respected Jewish literary language for modern times.

As my reading and research continued on the "big three"— Sholem Abramovitsh, Sholem Aleichem, and Peretz (often referred to as the three "classic writers" of modern Yiddish literature)—I began noticing another name popping up here and there: Jacob Dinezon. Dinezon's name showed up in letters to and from I. L. Peretz and Sholem Aleichem, in biographies and essays about Peretz and Sholem Aleichem, and in brief passages in books about the history of Yiddish literature. I also found him in photographs—a small, impeccably dressed, distinguished-looking man with gray hair and gray beard— standing or sitting beside Peretz, Sholem Aleichem, and even Sholem Abramovitsh.

Who was this Jacob Dinezon and why was there so little written about him? I wanted to know more, but except for a few chapters here and there, none of Jacob Dinezon's major works had ever been translated into English. Furthermore, almost all in-depth biographical information on Dinezon was also written in Yiddish. Where in the world was I going to find these books and how was I going to read them?

My first phone call was to the National Yiddish Book Center, a clearinghouse in Amherst, Massachusetts, for more than a million and a half old Yiddish books. With the help of the former collections manager, Aaron Rubinstein, I was able to obtain several tattered and worn books containing Dinezon's stories and novels. I remember when the package arrived in my mailbox I opened it with great anticipation. At last I would know more about Jacob Dinezon!

And that's when it hit me that I couldn't read a single word. Of course, I had known that the books were printed in Yiddish when I ordered them, but it wasn't until I was holding them in my hands that I realized that this amazing literary treasure was locked up in a language I could not understand.

If something wasn't done soon, Jacob Dinezon's stories might all be lost forever. But what could I do? What I needed was someone who could read Yiddish. So I turned to my family and friends, but translating an entire Yiddish book into English is a major undertaking: you not only need to know Yiddish with its unique characteristics, but you must also know Hebrew to understand all the words and phrases that come from biblical, Talmudic and other religious references. What I needed was a professional Yiddish translator. Again I turned to the National Yiddish Book Center, and sure enough, they had a list.

So in early 2004, I located and hired the Yiddish translator Ruth Fisher Goodman of Delaware to translate into English a biographical profile of Jacob Dinezon from *Leksikon fun der nayer Yidisher literatur (Lexicon for the New Yiddish Literature)*, edited by Samuel Niger and

Jacob Shatzky, and a lengthy biographical sketch by Shmuel Rozshanski in an Argentinean edition of Dinezon's two novels, *Yosele (Little Joseph)* and *Der krizis (The Crisis)*.

Then my friend Kathleen Southern made an important discovery: Jacob Dinezon had written what appeared to be his autobiography: *Zikhroynes un bilder: Shtetl, kinder yorn, shraybers (Memories and Scenes: Shtetl, Childhood, Writers)*. At last, I thought, we would have Jacob Dinezon's life story in his own words.

In the summer of 2004, a second Yiddish translator, Tina Lunson of Maryland, was commissioned to translate Dinezon's memoirs into English. Yet what we found was not a traditional autobiography, but a series of short stories based on Jacob Dinezon's memories from his childhood days in the shtetl and his early years as a writer; a collection assembled and published nearly ten years after his death. Slowly, the pieces of Jacob Dinezon's life began to fall into place.

*   *   *   *   *

Jacob (Yankev) Dinezon was born in New Zager, Lithuania in 1851 or 1852[2]. He was a bright, sensitive, conscientious boy who lived in a comfortable Jewish household with a doting mother and a father who was often away traveling on business.

As a child, Dinezon attended cheder, the traditional Jewish elementary school, where he studied Torah and Rashi's commentaries on the Torah (called "Khumesh with Rashi"). He was a precocious learner and advanced to the study of Talmud while still quite young, much to the delight of his mother and sisters. But for Dinezon, this was a mixed blessing, because he quickly learned that with his promotion to the study of Talmud, he was no longer permitted to sit with his sisters and enjoy the wonderful Yiddish stories they read aloud with their girlfriends on Shabbes, the Sabbath.

By the time Jacob Dinezon was twelve, his father had died, and Jacob was sent to live with an uncle in the Russian city of Mohilev near the Dnieper River. There he attended a prestigious Jewish school that was beginning to teach aspects of the Enlightenment. This was a transitional time for Jews and Jewish education. Learning was moving from the traditional yeshiva study of Torah and Talmud to the study of broader, more worldly subjects, and Dinezon was taught Hebrew, Russian, and German literature, mathematics, science, and world history.

While still a teenager, Dinezon became a live-in tutor for a wealthy Mohilev family named Horowitz. Though first employed to teach Hebrew to the Horowitz's daughter, he soon became a trusted member of the household, progressing from tutor to bookkeeper, and eventually to manager of the family business.

The Horowitz home was a meeting place for young people in the community who were struggling with the growing tensions between the prevailing Jewish religious traditions and the new "worldly" social values. Mrs. Horowitz became an advisor to several distraught young people who were in conflict with their parents over restrictive gender roles and arranged marriages. From these emotional situations, Dinezon found material that he would later incorporate into his novels.

It was also in the Horowitz household that Dinezon fell in love with the Horowitz daughter who was his student. Though smitten, Dinezon's sense of integrity never permitted him to reveal his true feelings to the girl or her parents. In all the years that he was employed by the Horowitz family, Dinezon always maintained the strictest teacher-student relationship, keeping his feelings to himself, even though he often traveled alone with the girl to other countries where she studied music.

Then one day, the Horowitz family asked Dinezon to travel to Vilna to arrange a marriage between his beloved and another man. Unable to express his true feelings, Dinezon did as requested, accomplishing the task, as always, with great skill. But the experience left the gentle and sensitive young man devastated. He would remain a bachelor for the rest of his life.[3]

It was also in Vilna on Horowitz family business that Dinezon met Mrs. Horowitz's sister, Devorah Romm, the owner of a major Jewish publishing house, The Widow and Brothers Romm. Through this association, Dinezon was introduced to one of Vilna's leading Yiddish writers, Ayzik Meyer Dik. Dik agreed to read two of Dinezon's manuscripts and was so impressed he recommended them for publication. The Widow and Brothers Romm paid Dinezon twenty-three rubles to publish his first work, *Beoven avos (For the Sins of the Fathers)*, a novel that dealt with a scandal surrounding an arranged marriage that ends in a tragic suicide.

The Czar's censor, however, finding too many similarities between the novel's characters and members of a prominent Mohilev family, refused to permit the book's printing. Fortunately for Dinezon, his second manuscript survived the censor's scrutiny and in 1877, the Widow and Brothers Romm published *Ha-Ne'ehavim veha-ne'imim, oder Der shvartser yunger-mantshik (The Beloved and the Pleasant; or The Dark Young Man)*, another emotionally charged, heartbreaking story about the devastating effects of arranged marriages. To everyone's surprise, including Dinezon's, the book became a best seller among Yiddish readers. The first ten thousand copies sold out quickly and several additional printings followed.

Even with the book's popular success, *The Dark Young Man* did not garner the critical attention Dinezon hoped it would receive from the Jewish Enlightenment press. In fact, the book was largely ignored or disparaged by the editors of Enlightenment journals who wondered why Dinezon had written *The Dark Young Man* in Yiddish and not in Hebrew. Further complicating matters was the sudden appearance of imitative writers who copied Dinezon's melodramatic and sentimental style without the depth and substance of his characters. This so infuriated and embarrassed Dinezon, he refused to publish another novel for ten years.

By 1885, Dinezon had settled in Warsaw, Poland to be closer to his sister and her family. His small attic apartment soon became a popular meeting place for writers, and Dinezon quickly became a prominent member of Warsaw's Jewish literary community. During this period the political situation for Jews in Russia and Russian-controlled countries, including Poland, had become very difficult. Czar Alexander II had been assassinated in 1880, and riots and pogroms quickly followed. By 1882, Czar Alexander III had placed restrictions on where Jews could permanently settle in the Russian Empire, an area that became known as the "Pale of Settlement," and the years that followed were filled with intense anti-Semitism, restrictive work and social laws, severe economic pressures, and limits on educational and cultural opportunities.

Yet in the face of these oppressive difficulties, interest in Yiddish literature continued to grow. In 1887, the popular Yiddish writer Sholem Aleichem who had just inherited a fortune from his recently deceased father-in-law, paid a visit to Dinezon's apartment to discuss his plans for a new Jewish literary journal to be written entirely in Yiddish. In addition to advice, Jacob Dinezon provided a story, "Go Eat Kreplach," to Sholem Aleichem's first issue of *Di Yidishe Folks-Bibliotek (The Jewish Folk Library)*.

Another early contributor to Sholem Aleichem's journal was I. L. Peretz who had found success writing in Hebrew and was just beginning to write seriously in Yiddish. Recently disbarred from practicing law by the Czarist authorities in his hometown of Zamość, Poland, Peretz submitted poems and stories to Sholem Aleichem to earn much-needed income. One long poem, "Monish," so impressed Jacob Dinezon, that he immediately wrote to Peretz to express his enthusiasm.

In 1888, when Peretz moved to Warsaw, the two men met and became inseparable friends. Two years later, with his own money, Dinezon published Peretz's first book of Yiddish stories, *Bakante bilder (Familiar Scenes)*. In the book's preface, Dinezon wrote that it was his intention to publish a series of affordable Jewish books that would elevate the level of Yiddish literature. This would become an especially important undertaking, because in the same year Sholem Aleichem was forced to end the publication of his *Di Yidishe Folks-Bibliotek* after losing a substantial amount of money in the Kiev stock market.

Also in 1888, with the encouragement of Peretz, Dinezon ended his ten-year hiatus, and permitted his second novel, *Even negef, oder A shtein in veg (Stumbling Block, or A Stone in the Road)* to be published in Vilna. In this novel, Dinezon again addressed family conflicts between the old ways and the new, this time between the Chassidim and the more liberal followers of the Enlightenment.

Three years later, Dinezon published his third novel, *Hershele (Little Hershel),* another heartbreaking story of young love thwarted by an arranged marriage. During this same year, Dinezon and Peretz joined forces to produce their own literary journal, *Di Yidishe Bibliotek (The Jewish Library).*

When Czar Nicholas II assumed power in 1894, a government decree prohibited Jews from publishing newspapers and journals, forcing *Di Yidishe Bibliotek* to fold. Undaunted, Peretz and Dinezon convinced the local authorities to allow them to produce special Jewish holiday publications called *Yontef bletlekh (Holiday Pages).* Thanks to the abundance of Jewish holidays, they were able to publish seventeen issues between 1894 and 1896.

In 1899, *Yosele (Little Joseph)* was published in Warsaw. Perhaps Dinezon's most influential book, the novella was a heart-rending look at poverty in the shtetl and a powerful attack on the severe form of corporal punishment being used by teachers in the traditional cheders of that time.

One of Peretz's protégés, the Yiddish writer J. I. Trunk, described *Yosele* as a book over which he and his whole family wept many tears. He said his own mother wailed aloud and even his hard-hearted grandfather broke into sobs and groped for his cane to beat up the cruel Hebrew school teacher, Reb Berl.[4] The book caused such a public uproar that sweeping changes were made in Jewish education and firmly established Dinezon as a defender of Jewish children.

In 1902, Dinezon organized a three-day celebration in Warsaw to honor I. L. Peretz's fiftieth birthday and twenty-fifth anniversary as a writer. For the occasion, Dinezon published, again out of his own pocket, the first volume of Peretz's collected works.

Over the next decade, Dinezon's own literary output diminished, but in concert with Peretz, he became a great champion and mentor for many young and talented Yiddish writers who were being drawn to Warsaw's thriving literary community: names such as Sholem Asch, Dovid Pinski, and Avrom Reyzen. The Yiddish writer and ethnographer S. An-ski said of Dinezon: "He was satisfied with his small room on a narrow street in a quiet courtyard. Whenever you saw a smile on his face, it was not about something done for him, but because he had given something to someone else. He looked after each new writer; he had something for each one and within each one of us there lies a piece of Dinezon."[5]

As Yiddish continued to grow more popular in literary and academic circles, Peretz and Dinezon were invited to participate in the *Yidishe shprakh-konferents,* the "Conference on Yiddish Language" to be held in August of 1908. Several well-known Yiddish writers, intellectuals, and academics gathered in Czernowitz, then the capital of the Austrian province of Bukovina. Their mission was to chart a future for the Yiddish language. Both Peretz and Dinezon signed the conference invitation. Though it does not appear that Dinezon attended, Peretz provided the keynote address. When the conference ended, there was a great feeling that Yiddish had finally arrived as a reputable literary language with resolutions in place to help ensure its development.

Across Russia, Eastern and Western Europe, and even here in America, Jewish audiences enjoyed a proliferation of Yiddish newspapers, novels, short stories, poems, plays, and songs. To Jacob Dinezon and I. L. Peretz, the future of Yiddish looked bright and secure.

But everything changed in 1914 with the outbreak of World War I. Both men were suddenly faced with the challenge of coping with the influx of refugees fleeing from the battlefront between Russia and Germany. As orphaned Jewish children poured into Warsaw, Dinezon and Peretz founded the Home for Jewish Children. Dinezon turned his attention to fundraising and directed all his efforts and financial resources to helping the children.

Then on April 3, 1915, tragedy struck when Dinezon's close friend and partner I. L. Peretz was found dead of a heart attack in his study. A year later, dear friend Sholem Aleichem died in New York City. By the end of 1917, Sholem Abramovitsh (Mendele) was also gone.

During the final few years of his life, Jacob Dinezon devoted himself to the development of the secular Yiddish school movement in Poland, which Peretz had also championed. Although he remained active in literary circles, he never published again.

In the summer of 1919, Dinezon fell gravely ill. On August 29, Jacob Dinezon died in his small Warsaw apartment, surrounded by several of the writer-friends to whom he had devoted his life. He requested only to be buried beside I. L. Peretz. On Sunday, September 1, the Yiddish newspaper, *Haynt,* reported: "His wish was fulfilled and he was buried beside his friend."[6]

Tens of thousands of Jews came out to mourn the passing of Jacob Dinezon. On that day, all opposing factions in the Jewish community set aside their differences to be a part of his funeral procession. At the cemetery, Dinezon's close friend, S. An-ski, made the following remarks: "It is a difficult and bitter task to speak at the grave of one who is still alive to me. . . . A great and beautiful poem has ended. The heart stands still that lived for the people, that rejoiced in its joys, and that suffered with its frequent troubles. . . .

"He spent his 68 years of pure life like a saint. He was a romantic and an idealist in his writing and in his life he was exactly the same. . . . He was always with those who suffered, for whom things were going badly, who needed something; who needed help. He gave away everything to them, he did not worry about himself, he asked for nothing."[7]

Ten years later, Jacob Dinezon's collected works were published in Warsaw. They filled eleven volumes.

*   *   *   *   *

Eleven volumes of novels and short stories, and yet the question remains: "Why had none of Jacob Dinezon's works been translated into English?" Why had this writer who was so central to the Warsaw Yiddish literary community, who produced such popular novels, and who was so close to all the major Jewish writers of his day, been so overlooked? Why had this man, so beloved by the Jews of Warsaw that tens of thousands of mourners lined the streets to pay their respects, been so neglected and forgotten?

One theory is that Jacob Dinezon's relationship with Peretz led to his demise as an author. Peretz's biographer, A. Mukdoni, writes, "The bold facts of the case are that Dinezon's fellowship with Peretz meant the end of his career as a writer. . . . Dinezon had been a writer of considerable talent with an individuality of his own, and an assured place in Yiddish literature. All this ceased with his intimacy with Peretz. His literary work was henceforth limited to memoirs, written listlessly and without his old-time fervor."[8]

But did Dinezon's gifts as a writer really cease in his later years, or did his temperament, his circumstances, and his conscious choices eventually lead to his diminished literary output? As modern Yiddish literature advanced rapidly during the first two decades of the twentieth century, Dinezon, with his nineteenth century sensibilities and values, may have felt out of step with the rapidly changing trends.

Another possibility is suggested by the Yiddish biographer Shmuel Rozshanski in his book, *Ya'akov Dinezon: Di mame tsvishn unzere klasikers (Jacob Dinezon: The Mother Among Our Classic Writers).*

Rozshanski's allusion to Jacob Dinezon as "the mother of our classic writers" is a reference to what has been called "the family" of modern Yiddish writers. Sholem Aleichem called Sholem Abramovitsh the *zayde,* the grandfather, of Yiddish literature and proclaimed himself the grandson. Scholars have added I. L. Peretz as the father. Rozshanski offers Dinezon in the role of mother.[9]

There is no doubt that Jacob Dinezon in both his stories and his life, provided the gentle, nurturing, "motherly" touch—the heart and soul—to that early period of modern Yiddish literature. But from all accounts, Dinezon was a strong advocate and mentor; he just never seemed comfortable in the limelight, preferring always to take a more giving, supportive, "behind-the-scenes" role, unlike Peretz and Sholem Aleichem who both greatly enjoyed the attention.

In his eulogy at Dinezon's grave, S. An-ski said, "He gave us everything. Our entire literature was brought up on his lap. . . . Perhaps the most precious gift that God gave him, his talent, he also gave away. He was always with us, not with himself."[10]

Whatever the reasons for Jacob Dinezon's drift into obscurity, it is now time for his work and talent to be recognized. I hope that publication of *Memories and Scenes* will begin that process.

I am still not sure why I have been so drawn to Jacob Dinezon, but like Sholem Aleichem, I have come to think of him as a beloved *fetter,* a beloved uncle, a quiet, gentle relative, always in the background, smiling, nodding, and maybe slipping the children a little gelt, a little money. Jacob Dinezon's gelt took the form of love and encouragement for his friends, his fellow writers, and for the Jewish people.

At last, through this English translation of *Memories and Scenes* by Tina Lunson, Jacob Dinezon's short stories will take their place beside the short story collections of his two great friends, I. L. Peretz and Sholem Aleichem. Perhaps one day, several of his other works, *Der shvartser yunger-mantshik, Hershele,* and *Yosele,* will take their rightful place on the shelves of translated Yiddish novels to be read, appreciated, and enjoyed by a whole new generation of readers. And when that happens, the world will finally come to know the small, quiet, loving Jewish writer named Jacob Dinezon.

NOTES

1 M. W. (Melech) Grafstein, editor and publisher, "The Sholom Aleichem Panorama," *The Jewish Observer,* Farlag Melech Grafstein: London, Ontario, Canada, 1948, p. 343

2 Tina Lunson, translator, *Haynt,* Warsaw, August 31, 1919. In coverage of Dinezon's death, the Yiddish newspaper *Haynt* reported his birth year as 1851. Others have suggested 1852 and 1856.

3 Sh. L. Tzitron, Archie Barkan, translator, *Dray literarishe doyres: zikhroynes vegn Yidishe shriftshteler (Three Literary Generations: Memories of Yiddish Writers),* Sh. Shreberk: Warsaw, 1920, Vol. 1, pp. 56-104.

4 Jehiel Isaiah Trunk, L. Dawidowicz, translator, "Peretz at Home," *Three Great Classic Writers of Yiddish Literature: Selected Works of I. L. Peretz,* Marvin Zuckerman and Marion Herbst, editors, Joseph Simon Pangloss Press, CA, 1996, pp. 64-71.

5 Tina Lunson, translator, *Haynt,* Warsaw, September 2, 1919.

6 Tina Lunson, translator, *Haynt,* Warsaw, September 1, 1919.

7 *Haynt,* September 2, 1919.

8 A. Mukdoni, Moshe Spiegel, translator, "How I. L. Peretz Wrote His Folk Tales," *In This World And The Next: Selected Writings of I. L. Peretz,* Thomas Yoseloff, NY, 1958, pp. 352-359.

9 Shmuel Rozshanski, Tina Lunson, translator, *Ya'akov Dinezon: Di mame tsvishn unzere klasikers (Jacob Dinezon: The Mother Among Our Classic Writers),* Alveltlekhn Yidishn kultur kongres, Buenos-Ayres, 1956.

10 *Haynt,* September 2, 1919.

ONE

MEMORIES

Two men, two Jews, unwittingly—and unknowingly—burned my first conscious awareness into me. They awakened in me a war from which I suffered for some time and which cost me many innocent tears. I mean that war in which the head is in opposition to the heart and reason cannot come to terms with feelings.

Reason has her clear, cold accounting, calculating what is good and what is fair. Feeling, however, does not want to know about that, and sometimes demands just the opposite. Both have their important claims, both pull with similar power, each to its own side. The human being stands in the middle, torn between the two until help comes from one side or the other and pulls this way or that. Then we are so happy with the resulting peace that we can barely imagine how we did not understand it earlier.

The first man, a poor Jew named Mayer Yeke, was the Talmud-Torah teacher. The other man, Kalmen Marinhof, was also a poor teacher. Mayer Yeke was a tall, strong Jew, if not as tall and strong as Og the King of Bashan, then no smaller and no weaker than Goliath the Philistine. I used to think that the only difference between Go-

25

liath and Mayer Yeke—not to mention them in the same breath—was Mayer Yeke's incredibly long *peyes,* his earlocks, which Goliath did not have. I had seen a drawing of Goliath in my mother's Yiddish prayer book and I could not picture any other.

I never saw Mayer Yeke—sitting, standing, or walking—except in the company of Borekh the Slaughterer and Arye the Judge. Mayer would stride, his energy carrying him forward, his *peyes* floating up, fluttering in the wind like two flags. The wide coattails of his *kapote,* his long black silk coat, would fill with air and spread out behind him like two billowing sails, carrying him along like a ship on the ocean.

No sooner did I see him in this company than I knew that something bad had happened in the town. Something was out of order: either there was a break in the *eruv,* the community boundary, or something was wrong with the mikvah, the ritual bath, or some other Jewish matter required repair or supervision, like the kosher meat in the butcher shops, or a suspicion of leaven at a matzo bakery. These men were always ready to reclaim or improve any place, and because of them, you could be certain that the Jews in our town would never fall into unknowing sin.

While praying at the big study house, I always saw Mayer Yeke's giant body tossing about like a tree in a forest during a fierce storm. And his praying was not some ordinary praying like reading the words from the prayer book. His praying was like a long wild roar from an excited lion without a moment's interruption between the opening psalm and the last "Redeemer of *Yisroel.*"

From his calling out, "His greatness is unsearchable," I thought that it was not only the windows of the study house that shook, but all seven heavens; and there above, among the angels, his words made a noise like a bomb falling or a marching army. His "holy, holy, holy" was the salute of a hundred cannons firing at once. That is the kind of voice Mayer Yeke had, and the kind of power with which he prayed.

It was not without justification that the pious women of the town prayed to have such saintly children, or that we cheder boys considered him the greatest saint in the world. Perhaps even more of a saint than our rebbe, who was known as a great genius. We all knew that in learning and wisdom our rebbe was better than Mayer Yeke. Had that not been so, Reb Mayer could have been a rabbi himself and would not have needed to teach Khumesh with Rashi to ragged and barefoot little children.

I do not recall who I heard it from, but I knew that Mayer Yeke was willing to be a sacrifice for the community of *Yisroel,* and would go joyfully into fire or water if his death would still God's wrath or redeem all Jews from an evil decree. If I wanted to conjure up someone truly holy, I would think of Mayer Yeke. I could not even imagine *Meshiekh,* the Messiah, without also imagining Mayer Yeke.

In my imagination, it looked to me as though *Meshiekh* was coming soon. Jews were preparing to welcome him, but before I could recognize *Meshiekh,* I could already see Mayer Yeke with his *peyes* flying, his wind-filled coattails, and right behind him I could see *Meshiekh* Himself surrounded by a crowd of elders and pious Jews.

When *Meshiekh* blows the great shofar to begin the grand war with Gog and Magog, Mayer Yeke stands up and strides ahead, and whole armies fall under his feet like straw in a field. He raises his right hand and gives a shout: "The Lord is glorious in his might!" and the enemy's teeth fall out from terror!

Later I see Mayer Yeke in Paradise, sitting by the eastern wall in the seat of honor. He dances and sings with such power and ecstasy that it seems to me that all of Paradise dances and sings with him, just as the whole shul, the whole synagogue, sings during Simchas Torah, with the rabbi and the elders standing there looking at Mayer Yeke with happiness, clapping their hands and singing, "Joy and gladness!"

Our forefathers, Abraham, Isaac, and Jacob, clap joyfully with the righteous as Mayer Yeke dances, his *peyes* leaping in the air, his coattails sailing behind him. He dances and sings and all of Paradise dances with him. Even Jeremiah the Prophet, who in his portrait on our wall weeps and laments, smiles and claps his hands, and the whole congregation is lively and merry and joyful.

All my cheder friends loved Mayer Yeke and often talked about his piety, saying that they loved him like life itself. It was a mitzvah to love him, they said, because it was likely due to his merit that we were all still alive. It was because he prayed with such energy and power that God did not destroy the world as He did with Sodom and Gomorrah for their terrible sins. So he was worthy of having the ground that he walked on kissed.

And I also wanted to be as pious as my friends and love Mayer Yeke as they did. But whenever I thought about loving Mayer Yeke and kissing his footsteps, I would tremble a little and my heart would tremble inside of me.

Then one day, he came to our house, probably for a charity contribution, and he patted my head with his huge hand, and I tore away from him and ran out of the house, and only went back inside when I saw him leave. My mother scolded me, saying that she had never thought that I would behave so badly when such a pious man gave me a pat on the head.

"Why, my son? Did he do something bad to you?" she asked.

I stood there in silence feeling unhappy; my heart clenched. I myself did not know what was going on inside me, but from then on I began to be afraid of Mayer Yeke, afraid that he might give me a kiss and afraid that he might ask me to give him a kiss in return, and it always made me tremble.

Why? Why didn't I love him? For his piety, for his praying, wasn't he worthy of my love? That question always presented itself when I was around Mayer Yeke. I never had a clear answer, but if it ever seemed as though he was going to talk to me or give me a pat, I ran away in anguish.

It was just the opposite with the other Jew, Kalmen Marinhof. Only his students called him Kalmen Marinhof; to the rest of the town he had no other name but Kalmen the *Apikoyres,* Kalmen the Heretic. Though I did not know what a heretic was, I heard from my friends that Kalmen was a kind of cursed Jew who had sold his soul to the devil, and now his only job was to commit all kinds of sins, day and night, in order to vex God, so that the Messiah could not come to release the Jews from the Exile.

I remember how cheder boys ran after him and called out the letters of the German alphabet with a certain melody: "kay, el, em, en, oh, pee, ar, es!" Yet Kalmen just went on his way, smiling to himself, as though he enjoyed it.

And he was so handsome with long curly hair that hid all glimpse of a *peye.* He was always immaculately dressed, not just in a short coat like the Germanized Jews, but in something so fine, it was always a pleasure to look at him. And on Friday evenings, he welcomed Shabbes so beautifully, leading the "German" minyan, which was in the house next door to ours, and where I often prayed on Shabbes. He read the Torah beautifully, and when he sang his melody for the additional prayers, his voice was heavenly to hear.

I did know that only "Germans" prayed in that minyan and that all the Jews who prayed there were considered lax in their observance, but the worst of all was Kalmen Marinhof. I would not have prayed there at all if my father had been at home. But when my father was away, my mother would send me next door on the Sabbath. "You may surely pray there on Shabbes," she would say. "In any case you cannot play there like you do in the big shul."

A friend of mine told me that *gehenna,* hell, was always open under Kalmen's feet, and I was afraid to go up to the Torah and stand beside him because I did not want to fall into *gehenna.* Nonetheless, I liked to look at him and always listened with pleasure as he recited the prayers and sang his melodies, and it grieved me that he had sold his soul to the devil.

"What does he teach his students?" I asked a friend who had cursed at him. This friend was three years older than I and had been studying Talmud for some time, while I had just started Khumesh with Rashi a few weeks earlier. I believed everything this friend told me and thought that he knew everything. He was not only studying Talmud, he was also a grandson of the rabbi!

"You call them students?" he scolded me. "You should not call them by such a respectable name! They wear their *peyes* tucked behind their ears and they bend the Law by running around in short jackets. They speak German like the goyim and their rebbe, the *Apikoyres,* even teaches them Torah in German! Do you get it?"

"Why are they to blame if their teacher teaches them that way?" I asked.

"It doesn't matter what he teaches!" my friend yelled at me. "They must not obey him!"

"But their fathers tell them to follow him!" I answered.

"Who would you sooner obey?" my friend asked me. "A father or God?"

I did not know what to say. Not because I did not know that one must obey God before obeying a father, but because I could not admit that these boys—such fine and smart boys—had committed such a big sin by studying with their teacher.

"You must remember," he said, turning to me again like an older, trusted friend, "that everyone should always obey God, more than a father, more than a rebbe. Even if a father and a rebbe tell you to turn away from God's path and commit a sin, you must not obey them. There is a mitzvah in not obeying them! But you must obey God always and in everything! I would obey God even if He told me to climb up to the top of the shul roof and throw myself off."

"You mustn't kill yourself," I gasped.

"I would do it!" he answered. "If God Himself said it, He would bring me right back to life. Do you understand?"

"Me, too," volunteered another boy who was cutting a bit of glass with a pebble. "See this piece of glass? I would swallow it if God Himself told me to do it!"

"Donkey!" my friend yelled at him, "Why would God tell you to do such a stupid thing? 'Please! Swallow a piece of glass?'"

"Why would He tell you to jump off the shul roof?" I asked.

"As a test of faith! Like He told Avrom to slaughter Itsik to see if he would obey Him!"

Only I still did not understand how throwing oneself off the shul roof was more of a test of faith than swallowing a piece of glass, although the latter seemed a lot more difficult to do. But my friend did not want to be questioned about it anymore, and began to tell us a story about the *lamed-vovniks*, the thirty-six righteous ones. When he finished, he told us that he was certain that Mayer Yeke was one of them. The whole world was sustained on his merit, and if Meyer Yeke would only will it, *Meshiekh* would come.

"So why doesn't he will it?" I asked, always willing to believe his answers.

"He doesn't do it because of Kalmen the *Apikoyres*. Why should such a wicked man experience the Messiah? Rather, let us all be pious and pray to God that Kalmen will perish, so that Mayer Yeke will have no reason not to bring *Meshiekh*!"

Meshiekh would come! And how I hoped for him to come soon. I had an important reason for wishing it. Just a year ago one of my brothers had died, a beautiful child who I had loved very much. My only comfort after his death was that *Meshiekh* would come, the dead would be raised, and my dear little brother would live again. So if I prayed to God that Kalmen would die, I was certain *Meshiekh* would arrive soon, my brother would live again, and my mother would stop crying quietly whenever she was reminded of him.

But something did not allow me to pray for Kalmen's death. Whenever I saw him, my heart—even against my own will—wished him a long life, even though I knew it was because of him that *Meshiekh* did not come and my little brother, poor thing, still lay in his grave.

It was not just us, the little cheder boys who held Kalmen guilty for *Meshiekh's* failure to come. Grownup Jews and Jewesses accused him of much worse things. I recall an incident that took place one morning just as we were finishing our prayers.

An old woman burst into the study house, her eyes red from crying. She went straight to the ark and yanked open the curtains, opened both doors, stuck her head inside, wrapped both her arms around the holy scrolls, and with a terrible wail, began her case: "Holy light-filled Torahs! Where is it written in you that because of the sins of that unbeliever Kalmen the *Apikoyres,* that my innocent child should be taken before her time? Such a pious child, such a young little sapling, raised and nurtured with such care and concern, given in a wonderful marriage and just delivered of her first child, poor baby, and now she must bid farewell to this bright world, to her dear husband, the brilliant scholar, and her first child that she just bore three days ago, only to go into a dark grave.

"Why? For whose sins? For Kalmen's, may he see no good for what he has done to us in this town! Innocent babies perish in their cradles; women die in childbirth. Children are taken from their parents and young mothers are taken from their children! Don't be silent, holy Torahs; fly up to God, beg Him to still His wrath. Cancel the bitter sentence against my child. Give me, the unworthy mother, my child back. Send healing to the young mother and may He send punishment to the guilty, to Kalmen. May His first strike find him and those who follow in his ways, so that we may not know any more sickness and grief!"

Those who heard the woman's pleas wept. Even my eyes filled with tears. My heart clenched and it seemed that I would choke from anguish.

There was a commotion in the study house. "How long are we going to have to suffer because of him?" one man yelled. "When did we know such misfortune or hear such lamentations? Since the devil sent that *Apikoyres* to us, it has been a new calamity every day. Every hour another misfortune!"

"It would be a good deed to tear him apart like a herring!" shouted a tall Jew. "In another town he would have been a sacrifice for the community long ago, so what kind of people are we here? Will anyone lift a finger against him?"

"So go ahead," called another, "if you are the man you say you are, do what you will with him, and make him the atonement for everyone's sins!"

"I? Why me? Do you think that I am afraid of him?" cried the tall Jew. "I could make a pile of rubble out of him with one punch. But I am afraid of his supporters, the rich parents who give their children to him to teach. I make my own living from them and my livelihood is tied to Kalmen's success, understand?"

The others each had similar excuses. And who wanted to tangle with the rich and powerful people who believed so much in this heretic?

"But we can't be silent about it either," someone said. "We must ask Mayer Yeke. He is not afraid of anyone, rich or poor. Since it is an issue that is important to the whole community, he may take the duty upon himself, and tonight he can make a pile of rubble out of Kalmen the Heretic!"

Everyone liked this idea. No one had any doubt that Mayer Yeke could make a heap of rubble out of someone like Kalmen, who was about half his size. I imagined that with one good blow all of Kalmen's bones would be scattered and I had no doubt that Mayer Yeke could do it.

Mayer Yeke had long wanted to be a sacrifice for the community of Israel and why should he allow this young wife to die, this beloved daughter whose mother mourned her so? Why should he not save little infants who were dying like flies in their cradles?

Leaving the study house, I felt something pressing on my heart. I had pity on the poor crying woman, on her daughter who was suffering so and perhaps was dying at this very moment. The woman was in the right; the whole world was in the right. Why should innocent children die? Why should a pious woman who just gave birth to her first child have to leave the bright world for a dark grave while he, Kalmen, the one who was guilty, went happily through the streets with his walking stick and his polished boots? Perhaps I was angry with him myself and wanted to tear him apart like a herring.

I imagined how Mayer Yeke would go to him and throw Kalmen to the ground. Kalmen would plead to be spared, but Mayer Yeke would not listen and would shout back, "Criminal, heretic!" And then he would beat Kalmen to a pulp. I shuddered at the thought and my heart pained me even more.

"But why does God do things like this?" I suddenly wondered. "Why allow Kalmen to commit sins that make Him angry, and then take out His anger on innocent babies and young mothers? Why can't He punish Kalmen Himself? Was He afraid of the rich families, too? No. He could punish Kalmen, but He didn't want to. Better to punish the innocent, many of them, than one heretic!" And then I felt angry with God. I hated Mayer Yeke, but I was even angrier with God!

"Wicked, wicked!" I could hear my *yetzer tov*, my inclination for good, screaming at me, "You're angry at God? You're so pious? You listen to the *yetzer hore*, the inclination for evil, and feel sorry for Kalmen the Heretic?" I straightened myself up and asked God to forgive me.

I calmed down a little, but why did my heart still trouble me so? Why was I so sad and without any appetite the whole day? I asked God to help me be pious like all my friends who were out running and playing, laughing and singing like any other day, just as though there were no women sick from childbirth and Mayer Yeke was not going to make a heap of rubble out of Kalmen.

My faithful mother remarked that I was not my usual self. She asked me how I was feeling. She felt my forehead. I had to show her my tongue. "Do you have a fever? Did you fall and break something?

Do you have a chill?" When she could not find anything wrong with me, she said, "It must be that the rebbe hit you for something!"

I had been searching for a reason to cry. My mother's words gave me the opportunity. I broke into tears and though my mother pleaded with me, I could not eat anything. She said that in the morning she would go and give the rebbe a piece of her mind, but I swore that neither the rebbe nor any of my friends had done anything to me. But I could not eat and I went to bed without any supper.

All night long after such a fractured day, I saw Mayer Yeke in my dreams. He was in various poses that I had seen him in, both in reality and in my imagination. I saw him with Arye the Judge and a whole company of saints when up ran the woman who had lamented that morning over the Torah scrolls in the study house. She falls on him and cries, "Reb Mayer Yeke, save my daughter! Only you can make Kalmen the *Apikoyres* into a heap of rubble! Go quickly, take revenge for my child!"

"Come, Mayer Yeke!" shouts the tall Jew from the study house. "I'll show you where the heretic is hiding!" The tall Jew runs off and Mayer Yeke follows him.

"There in the shul, in the vestibule!" shouts the tall Jew.

Mayer Yeke strides in and drags Kalmen out by his curly hair. He springs up into the air with him and suddenly they are on the roof of the shul. Then Mayer Yeke lifts Kalmen up and throws him down. Kalmen lands near my feet, beaten and bloodied.

I want to go to him, but there is Mayer Yeke again, and Kalmen pleads with him in a very touching melody. It is the melody from the prayers that I just heard him recite last Shabbes in the German minyan. My heart melts with sweetness and pity. But Mayer Yeke shouts, "His greatness is unsearchable!"

There is a clap of thunder and a ringing. I see that the shul's windows have fallen out and shattered into splinters. Mayer Yeke bends down and picks up a piece of glass, a big piece, and serves it to Kalmen. "Swallow this, you heretic!" he roars. "God has commanded you!"

"And if God told you to commit such foolishness," asks Kalmen, still in the lovely melody, "would you obey Him, Reb Mayer Yeke?"

"Of course!" Mayer Yeke roars, and the roar echoes from all sides, until it seems that the whole world around me is roaring like a fierce windstorm, and to my horror I see that Mayer Yeke has grabbed a pointed piece of glass, opened his own terrible mouth, and is swallowing piece after piece of broken glass.

He swallows and swallows, but nothing happens. All of a sudden, Kalmen is gone and I am all alone with Mayer Yeke. I tremble with fear as he gives me a piece of glass. "So, boy," he screams, "swallow a piece of glass. God will see if you obey!"

I start to run, but my feet are as heavy as logs. I try to scream, but my voice is choked. Oh, no, he's catching me! He's got me now! But in that very moment, I feel a soft warm hand on my forehead. I open my eyes: my faithful mother is standing by my bed with her hand on my forehead. She asks me if I am so terrified by the window shutter that is flapping in the wind and has broken three panes of glass.

"It's that servant girl," my mother says, "she didn't latch the shutter properly, but you shouldn't worry about that, my dear child! Why are you still shaking? It's just the wind. It's going to rain; it's already thundering." And before I can even say another word, the whole room is filled with a blinding white flash and there is a huge clap of thunder that seems to split me into a thousand splinters.

"Be benevolent, God in heaven," I hear my mother say with quiet piety. "Be benevolent to everyone and protect my dear child, my innocent child!"

That made me even more frightened. There was more lightning and a long roll of thunder, deep and mean. My dear mother bent over me as though to protect me. I cuddled up to her and trembled as in a fever. I knew for whom it was thundering: for Kalmen the Heretic.

And I, too, had sinned badly. I had thought badly of God Himself and now I regretted it. I begged God to forgive me. I promised not to do it again! But the thundering did not stop. God was still angry, and though I knew one could not hide anything from God, I nevertheless hid behind my mother and could not stop shaking.

"What are you so afraid of, my child?"

"God is angry, mama!" I said quietly.

"May the one who made Him angry shake!" she comforted me. "The one who carries a sin in his heart should be afraid. You, my son, do not need to tremble. We are always in God's hands and can sustain His punishment whether it thunders or not."

"Forgive me, dear mama!" I stammered in an effort to lessen the sin that lay so heavily on my heart. I wanted to tell her everything, but she did not wait for my confession and answered with a kiss.

"Forgive, forgive, my precious child, I will as easily forgive anything you do in your life as I forgive you your latest little whim! But there must be something that has made you so sad. As long as you are sorry for it, you will be forgiven! And see, God has already forgiven us: the sky is growing brighter now. Tomorrow will be a beautiful day!" My good mother licked my forehead three times, spit three times, whispered some kind of healing melody, told me to go to sleep, and went back to her own bed.

In the morning, I heard in cheder that last night's storm had broken the vanes off the windmill and that one of the miller's valuable horses had been killed. "And Kalmen?" I asked.

"You mean the *Apikoyres?*" one of my friends asked back.

"Yes, is he still alive?"

"Was he at the miller's? Why wouldn't he be alive?"

"I thought that the storm had struck him," I said innocently.

"If it were only true! But such a heretic has no fear. I saw him this morning coming from his bath. He is as healthy as Esau."

He was alive, I comforted myself. The storm hadn't struck him and Mayer Yeke hadn't killed him! But being reminded of Mayer Yeke reminded me of my dream, and I imagined Mayer Yeke like some wild bandit, some crazy beast, that swallowed glass. I shuddered and felt that I hated him now and loved Kalmen. I saw Kalmen as someone who had been beaten, wounded. My heart felt pity for him. If I saw him now, I thought, I would tell him that he should protect himself from Mayer Yeke. But then I remembered last night's thunder and something in me cried out, "Do not heed the evil inclination that tries to convince you to hate Mayer Yeke, the saint, and to love Kalmen, the heretic! Do you think that just because it is not thundering now that you don't need to hold God in awe? We are always in His hand, whether it's thundering or not."

We can always meet with punishment, my mother said, and I had remorse, but what should I do about my heart that gnawed and had pity; that did not want to suffer because of that wild man Mayer Yeke who ate glass like some kind of beast? I pondered this until the rebbe called us into cheder and while I was studying I forgot about these thoughts for a while.

A few hours before afternoon prayers, the rebbe told us that the preacher of Kelm would be speaking today in the big shul and that those who wished to hear him would be allowed to go. "Whoever wants to go home now may do so, and whoever wants to hear the preacher may come with me."

I decided to go with the rebbe, but by the time we arrived, the preacher was already speaking and the shul was packed full of people. Due to the rebbe, who was very respected by the crowd, we got to stand on a bench near the bimah, the speaker's platform. From where I stood, I could clearly see the preacher's face, watch his gestures, and hear his words.

I do not remember if I understood everything, but I do remember that every few minutes something like a storm passed through the whole audience of Jews, and that from the seat of honor by the eastern wall all the way to the vestibule, a cry began, a lament. And above, in the women's balcony, there was a sobbing lament that would get quiet for a while and then begin again, get quiet and then begin anew.

It seems that in every place and in all times the Jewish heart is filled with troubles and tears. One just needs to know the right word or the touching melody, and the thick ice that forms around the Jewish heart by cold life breaks open and out pour tears. The Kelm preacher had both virtues. For me the melody by itself was enough, even without understanding all his words. Looking at the grownups, I cried, too.

Suddenly the preacher shouted, "Water!" Someone brought him water and the whole crowd watched as he drank. I could not stop looking at how much and how long he drank. When he stopped drinking and the audience was calmed down a little, the preacher began to describe with a new zeal the many levels of sin.

"There are sins," he said in his melody, "very small sins, that people do not consider as sins, and do not beat their chests over them on Yom Kippur. But they are still sins, my brothers!

"There are also sins that everyone knows are sins, but the one who commits them thinks nothing of it. He sins with every step and feels nothing. But there, above, dear brothers, they are written in the big book and collect into whole mountains!

"There are other sins, Jews, heavy sins! And other sins, even more terrible, really frightening sins, may heaven preserve us, that can destroy whole worlds! Seven types of sins, which are divided into seven levels. Remember, brothers, do not forget: there are seven levels of sin!

"Contrast this, brothers, with the seven circles of *gehenna*, the seven circles of hell!" And then he began to describe how large, how wide, how deep and how high *gehenna* is, with its sixty-times hotter fires; with its terrible river of pitch and sulfur; with its great pots, big as the whole world, full of molten lead in which souls are cleansed and refined. He presented it so clearly and in such detail that the skins of all the listeners crawled.

"That *gehenna*, brothers, is only the first circle of hell! All, almost all souls fall into that level. Since Adam, there has been no saint on earth that is completely good and without sin! There is no person who will not sin, and that certainly includes Jews! How many times does a Jew come into his home without washing his hands! How many times does he neglect to say *asher yotser*, the blessing after natural functions? How many blessings does he allow to go by without saying, 'Amen?' Ay, brothers, cry out, Jews! A thought, a glance, a touch, even a smell can be a sin, and each sin is recorded in the Book of Life for the Jew. But the Jew knows nothing and does not account for them on Yom Kippur. For just such sins they fall into the first circle! Think about it, brothers, the first circle of *gehenna!*"

After that he enumerated the sins for the other levels of hell for which the second circle opened, and the third, and so on to the last circle, each more and more terrible, so that the whole future seemed black. And I felt that my hands were the hands of a thief and my teeth were the teeth of a wild animal.

Life was so complicated and I was so confused. Why, while my soul was still in Paradise, did I say that I wanted to be born when they asked me? Better that I had not been born because then my pure little soul would still be flying around freely in Paradise with all the other little unborn souls, singing praise songs with the angels. But now, now I am full of sins and will have to suffer in *gehenna*, and God only knows into what circle of hell I will fall!

While I was thinking this, the preacher took another almost endless drink of water, rested a moment, and then went on: "Jews, do you think this is all? No! There is yet another *gehenna*: a bigger, deeper, and wider *gehenna!* Bigger than the whole world, deeper and wider than the abyss, wider than all the seven heavens! And its misery defies description! This hell is called Sheol, the lowest hell, the hell that is underneath all the seven levels of hell, and from which there is no way out! Do you know for whom this level has been prepared? For heretics, heaven forbid! For Kalmen the *Apikoyres*, may his name be blotted out!

"Ay, Kalmen, woe to you, heretic!" shouted the preacher. "You can already see your end, your bitter end, your dark end, heretic! And do you think that your body will be tormented there for twelve months, or twelve years, or one hundred years, after which you will be released? No, Kalmen, one hundred years is nothing, a thousand years is not even the beginning! You will be tormented there forever! Forever and ever! Hell without end, the hell that will never be destroyed, Kalmen, the fires that will burn you, that will roast and torture your body will never go out! Repent, Kalmen! Repent, atone, remedy yourself, mortify your body now. That is repentance! Be warned Kalmen and repent!"

These last words were not spoken but screamed with the preacher's last ounce of energy in such an alarming voice and with such penetrating words, that it seemed as though a raging storm was rising and washing over the audience in bigger and bigger waves. Tears were falling. There was not one person who was not crying and sobbing, and still the preacher continued: "What do you think of yourself, what do you think of yourself, Kalmen?"

My heart had long since died inside my chest. It was so clenched that I could not utter a word to the rebbe when he asked me as we were leaving if I had understood the lecture and if I had liked it. I was angry at the rebbe for taking me to shul. It would have been better if I had not heard the preacher, had not known about Kalmen's dreadful end, had not known about the impending fires, torment, and misery of even the first circle of *gehenna* into which I, myself, would certainly fall, even if I were as pious as Mayer Yeke himself.

And my heart wept for Kalmen's troubles in Sheol and trembled for my own torment, although it would only be in the first or second circle: "A turn, a touch, a glance, a thought!" Already a sin! Already in *gehenna!*

But how can one protect oneself from such sins? And what can I do for the Master of the Universe if sometimes I forget and leap up from bed without washing my hands? And am I guilty that my eyes see, that my ears hear, and that my thoughts sometimes wander un-willingly, even during the *shmone esrey,* the eighteen blessings in the daily prayers? And God has already registered this, already collected a whole mountain of sins and will throw my soul into *gehenna,* into whatever circle He decides, and torture it as much as He wants, and for as long as He wants. Why? Do I want to commit sins? Do I want Him to be angry with me?

Everyone says that God is good, a Master of Mercy, who only wants people to be good. Some good soul He is with that fiery *gehenna.* Some Master of Mercy if a thousand years of Sheol is nothing, if a million years in such torment is just a beginning!

These were the complaints of my heart, of my *yetzer hore,* my evil inclination, as I walked home from shul. I lay down on my bed to sleep, embittered and defeated. I wanted to forget my bitter fate by sleeping, but the words of the Kelm preacher, "A warning, Kalmen, what do you think of yourself?" rang in my ears like an alarm bell.

Once again my *yetzer hore* jumped in and pointed out to me how bad God was, what a hard heart He had. I felt angry at God, at the Kelm preacher, and at Mayer Yeke. How he arrived in the picture I do not know, but he was always getting mixed up in my thoughts.

But my anger did not last for long. "Scoundrel, scoundrel!" yelled my *yetzer tov,* my good inclination. "You are sinning against God! One must not question God! If He created a hell, He knows why! A real Jew knows and believes that God is good!"

I began to shudder at my sinful thoughts. I wanted to be pious. I wanted to believe in the goodness of God.

"You must repent!" said my *yetzer tov* in the same tone and melody as the Kelm preacher. "Atone!"

Atone? I could atone, but how should I do it? "Mortification and fasting," said the Kelm preacher. Good, tomorrow I will fast; I will not even let a sip of tea into my mouth. But what will my mother say? Will she let me fast? Will she not demand, "You must eat!"

I knew that one must obey God first before a mother. But not obey my good and pious mother? No, I could never do that!

"Self-mortification," the Kelm preacher had said. "In the summer roll in ants and in the winter roll in snow. This is also repentance." Good. Now it was summer, tomorrow was, in fact, Rosh Chodesh, the New Moon. I could go into the woods, find an anthill, lay on it, and let the ants crawl all over me and bite me as much as they wanted to, and I would not stop them! But what would I do if one of the ants happened to crawl into my nose? And what if it started to tickle just from going in? And what if I sneezed?

Winter was no better. How could I lie in the snow and roll around in it? And where would I do it? In the street? How could I undress in the middle of the street, naked without even a shirt on, and roll around in the snow? Wouldn't people think that I had gone crazy? And what would I do if I got a chill and then died? It is actually good to die of repentance, but how can I bear it in the next world if my mother mourns and cries for me in this world?

So I was left having to mortify my body another way. I took my arm and bit it as hard as I could and the pain felt good. I did not let up until my heart clenched and tears sprang from my eyes.

"Good, good!" said my *yetzer tov*. "Just like that every day and God will forgive you!" I bit harder, and though it hurt even more, I enjoyed it. I felt comforted and my heart was lighter. It seemed to me that God Himself saw it and said with a smile, "Good boy! Do it for my sake, it makes me proud!"

But right in the middle I remembered the seven circles of hell with all the sinful souls who were being tormented in them. And there, in the deep dark Sheol, Kalmen hangs by his tongue from a burning hook. I see the wounds burned into his body and the pieces of torn off flesh. Thousands of snakes and lizards are biting him and sucking his blood. Beneath him, kettles of pitch and sulfur boil and seethe. He falls into them, struggling and screaming, but an angel as black as the devil himself grabs a long fish-hook, jabs it into Kalmen's side, drags him out and hangs him up again, while the Kelm preacher stands off to the side and shouts, "What do you think of yourself, Kalmen? What do you think of yourself now?"

And high above sits God Himself with his long, snow-white beard and asks that the fires be made hotter and hotter, and laughs in revenge at the heretic.

"Oy, what a murderous heart he has!" a voice cries out inside of me. "What did Kalmen do to Him to make Him so angry? Who can do anything to Him? Isn't He stronger than anyone?"

"Scoundrel!" shouts the *yetzer tov.* "You do a little repentance and off you go sinning again. You are worthy of hell yourself!"

I did not ponder this for long before I bent my head down and gave my arm another hard bite, but this time I did not feel the pain. Everything was all mixed up in my head. I no longer knew where I was. I could think of nothing and I passed out for several days.

I was very sick. The Kelm preacher was to blame: his lecture had so shattered my nerves that I fell into a nervous exhaustion and lay unconscious with a high fever, babbling nonsense.

Later, when I was well again, my older sisters teased me by throwing taunts in my face: "An ant in my nose!" "In the lowest circle of *gehenna!*" "God is terrible!" "What do you think of yourself now, Kalmen?"

I started to cry and my mother comforted me, "Don't listen to anything they say. You didn't say anything, don't believe them."

But I must have said it. How else would they have known what I was thinking? Hadn't the evil inclination said the very same words? Wasn't it still sapping my blood with its complaints against God for His horrific *gehenna?* Wasn't it still pestering me to hate Mayer Yeke and to love Kalmen the *Apikoyres* for his sins?

And was the good inclination any better? Did it take any pity on me? Did it not remind me that a turn, a touch, a thought, a look, is a new sin? Did it not show me my own hell? Did it not scream at me in the voice of the Kelm preacher: "What do you think of yourself?"

Both tore at me and I suffered from them both. I was pale. I lost my childish merriment. I didn't play anymore. I was no longer a happy little boy. I spent all my time brooding, always sad like a depressed old man.

I saw boys playing, running, dancing, singing, and joking. I did not have the same taste for it as before. I knew how good it was, I was jealous of them, but I could not run after them. My heart was weeping. Not only for myself, knowing that I would suffer in *gehenna*, but also for them, for *their* suffering in *gehenna*. They were unaware; they knew nothing.

I said to myself, "If they had heard the Kelm preacher as I had, they would not run and sing either!" And the *yetzer hore* started its complaints against God again: "What are those happy children doing to You, God? What am I doing to You? You know that I want to obey You, that I want to repent by fasting, by rolling in ants or snow, but I cannot, I cannot act like a crazy person in front of my own mother, in front of my own sisters! They laugh at me already and my mother weeps at my paleness and my sadness." And this is how things stood until an unexpected event suddenly opened my eyes.

One Shabbes, on my way to afternoon prayers, I saw a crowd of boys shouting about something in the street, and I went over to see what was going on. Zalke Pianitse lay drunk in the gutter and the boys were spitting on him, throwing mud, and yelling, "Zalke the *shiker!* Zalke the drunkard!"

I knew Zalke. I knew that he was once a distinguished scholar and had more education than our rabbi. Everyone said that if he had not been such a heavy drinker, he would have been a great genius for our time. I had also heard it said that in his youth he was a student of a famous rebbe, a genius and a saint, but that he, Zalke, had once posed a very difficult question that the rebbe could not answer. The rebbe was humiliated and cursed Zalke, saying that he would never be a normal person again and that his excellent mind and reasoning would never bring him any honor.

Indeed, Zalke became a drunkard, and whenever I saw him, my heart melted with pity for his misfortune. I was sure he did not want to be a drunkard, but what could he do when the great teacher had placed such a curse upon him?

My mother had pity on him, too, and when he came to our house she would set a place for him, and say, "Have a seat, Reb Zalke!"

She would always give him something to eat, and sometimes she also gave him clothes to wear so he would not go around in tatters. But she never gave him any money.

"I must not give you money, Reb Zalke," she would say. "Giving you money is like putting a knife in a small child's hand."

When he left, I often saw tears in her eyes. Sometimes I heard her say under her breath, "A person should not have to bear such a curse, dear God. Such a mind, such a scholar, such wisdom, and with such a curse!"

Recognizing him now as he lay there in the street with the boys making fun of him and treating him so shamefully, I became so angry I wanted to tear them to pieces. But there were so many of them and only one of me, so I asked them nicely to have pity on such an old and unfortunate Jew. I told them that it was a great sin to abuse him, but they just laughed at me and one of them yanked my ear.

As I looked around for a grown-up Jew to assist Reb Zalke, I spied Kalmen the Heretic with another of the "German" Jews coming down the street. I dared to approach them and asked if they would please help Reb Zalke. They came over, saw what was happening, and began to laugh.

"This would be a good end for all our pious and saintly Jews!" said Kalmen to the other German. "I would love to see Arye the Judge and Borekh the Slaughterer in such a state, wallowing around drunk in the gutter!"

He did nothing to chase away the children who shoved and picked at Reb Zalke, their laughing and shouting so loud you could hear it in the marketplace. Kalmen strolled away with his German friend and at that very moment, I really hated him and wanted to yell after him, "Burn in hell, Heretic!"

But just then I saw Mayer Yeke walking to the study house for afternoon prayers. When he saw Reb Zalke, he quickly drove the boys away, and I saw tears in his eyes.

"Oy, children," he said so softly and so kindly. "How can you have such mean hearts to abuse such a sick old Jew? Go home! God will forgive you. You have no idea how great your sin is!"

Suddenly the children regretted their actions. No one said a word back to Mayer Yeke as he bent down and tried to wake up Reb Zalke.

"Reb Zalke, stand up! Come, Reb Zalke, let's go home!" He lifted Zalke to his feet, and what trouble Mayer Yeke went through getting the drunkard under control! Reb Zalke hit him, spit in his face, pulled away from him, and kept shouting, "Mayer Yeke, you're a savage! Leave me alone!"

And Mayer Yeke said only, "Reb Zalke, Reb Zalke!"

Grown Jews who passed by and saw Mayer Yeke's struggle, shouted, "Leave the drunk alone! A Jew who has no respect for his own honor does not deserve sympathy! And you are not obligated to lay down your life for him!"

But Mayer Yeke answered, "Don't forget, my dear Jews, that even a torn page from a holy book may not be allowed to fall on the ground, and especially the broken tablets on which the Ten Commandments were written. You have nothing like the fine palace that Reb Zalke has in store for him, because even the broken tablets are kept in the ark with the Torah! You should tear your clothes in mourning to see such a great scholar in such a condition! You should weep when you see what can befall such a great and noble mind!"

And I heard in Mayer Yeke's voice something so deeply heartfelt and touching, and saw in his eyes something so kind and loving, that in that very moment I saw an entirely different Mayer Yeke. In that moment, the fear that I once had for him fled completely, and I felt a joy and love for him that I had never felt before for any other person.

And it was not only for the great scholar Zalke that I saw Mayer Yeke show such deep respect and compassion. I saw him behave in a similar way in an entirely different situation.

It was a market day. There was a drunken peasant lying in the road near the tavern and several coarse Jewish wagon drivers were tormenting him. Whenever the peasant tried to get to his feet, the drivers pushed him down again. Still he managed to get up and tried to get away, but they tripped him and he fell back into the mud.

Suddenly Mayer Yeke appeared. "Oy," he said to the wagon drivers, "is this fitting for Jews? What are you doing?"

"He's just a drunken goy!" the wagon drivers laughed.

"No, my dear Jews, take pity on him. He is a person, too. He is also made in the image of God and whoever insults him is insulting God's image in general, and has committed the sin of taking God's name in vain!"

Then Mayer Yeke took the drunken peasant back to his wagon and made him lie down. He then asked another peasant to watch over him so that no one else would bother him.

Another time during Sukkot, there was a great distress in the town. It was the cholera or some such terrible illness and it was said that people were dropping like flies. I remember walking in several funeral processions. The deceased was carried in a coffin and barely a minyan followed behind. I went as far as the river, washed my hands and started for home, but before my hands were dry, I saw another coffin being lifted and carried on men's shoulders. The street was full of people going to this funeral. It was heartrending to hear the crying and wailing of the women who followed at the back of the crowd. It appeared that someone very wealthy had died.

At home we were protected by my loving mother who watched over my sisters and me. She made us promise that we would be very careful. But I had to go to shul. Who would carry father's *etrog*, citron, back for Psalms if not me?

One day on my way home, I saw Mayer Yeke sneaking—better said, *stepping*—over a picket fence. I stood there in amazement. What was he doing? There were a lot of chickens in the yard and with one swipe he snatched one up and was ready to step back over the fence when a Jewish woman ran out of the house shouting, "Reb Mayer, what are you doing? Dear God, that is my chicken!"

"I know, I know, Miriam," he answered, trying to quiet her down. "I know all your chickens, the white ones, the gray ones, the black ones, and the spotted ones. There they all go and may you use them in good health."

"But that one! The one you are holding is also mine!" she shouted.

"Yours, yours, Miriam. And it will also be your mitzvah when the patient who eats it gets well and regains her strength!"

"But why didn't you ask me?" she complained as she tried to pull the chicken out of Mayer Yeke's hands.

"I didn't want to bring you to a sin," he answered. "The sin of not giving charity while God helps you, since you can and must give—especially in times like these, when it could save a life."

"And stealing is not a sin?" she asked angrily.

"It is a sin, a grave sin, Miriam, may God protect and save us! But do you see my big, strong shoulders? Better that the sin should fall on them than on you with your weaker shoulders! Better for you to have the mitzvah of saving a life, and better that any punishment come to big, tall Mayer Yeke!" And without saying another word or listening to the woman's protests, Mayer Yeke was back over the fence in a single step and off to the slaughterer with the chicken.

And how people talked later about the concern and devotion with which Mayer Yeke cared for all the sick people in the town's makeshift hospital where he spent his days and nights. No task was too difficult for him, no danger too great, and no work too menial! And how many people had Mayer Yeke to thank for their recovery and even their very lives?

I also saw Kalmen during that uneasy time. He was strolling as usual with his walking stick in hand, when suddenly I heard a terrible scream. A disheveled Jewish woman ran out of a poor, rundown little house and cried out, "Oy, my child, a boy of fourteen, is wasting away! He came in from outside and didn't feel well! Come in, sir, have God in your heart, sit with him a minute while I run for the doctor!"

And as the woman grabbed Kalmen by the hand and tried to lead him into the house, he cried out, "Get away, woman, get away from me! Don't come near me! It's an infectious disease!" Another Jew came along and went into the woman's house and Kalmen hurried away rubbing the hand where the woman had touched him.

Now I clearly recognized my earlier error, and while I still did not hate Kalmen out of piety as I had once wished to hate him, I had come to love Mayer Yeke much more than I had ever thought possible. And my heart was pressed as with a heavy stone whenever I recalled how unfairly I had been in fear of him, and even more so in my unjustified hatred of him.

I got no rest from my *yetzer tov*. And my *yetzer hore* was not silent either, though I stopped listening to its complaints against God. "What can I do?" I finally decided. "I'm not the only one. Everyone is just as sinful as I am. Let God do with my soul what He will, how can I help it?"

But my *yetzer tov* kept saying, "Do repentance! You sinned against Mayer Yeke; you must apologize. He is a good person, he will forgive you, and you will have one less sin to repent on Yom Kippur."

I really wanted to apologize to Mayer Yeke, and not only apologize, but tell him that I now truly loved him; loved him like my own life and would share anything I had with him. But how could I apologize to him? When did I ever see him alone? I would not be ashamed to tell him the truth alone, but there was always a big crowd of Jews in the study house, and when did I ever see him alone on the street?

Then one day, when my mother and sisters had gone away and I was all alone at home, Mayer Yeke came to the door to ask for a donation, probably for the sick and the poor. He looked down at me and asked, "Son, where is your mother?"

"She went out, Reb Mayer, but she'll be back soon. Please have a seat!" I said it all in one breath and my heart danced with joy that I was about to speak with him in private.

"She'll be back soon?" he asked, trying to decide whether it was worth his time to wait.

"She'll be back soon. She's never late."

Mayer Yeke sat down and his big, awkward body seemed to disappear. All I could see were his eyes. I looked into them, deep into them, and they were so soft and kind!

The words, "Forgive me," were on the tip of my tongue, but my heart pounded and I could not say a word.

"Are you studying?" he asked me.

"I am!" I answered happily, although I had never answered my mother with such conviction.

"What are you learning?"

"Khumesh with Rashi!" I answered, even more bravely.

He asked me about the Khumesh, about Rashi, and I easily answered all his questions. To show me how pleased he was with my answers, he reached out his big hand to pat my head. I do not know how it happened, but in that moment, I pulled his hand to my lips and covered it with kisses and tears.

He pulled his hand away in surprise. "What are you doing, son?" He looked at me. "Are you crying?"

"Forgive me, Reb Mayer, dear Reb Mayer!" and I spilled out my whole heart to him.

"Forgive you? For what? What have you done against me?"

"Well, once I hated you," I stuttered tearfully.

"Hated me? Forgiven, my son, forgiven! Completely and absolutely forgiven. Always forgiven for the past and for the future. You may continue to hate me, I forgive you everything!" He lifted me up in the air and gave me a big kiss.

"No, now I love you, Reb Mayer, as I love my whole life," I said.

"Good, very good!" he said. "I have always loved you and now I love you even more. I certainly forgive you, forgive you with my whole heart."

"And God?" I asked him.

"Of course God forgives you, my son. God is absolutely good and certainly forgives you. Whoever asks is forgiven."

"And will my soul not be tortured in *gehenna,* not even in the first circle?" I asked him.

"What *gehenna?* What kind of foolishness are you talking about?"

"The Kelm preacher said—"

"Oh, the Kelm preacher's *gehenna?* Do you think I understand that stuff? *Narishkayt,* foolishness! How would you get to *gehenna?* The Talmud tells us that even an irreligious Jew will not go to *gehenna.* Isn't it is better to believe the Talmud than that fool the Kelm preacher?"

"And Kalmen the Heretic?" Will he go to *gehenna?*"

"It is written that all Jews are worthy; that means even Kalmen. He is a Jew, just not a very smart one, may he forgive me. He has learning, and in the silly role he has invented for himself, he appears to be a heretic. But if he ever does anything that is not right, he regrets it right away! The Master of the Universe who knows the human heart sees Kalmen's heart, too, how broken it is from every foolishness he commits."

"Will he be in the World to Come?" I asked.

"Of course!" he answered. "All Israel has a share in the World to Come. Even Kalmen. Even people much worse than Kalmen will have a share in the World to Come. As it is written, 'All your people are righteous.' All Jews are righteous, my son, some more, some less, because all Jews are one people. But in this world of illusion in which we live, people think that there is great and small, poor and rich. People think that *mine* is really *mine* and *yours* is really *yours.* But in the World to Come there will be no more mine and yours, only every-one's! In Paradise there is a share for everyone, for the smallest as for the greatest! Because all Jews are equally righteous."

"Even the ones who do not pray?"

"Even the ones who do not pray," he answered with a sigh, "be-cause for each Jew who does not pray, ten other Jews are praying for him! Do you understand, my son?"

"But we should hate such a Jew!" I burst out angrily.

"God forbid, you must not hate anyone! There are Jews in the world who do not earn a living and come to beg for a piece of bread. Do you hate them when you give them something to eat?"

"No."

"And so you must not hate the one who does not earn his place in the World to Come and has others do him a favor! Good and well for the one who earns his own bread, and good and well for the one who does not wait for others to perform his mitzvahs for him. He does it himself and earns his World to Come for himself. Be smart, my son, and always earn your way in this world and in the World to Come!"

While we were talking, my mother returned home. She gave Mayer Yeke a contribution and he headed for the door. But before he kissed the mezuzah on the doorpost, he turned back to me and called out in a voice filled with love and affection, "Remember!"

I still remember that precious "Remember!" to this day. My de-pression lifted and I went back to being a happy little boy again. My mother believed that Mayer Yeke had broken a spell and from that time on she always wished him long life and everything good.

Ah, innocent childhood! How deeply I desired to find the truth and how badly I suffered for my doubts. How honestly and open-heartedly I recognized my error, and how earnestly I strove to correct it. I wish it were so easy today when I sometimes suffer from a false concept or make a foolish mistake.

Once I hated someone who I needed to love and loved someone who was not worthy of my love. And when it happens that I am able to discern my error, why can I not correct it in the same openhearted way I did back then when I kissed and cried on Mayer Yeke's hand?

Have I become so different now? Is today's Mayer Yeke so different than he was back then?

Two

THE LITTLE FLASK

Sholem Yoyne was not one of the great masters, but he was no bungler either. You could be happy with every piece of work he stitched. If he sewed on a button, you could not tear it off. "Sholem Yoyne's seams outlast the material," people said. "You can wear it and wear it."

His father, Avreml the Tailor, had taught Sholem Yoyne the trade. He inherited his father's shop, his manner of working, his pricing, and his tailor's sayings.

Sholem Yoyne knew how to sew everything. He took measurements on the same piece of paper for a new satin coat for the rabbi, a new silk jacket for the rebbetzin, or a makeover from an old wedding dress for the shopkeeper. With the same needle and kosher thread, he sewed frockcoats, waistcoats, overcoats, and trousers for the town's householders, and brassieres, jackets, and undershirts for their wives. It made no difference to him what he sewed and for whom he sewed. He used to say: "When you're a craftsman, who you sew for is irrelevant."

And on selecting customers: "A tailor only sews for free when he has forgotten to make a seam. Everyone pays, and the poorest pauper,

I can tell you, has come by his poor article of clothing with more difficulty than the rich man with his silk and satin."

Sholem Yoyne did not believe in magazines or the latest fashions. "One has one's own good sense," he would say. "An artisan understands what suits, what is necessary, and what is desirable. But if you have a screw loose in your head, no magazine or fashion will help you! I don't understand how they fit them in the magazines! A painted person will never get taller or heavier, but a living person is here today and in the grave tomorrow! As long as we live the figure changes, and an artisan—especially a Jewish tailor—must bear in mind that a Jew does not buy new clothes every day. Thus one must sew so that it will still fit a year from now!"

If someone mentioned a flaw while being fitted, "It seems a little too big" or "a little too long," he always answered: "Wear it in good health, it's not a problem! My father, may he rest in peace, used to say to his apprentices, 'Children, there is a rule: from youth you must get old whether you want to or not. You can make something that is wide more narrow; you can make something long, shorter; but you can never make narrow wide or short long! No obligation and no goodwill can help you there either!' And how right he was, my father, may he be happy in Paradise, and may I live out my few years by the same rule."

After such a declaration about his own expertise, the clothes could have no other flaw. It was awkward to ask him to take it home and make it right, to take it in or make it a little shorter. And in such cases when someone did, Sholem Yoyne would suddenly fall silent, and would not speak to the customer for a whole year. He just wouldn't answer.

Seeing him at home, sitting in his workshop with his legs folded under him, completely absorbed in his work, belting out some melody the cantor had sung, or something his apprentices were singing, he seemed like a skinny little tailor who couldn't count to two. He was not concerned about the world or what happened in it. And in truth, he was a quiet man by nature. Neither his wife, nor any of his apprentices—he had no children—ever heard him raise his voice. But he did have one fault: he loved a drink and could not be separated from his flask of spirits.

It was a flattened flask that could not contain more than a pint of whiskey, but it was never allowed to go empty. When he had drunk a little, he went right to the tavern and filled it up. Without his flask he was as if without his soul. Even if he didn't drink a drop he had to feel it in his breast pocket.

He carried the flask wherever he went. If there were a Shabbes when the *eruv*, the community boundary, was broken, he would sit at home the whole day and study alone or read psalms rather than go out without his flask.

People said that there was magic involved with the flask. One sip from it and Sholem Yoyne would light up like a match and burn with a wild fire, not sparing anyone—not the rabbi, not the head of the community council, not even the householders who gave him business. He had quite a tongue, sharp as a razor, and pitch and sulfur dripped from it. Even the local ringleaders trembled when Sholem Yoyne lifted his flask, afraid that he would drink and then spill out all their secrets and crimes.

Scolding him, even throwing him down the stairs, did not help. Just a sip and he was already gone. Soon he was talking more heatedly and more sharply. Lock the door and it was even worse: he talked in the street, gathered a crowd around him, and the whole town buzzed about it.

But whose business was it if a drinker should howl? Who was without enemies? Better to suffer through such madness by yourself and keep his slanders within your own four walls. In the morning when he had sobered up he did not even know whom he owed an apology. He was at a loss. Today he did not remember anything about yesterday.

Once on such a drinking spree, he lit into Reb Elkane, the wealthiest man in town and the head of the community council, and came up with such a list of crimes and misdemeanors that everyone had long forgotten, or at least never referred to anymore and were afraid to mention. People thought that Elkane would take revenge and that this would drive the drinking and the mental confusion out of Sholem Yoyne.

It happened in the middle of shul. Elkane had taken over a brothel from a poor widow, probably for a percentage. But was this any of Sholem Yoyne's business? Not even as much as a nail in a horseshoe. Yet Sholem Yoyne's flask had lit a fire in him, and while another person might have backed off, Sholem Yoyne took the bait. He approached Elkane and he scolded, bullied, and roasted him. Sparks flew.

Elkane, however, showed a lot of fortitude and did not answer a word of the accusation, but let Sholem Yoyne know that he would never give him another piece of work, never pay him another ruble: "You will never get another kopeck's worth of business from me! Your foot will never cross my threshold again, you drunkard! It is a sin to give such a person any business!"

Someone else, even if he were drunk, would have sobered up from such a threat, and would have asked Elkane's forgiveness. He was the richest man in town, and he had children, sons and daughters, and sons-and-daughters-in-law. One could get a lot of work from such a household in a year. But Sholem Yoyne took another swallow from his flask and replied, "God is with me, I am not afraid! Translated into plain tailor's talk: God is first, and after that my flask! And listen brothers to the idea that can occur to a tailor! This has been going on for some time already. My father, may he rest in peace, died and I made the workshop my own. It was before Pesach. Shmuel the Watchman had not slept at night the whole winter, but had stood frozen, guarding people's shops. He had saved up a few rubles from his earnings and wanted *me* to make him a new coat for Pesach. Around the same time, but a few days later, someone sent for me to come to Reb Elkane's. He had just returned from abroad and had brought back some expensive fabric from Manchester, a kind you almost never see. I don't even know how much it would cost.

"'Take the measurements,' said Elkane, 'and let me know what you can do. Make me a coat that is unique in this town!' I took the measurements, cut the fabric, sewed it, quilted it, and put all of my energy into that piece of work. Because of my joy at working for such a customer as Reb Elkane, I put less attention into Shmuel's poor coat, and sewed it in a hurry and got it done. In a few days, both coats were ready. I probably took Elkane his expensive coat first. After that, I delivered Shmuel's. Both of them paid me. Coming home so happily, a certain tailor's sense of things gave me the idea of breaking both paper rubles into coins and counting them, just to see how many kopecks Reb Elkane's rubles were worth against Shmuel the Watchman's rubles.

"I counted this way, I counted that way, with the chalk like this, or the other way around. But no matter how I counted, both rubles were exactly one hundred kopecks, not a half a kopeck more or a half a kopeck less. I was surprised at the idea. So, I said to myself, let's see, how can both rubles—Elkane's and Shmuel's—be exactly the same, no more and no less than one hundred kopecks, when I laid down my life and put all the brains in my head into Elkane's coat, and threw together poor Shmuel's little coat without a thought? I was red from shame at myself and white from grief when I saw Shmuel later in his coat, whose defects only I knew.

"Where was my sense? I questioned everything. What had I, Sholem Yoyne the tailor, come to with Elkane, who lives in his own big house like a palace, and eats fish and meat and stew even on weekdays, and sleeps in a soft warm bed, and gets up every morning and pats his belly with satisfaction? And, then what was I doing with Shmuel, who lives in a shared, damp cellar with his wife and child, who doesn't eat fish or meat or stew even on Shabbes or the holidays, and who grabs a nap on a pile of snow someplace outside someone's shop, shivering from the cold?

"Woe to him, to Shmuel himself, poor thing, and to you, Sholem Yoyne the tailor, who was not concerned about this. Now tell me, you tailor, you stupid fellow, how you figured that Reb Elkane's piece of work was more important than Shmuel the Watchman's? What are you going to tell me, that Elkane is a rich Jew, who is always ordering new clothes, and you can make a good ruble from him three times a year, and Shmuel the Watchman earns that ruble once in a blue moon? That is also a grave error.

"First of all, Elkane still wears that Manchester coat three years later. Second, consider brothers, how many rich men like him, or smaller or greater, all of them pigs, do we have in this town? Twenty, thirty, as many as fifty! And how many paupers, greater or smaller than Shmuel, do we have to weigh against them, who don't go naked themselves—and how many poor children do they raise, a half dozen or a minyan—who also don't go naked? And tailors have to make all those clothes, too. And they don't make them for free! So, your threats are foolishness, Reb Elkane! A hundred paupers have more power than you, although all of them together have one-hundredth of your possessions!"

The audience was pleased to hear such a sermon in the middle of the week in the study house, although they probably agreed with Elkane that it was a sin to give work to such a drunkard. The Rabbi himself said, "It would be fair to excommunicate you for even half a year, just for you to learn to be civil!" But the Rabbi carried a grudge against Sholem Yoyne, too, from a time when he, the Rabbi, refused to take action against the new tax collector. And when he joined the slaughterers to declare more things treyf, unkosher.

Sholem Yoyne had said, "Rich people can afford to slaughter a chicken. If not, they make a few fish, baked or fried. Householders who have their own cows have cheese and butter and can put dairy stews in the oven and make dairy meals for Shabbes. But what do poor people do? They are depressed. Even on Shabbes they have to make do with a herring or with borscht. If the Rabbi says it's treyf, it's treyf."

Sholem Yoyne's flask got the better of the Rabbi that time. Though he was drunk, Sholem Yoyne spoke to the point. In fact, when he was drunk he acquired a special articulation, and he made ashes of the Rabbi and all his learned judgments.

Thousands of poor Jews, shoemakers, tailors, and other craftsmen, who could speak better, spoke only amongst themselves or at home; but once Sholem Yoyne, the smart aleck, threw himself into the fire and sipped from his flask, his talk ignited everyone. The Rabbi and the council were shocked about the fight and that same day everything that was slaughtered, large and small, was declared kosher. From then on there were no more tricks. And whom did they have to thank? Sholem Yoyne. And not only him, but also his flask, because he himself had no idea about it the next morning. And if people had not sworn to him that there was finally kosher meat for Shabbes because of the scandal he had caused the day before, his wife would have made a dairy stew as she had for the last few weeks.

But this was something that only Sholem Yoyne could forget because he was drunk at the time. But the Rabbi, who was sober and had an iron memory, could carry a grudge forever. And indeed, because of his memory, he could not forget his anger toward Sholem Yoyne, and when anyone else mentioned Sholem Yoyne in anger, the Rabbi helped them along, shouting that it would be fair and a mitzvah to impoverish such a person.

Besides the mitzvah, there was a prohibition against giving an ignorant person any Jewish work, because he could, heaven forbid, bring about the mixing of fibers. Not because Sholem Yoyne was not pious and observant. No tailor was more pious than he. But no tailor was such a drunkard as he, and the Rabbi feared that while Sholem Yoyne was drunk, he might be unable to tell the difference between wool and linen thread!

People even said that the Rabbi himself had sent for a tailor who would, in the Rabbi's presence, rip out all the seams in the clothes that Sholem Yoyne had sewn for him. In truth, they found no *shatnez*, no mixing of threads, but that was no proof of anything, said the Rabbi. "It could be that the drunkard was sober at the moment he sewed my clothes. He is a Jew after all and not some apostate out for spite. But what about the flask? Who can believe him when he is drunk, may God preserve us?"

The Rabbi further maintained, "Does he even know what he's doing? Does he know what he's saying? And it could be—we should not, heaven forbid, suspect him of speaking from hatred—but it could be that there is a migrant soul in him, may God have mercy, from Koyrekh's followers. And that little drink of whiskey that he takes awakens the evil spirit in him and makes him scream and bark, and he himself disappears. The problem is not what he says, but that his audience listens to what he says. Koyrekh and his followers are dead and gone, but their evil spirits remain, and they still want an audience today. Therefore, it is my advice that we drive the evil spirit from him in a natural way, and this can be done simply: Do not give him any work. He will not have anything to buy whiskey with, and the spirit will be destroyed and obliterated."

Pious Jews, especially the town ringleaders and do-gooders for whom Sholem Yoyne was like an annoying whip, followed the Rabbi's advice at first. They not only did not give him anything new to make, they did not give him any work at all. But after a while, when there was a special occasion coming, or a holiday, they sent for him to come and take measurements, and forgot about their old quarrels and about the Rabbi's warning against the danger of his mixing fibers.

When you need the thief, as the saying goes, you let him out of jail. True, he had faults that should prevent him from being allowed into Jewish homes: the flask, his drunkenness, and his angry mouth that could scorch a whole world. But he also had his merits, too, which sometimes outweighed his faults. It seemed that God's supervision and loving-kindness came to him more than to many others. Some said that you could find ten more craftsmen in town who were as good or better than he, but finding a Jewish tailor who kept his word, whose "today" really meant today, and whose "by Shabbes" or "by the holiday" did not mean "when I have time" or "when I feel like it"; a tailor whose oath was worth more than last year's snow. Well, you can search the entire community of Jews and not find another.

For when Sholem Yoyne said "by Shabbes," you could be certain that before it was time to go to the bathhouse, the clothes would be ready and brought to your house, fitted, adjusted and wished, "Wear it in good health, wear it out in good health, and go about your business!" And it goes without saying how much that service is worth to a Jewish businessman or proprietor, who first thinks about the clothes when the knife is already at his throat; that is, when the wedding is tomorrow or it is one hour before lighting the candles for a holiday.

Sholem Yoyne had another merit, too. He did not keep the remnants of the customer's fabric. He had his own set of rules. He would argue with his own customers, "Keeping the remnants is a type of robbery, like other robbery, but even worse. A thief does not rob because you put your key in his hand; and so a tailor who makes something else with someone else's material is not playing fair either!"

The other tailors could hardly imagine such a thing and called him Reb Righteous. They also said that he was fooling people, because any tailor who could hold a scissors in his hand had always, since the beginning of time, kept the remnants, and the fact that Sholem Yoyne did not keep them was no proof of anything. He was a drunkard; it made little sense to him what was permitted or prohibited. And what would he use it for? Who did he need it for? For the children that he did not have? His flask was enough for him. Could he conceive of anything more? But for the householders, and especially the wives, the mothers of children who put every scrap of cloth to use in an outer garment or a lining for something, this practice erased his flaws, and Sholem Yoyne never lacked for work.

Overall, the only ones who hated him were the ringleaders, the ones who ran the city, or the very rich who received honors everywhere and exerted broad influence. Ordinary householders were used to Sholem Yoyne's *mishegas*, his craziness, and had nothing bad to say about him.

"Is it news that a tailor drinks a drop of whiskey?" they said. "A tailor's soul is not a raisin, and it has the same temptation to strong drink as anyone else. Even our rabbi, may he live and be well, takes a drink now and then. But Sholem Yoyne's madness comes out through drink."

Still it was to his credit that he was not greedy about it and he drank only the whiskey from his own flask. When he went to a wedding, a circumcision, or just to a dinner, he only drank from his own flask and never drank a drop of anyone else's. And he always served himself. He sat at the table like everyone else and no one looked askance. As was his whim, he called out, "Mine, mine! Yours, yours! I don't bother your whiskey, don't bother mine!"

But no one could ever get anything out of his flask, either. You could die in front of him and he would not let you even touch his flask. So is it any wonder that his nickname was Sholem Yoyne Flask? And he knew that people in town called him that. Sometimes children trailed after him calling, "Sholem Yoyne Flask, Sholem Yoyne Flask." But it appeared that he actually liked the name.

"Long live Sholem Yoyne and long live his flask," he would call out in reply. "What am I without my flask? A tailor, a stitcher with a silent tongue, a dead creature! But the flask has fire. That spot of whiskey returns life to the dead! Do you understand? This is Sholem Yoyne's flask!"

He spoke the truth, because when he was sober no one ever knew what kind of person he was or whether he was good or bad. He was neither here nor there. But once he had a drink, you never saw such a good-natured person. Then, if anyone looked uneasy, he was ready to offer his soul to help. Like a good brother, nothing was too much for him to do. Ask him for money and if Sholem Yoyne had it he gave it to you. If not, he would offer to take the shirt off his back and give it away.

When that happened, his wife would protest, screaming that he did not know what he was doing. She would have to go begging because of his flask. She would be reduced to charity, may the day never come. But Sholem Yoyne calmed her down: "Wife, you have long hair but are short on sense! What are you yelling about? You will not fall into your stewpot and I will not fall into my flask! If God, blessed be He, hadn't wanted me to be this way, he wouldn't have made me this way. Understand, wife?"

"What are you then?" she asked angrily.

"I am Sholem Yoyne Flask. So sue me!"

People knew about his weakness and on several occasions took advantage of it. If someone was sick and they needed someone to stay awake with the patient all night, they came for Sholem Yoyne. If he were unwilling, they would mention his flask. "What harm would it do to take a little nip?" he would ask. "A sip of the juice is not a sin or a crime is it? Unless I can have some whisky, I will not go! I don't have the time or the strength for it!"

But as soon as he took a sip, he became a completely different person and forgot about time or strength. Sholem Yoyne sat near the patient, carried things in and carried things out, and did whatever was needed. Nothing was too hard or distasteful for him.

There was a famous doctor in town who specialized in obstetrics. He would not go to a woman in childbirth for less than ten rubles per visit. He was so proud and important that only a wealthy man could afford to bring him forth in the middle of the night.

But what could a poor Jew do when his wife or daughter had difficulty in childbirth in the middle of the night? One's heart went out to them, but what could you do?

But of course there is a cure for every plague. Someone would go to wake up Sholem Yoyne in the middle of the night. It seemed like nothing, they just told him: "Sholem Yoyne, how can you sleep the whole night without a drop of whiskey? We came to remind you that it's time to take a drop!"

"You're so kind," he answered, rubbing his eyes. He did not have to look far, the flask was under his pillow, and of course not empty. As soon as he was on his feet, he went to the kitchen to pour water over his hands. He perfunctorily wiped his hands, pulled the cork, toasted "L'chaim!" and was ready to go through fire and water. He banged on the pharmacist's door and entered the pharmacy. Or he headed off for the doctor, even the proud obstetrics specialist, and was not even afraid of the huge black dog the doctor kept in his yard or the lackey who answered the door.

Both the lackey and the doctor himself knew that Sholem Yoyne was stubborn and that it would not help to throw him down the steps. Sholem Yoyne would take another sip and go right back up again, banging on the door with even more impudence and more power. The doctor might even be ill, but the little Jew with the energy from a little whiskey in him, always found a way to get him out of bed and off to the birthing woman. That was the power in Sholem Yoyne Flask.

And that was not his only talent. His entertainment of the bride and groom and the poor relatives and guests at a poor family's wed-ding cannot be described. He took a sip from the flask and out poured witticisms and rhymes that could stand up against the best jesters.

"Pearls drop from his mouth," said the poor folk. "There must be true balm in his very flesh! May they both live long, Sholem Yoyne and his flask!"

As the big day of the wedding with its special dinner drew near, Sholem Yoyne did not touch a drop of strange whiskey. He even brought his own cake and cookies from home and did not try any of the wedding dinner. And indeed he had no time to do so. He had to serve the guests and entertain them. You could see that he got his well-being from it. Such was his nature and it never did him any harm.

And how the people loved him, the poor and the lonely. They would not trade him for anything and would not tolerate any harm coming to him.

One time it happened that he drunkenly attacked the tax collector, who had, out of the clear blue sky, added a half-ruble tax to each pound of kosher meat. "The Jews are used to it," he said, "so they may as well suffer."

Of course, when the tax collector added the half-ruble per pound for the butchers, the butchers added an additional two kopecks per pound for the customers. And would they weigh the meat on a correct scale? They kept that for the big fish—for the aristocrats—from whom they got a ruble as a percentage.

But for the poor people, only the carcass and the bones were left. They brought it home from the butcher shop and it broke their hearts to look at it. Why did they pay two kopecks more than usual for this? Apparently Sholem Yoyne did not like the smell of it either, because he gave the tax collector such a tongue-lashing that it had everybody in the town talking and he was served with a citation for libel and creating a scandal in the middle of the marketplace.

Sholem Yoyne was called into court and they found a hundred uninvited witnesses from among the "folk," as the aristocrats called them, and they told the judge the whole history from A to Z, thereby digging the tax collector ten feet into the ground. The tax collector willingly dropped the case and was lucky to get out of the court alive and to just go home in embarrassment.

But the end was even better. The next morning, the police introduced charges against the tax collector and the same judge pronounced the sentence: he must return the overcharged half-rubles to the butchers. That incident cost him hundreds of rubles. In truth, the butchers did not care a bit about the poor people and did not even give them back a kopeck, but it was a lesson for tax collectors for generations to come.

The tax collector was made an example for others and Sholem Yoyne had gotten off that time and owed nothing to God or to people. He had a lot of enemies in the town, but of good friends, he had even more.

Meanwhile even his enemies had something good to say about him. "He only drinks because he was punished by God in not having any children. He douses his pain, his loneliness, with whiskey. And who knows whether another in his place might not be even worse?"

And Sholem Yoyne might have lived out his years without ever changing his style or his flask, had it not been for the strange luck that neither he nor his people were able to put right. Here is the story.

Reb Elkane, the wealthy head of the community council, was marrying off his youngest daughter, Rivkele, who was the apple of his eye. Naturally, Elkane was giving his own dowry, some twenty thousand rubles, and why not more? Was he a small-time rich man?

Perhaps half of the houses in the town were his for which he was paid interest, and it was said that he was easily worth a quarter of a million. He had accomplished it, they said, with some hugely wealthy man from Vilna, someone who was even more important than Elkane and on the peak of aristocracy. So when someone like Elkane is making a wedding for his youngest daughter, the merchants expect to sell expensive things, tailors expect to be busy with work, and everyone expects to lick the bones of a sumptuous turkey.

That is no sin. Elkane was a town councilman with great wealth! But who has rights with a rich man? Three months before the wedding, he sent the bride off to an aunt, probably someone as mean as the bride herself, in Warsaw of all places, and there she stayed for the entire summer.

Here in town, the shopkeepers and the tailors were banging the doors down. They wanted to sell; they wanted to earn something. But there was no bride to purchase the expensive wares, no one to measure and sew for! Their eyes rolled while they were waiting, and what were they waiting for?

A week before the wedding the bride returned from Warsaw with her aunt and a whole army of children, daughters, and sisters-in-law, all decked out in new clothes, new from head to toe, and especially the bride who had already purchased her entire wardrobe. It struck everyone like a thunderclap. The town had never heard of such a thing before. Not only that, Elkane had the nerve—perhaps at the suggestion of his new Warsaw relatives—to order musicians, waiters, religious functionaries, and kosher meat from Warsaw. He even brought a new chuppah, a wedding canopy, from there.

Fortunately, the local relatives and ordinary proprietors that encircled such a rich pot as Elkane had gotten a little inspiration from the wedding and needed some articles of clothing made. If not for them, the shopkeepers and tailors would not have enjoyed any part of the huge, joyful event.

Nor did Sholem Yoyne go lacking for work. Elkane himself ordered a suit of clothes from him. It was even said that Elkane was so happy with Sholem Yoyne that he told him who all the new relatives were, who the groom was, and named all the religious figures and other important people who had been invited to the wedding. But his heart compelled him to make Sholem Yoyne promise not to drink too much during the days of the wedding, because all the Vilna relatives and rabbis would be here in honor of the joyous occasion.

And so they came. Relatives started arriving from every direction. Rabbis came from Vilna and from Kovne—the most important figures in the land—fine Jews on whom the light of God seemed to shine. And Sholem Yoyne was at the wedding, too. First of all, Elkane himself had invited him. And second, who was not there? Who did not want to see a wedding for which such a fortune was being given in a dowry? Who did not want to see all the fancy relatives and important rabbis from Vilna, or did not want to hear the famous Vilna wedding jester who Elkane had hired to guide the bride to her seat and to entertain his guests?

The whole town—great and small, rich and poor—was at the wedding. It was of no help that attendants and bouncers stood at every door to keep out the uninvited, people just pushed in, cheek by jowl, and stared at the beautiful tables and the fine guests sitting around them.

The town rabbi delivered a long sermon at the wedding dinner, displaying his sagacity in front of the important people. Those from Vilna, it was reported, chuckled at him, and even the great rabbis smiled. And why not? It was a happy occasion, and when you are happy, you laugh at anything.

When the Rabbi finished his sermon and wiped the huge drops of sweat off his fleshy forehead, Sholem Yoyne slipped in, holding his flask in his hand, and asked the Rabbi, "Tell me, Rebbe, what did God make before heaven and earth?"

"The holy Torah!" answered the Rabbi.

"Aha, his best merchandise!" Sholem Yoyne said to himself, but loud enough for everyone to hear. "And after the Torah, what did he make?"

"Heaven and earth!" answered the Rabbi and threw an angry look at Sholem Yoyne.

"No!" cried Sholem Yoyne, and held up his flask. "This is what God made before heaven and earth: what is in this flask, this little bit of whiskey, Rebbe!"

"Where did you get that from?" asked someone at one of the tables.

"From the Torah itself," Sholem Yoyne answered. "In the beginning, God created the heavens and the earth. The Targum says, '*Borey hashem yas.*' *Yas* is *yas!* It's whisky. Even a tailor knows that, but our rabbi, may he enjoy long life, drinks spirits and does not know that God created whisky before he created heaven and earth." There was laughter and Sholem Yoyne took a sip from his flask.

The Rabbi did not conceal his anger. "Ignoramus! Boor!" he shouted, "'*Yas*' in the Targum is spelled with a '*sav,*' and whisky is '*yas*' spelled with a '*sin.*' It's an abbreviation. '*Yas*' means '*yayn soref.*' Whisky on the other hand—"

"But the whisky in my flask is certainly spelled with a '*sav,*'" Sholem Yoyne retorted. "And *yayn soref* does not make it *yas* any more than it makes the blind to see, the deaf to hear, or makes a dumb tailor speak. Leave off your barking, Rebbe. As our Reb Elkane, may he be well, has said, a dog does not bark for nothing. L'chaim, bride and groom! L'chaim, rabbis and relatives! L'chaim to the princes and paupers, the rich and poor, all are equally important!"

"L'chaim," answered the people at the tables.

"L'chaim and peace," Elkane himself added and remarked, "So, Sholem Yoyne, you've had your say, let that be enough. Go and be well."

"No, that's not what I mean," yelled Sholem Yoyne. "When else could the Vilna rabbis and these important people hear my sermon? Maybe it is the hand of God who has brought them here to allow us to pour out our bitter hearts to them, and to not let them leave without doing something to repair us poor people?"

Sholem Yoyne wiped his moustache and went on: "Hear me out leaders and teachers, we have become slaves to the ringleaders, to our town leaders, to our wealthy citizens, those who live on interest!"

"Be quiet, you scoundrel!" Elkane interrupted. "Throw him out, the drunkard, the hooligan!"

But one of the Vilna rabbis reminded Elkane of a teaching that one may not drive a Jew away from a feast of rejoicing. So Elkane had to hold his anger inside.

Sholem Yoyne started in again: "Perhaps the esteemed rebbe thinks that I would denounce him, heaven forbid, if they threw me out? That would not happen! On the contrary, I would protect him, and it is because of me that others do not denounce him, and it is better to make these complaints here in the open. You, great rabbis with Torah and with justice, and you, the wealthy families whom God has blessed with everything good, do not forget that despite everything, you are Jews, and Jews are merciful! Let your pity awaken and fulfill what is written in the scriptures: look after the orphans who are wandering around naked, barefoot, and hungry in the streets with no proper school for them to study in. There is a Talmud-Torah here and three thousand rubles a year are designated from our taxes to provide for it, but where are those three thousand rubles from year to year? Maybe Reb Elkane, the father of the bride, can tell us!"

Sholem Yoyne laughed good-heartedly and went on: "We, the poor people, have never seen it and the poor orphans know nothing of it. As for the widows, if a Jewish proprietor dies and leaves his shop as a little inheritance for his widow and orphans, what happens right after the funeral, or even during the funeral? Not the collection of contributions to buy food for the family as is the custom among Jews of mercy, but along comes the merchant, who the deceased had bought from on credit, to take the shop as payment. The shop's inheritor must then go searching for our father of the bride, Reb Elkane, or his son or son-in-law, and the widow and her orphans are cast out into the world to go begging door to door with or without a pack of belongings. And for what? For the interest! Probably Elkane never gave the whole principal, or it was paid back long ago!

"You may ask, how can it be? Elkane is an observant Jew, he knows better than Sholem Yoyne, the drunkard, that the holy Torah tells us that we must not charge interest. But here's the excuse: our Rabbi, who is a judge for the Torah and protects the Jews from even the dust of *chametz*, leaven, on Pesach or from a drop of milk in a meat pot. Every year the Rabbi makes new decrees about meat, chicken fat, oil, butter, and what else? From this he gets a percentage for himself. Really in fairness, a total of two kopecks a week for every ruble, which he directs to his wife as a pledge. And he has a receipt for it, a little note printed in Aramaic, a special rabbinic permission. He sells that note along with all the holy books and religious paraphernalia that he deals in, and that little note, friends, swallows up all the big, thick books and all that is written in them just as Pharaoh's seven skinny cows swallowed up the seven fat cows, and no one knows how they did it!"

And so people told of his heroism that evening at the wedding, when Sholem Yoyne talked and talked, pitch and sulfur spewing from his mouth. He presented pictures, vivid images of local happenings, to the guests around the tables. He cried tears himself and drew tears from his listeners. Sholem Yoyne had never spoken with such fire. Until now, people had never known what power he had in himself and in his flask.

People were surprised. Where did he get a mouth so articulate and so to the point? And with such details: all the names mentioned, all the witnesses called, who, what, when, and how. Sparks seemed to fly from wrathful eyes and dark murderous expressions appeared on Elkane's face and on many others who were sitting around the tables. Hands and fists were balled up ready to strike at the skinny little Jew whose mouth was scalding people worse than boiling water.

But hundreds of poor people, paupers, shoemakers, butchers, tailors, and such bitter souls forced themselves in and circled around Sholem Yoyne like a fence. If anyone had laid so much as a finger on him, there would have been a fist fight with blood and the wedding would have turned into a war with each side risking its lives. Everyone clearly perceived this and so they let the drunkard talk on and on.

"Every town has its afflictions," Elkane explained to his new relatives. "One town is famous for its madmen, a second is known for its thieves and pickpockets, another is cursed with denouncers and chicaners. God has punished us with this plague, this drunkard, and we are used to him by now. This isn't the first time and it won't be the last. But we, the calm, quiet proprietors can be tolerant and bear everything, we can quiet the drunkard and take care of him, he will not lack for work or for food!

"It's like the other scoundrels, young hoodlums, idlers, and hooligans that burden the community. For the sake of God's name, we must bear the trouble and be quiet. In some other town they would not put up with this drunken little tailor, they would send him off to Siberia for hard labor; or he would eventually be a suicide. But we, we can take it, and the Master of the Universe will include it in our account."

Sholem Yoyne heard Elkane's remarks and took a big gulp from his flask. He began to answer him with even more heat and fire, and began to depict the quiet, calm little lambs with the satisfied faces and fat bellies, "poor things," who were sitting around the tables, who could not even count to two, let alone see anyone's tears or hear a despondent sigh. After that he began to paint the terrible lions, tigers, and wild beasts, ragged, hungry, sick, with sunken faces, who were standing by the door and in the street outside the door who, out of their goodness and merriment, want to bite those poor fat, satisfied, and pious little lambs.

He was so overheated that he was almost swept away by his speech, as though by a windstorm, and for a moment he forgot about his flask. Someone at the table had noticed it and quietly taken and hidden it. Sholem Yoyne apparently needed a drink, because they saw how his hand was searching for something. It looked eagerly for the flask as the storm of his talk carried him further along. Sholem Yoyne kept talking and looking for the flask.

When a friend of his noticed that someone had hidden the flask, he grabbed a flat bottle from another table and quietly slipped it into Sholem Yoyne's pocket. Sholem Yoyne did not hear or see the world around him. Apparently he was really drunk by then, and had not noticed the switch. But when his throat got dry again, and he started looking for the flask, he felt the bottle, and took a big swig into his mouth.

Suddenly he turned red. It had apparently gone down the wrong pipe. He coughed, choked, and could not catch his breath. His eyes became glassy and bloodshot and he fell over like a cut sheaf.

There was a great tumult and shouting. "Pour water on him, cold water!" someone shouted. "The whiskey has ignited inside of him!"

They poured water on his hot, sweaty body. He seemed to be a little less in distress, but he still could not open his mouth.

"Home, home," he could barely say, and he pointed to the door with his hand. Good friends carried him home, but there at the wedding, a kind of black mood hung behind him. People looked at one another with questioning eyes: "What was that? What does it mean?"

Anger burned in the hearts of Elkane and the aristocrats like the fires of *gehenna*, the fires of hell. In others, maybe in the Vilna rabbis and guests, pity and empathy had awakened, but no one spoke a word.

"In the end the cow goes to the slaughter, the thief goes to jail!" said Elkane, trying to perk up the audience. "And the end of a drunkard like that is better left out of the story! He will burn in his own whisky! A beautiful defeat!"

"The dog earns the stick!" others tried to help him along.

"For the honor of the Torah!" said the Rabbi with vengeance. "He was toying with the honor of the Torah!"

Sholem Yoyne was ill for many days after that evening. He had gotten a bad chill from the water they had doused him with during his unfortunate incident, and he lay suffering for several weeks afterwards.

Good friends from among the town ringleaders asked the doctor who was treating him, to make Sholem Yoyne promise not to taste a drop of whisky again because his life hung by a hair. They wanted him to say that even a little could be fatal. They were not looking after Sholem Yoyne's best interests, but after their own peace of mind. When he did not drink, he did not even bother a fly on the wall.

But all that was over now. For one, all they found in Sholem Yoyne's flask was a bit of pure, cool water that did not even smell of whisky. And two, the doctor swore by every oath possible that his examination of the drunkard's entire body, even of his inner organs, showed clearly that Sholem Yoyne had never drunk whisky or even beer in his whole lifetime, in the way that a pious Jew would never, heaven forbid, touch anything treyf.

The news spread all over the entire town that the whole production with the flask was nothing but Sholem Yoyne's device. He drank nothing but water from it and only used it to give himself courage, and so that people would think that he was drunk.

Sholem Yoyne recovered, and went back to his trade. But he did not get a new flask. He became as quiet as a dove and no one ever heard him raise his voice again. With the drunkenness gone, there was no more audacity, no more merry Jew, no more flask; just the good-natured, good-hearted man he was before.

Sometimes people asked him: "So now that you are yourself among your own Jews, and you can still see all the sins and crimes that are perpetrated in the town, why are you silent? Isn't there enough water in the river?"

"Children," he answered with a heavy sigh, and tears appeared in his eyes, "Children, remember how Samson the Strong had all his strength in his long hair? But when they took away his long hair he lost his strength? His enemies were able to tie him up and lead him around like a sheep. My strength was in my flask. That is, in my secret that I had put into the flask. But once the secret was out, my whole act was over. Without that strength, I'm back to being a tailor like any other tailor. But meanwhile, brothers, I have not been put into chains yet, they have not put out my eyes yet, but I do not have enough strength left to pull down the middle columns of the town council's structure and toss out the whole lot of them, and yell out like Samson, once and for all, 'Let me die with the Philistines.'

"Maybe, maybe, someday, but no one can swear about himself. No one knows when his hour may come. But God is always about, and who knows?"

So Sholem Yoyne sat deep in thought and sewed. Whether he was thinking about his work or a new device to bring his enemies to an accounting, no one knew. But everyone did know that his enemies had taken the flask, smashed it, and thrown the pieces into the garbage heap. Everyone also knew that the name, "Sholem Yoyne Flask," would never be forgotten, and that someday, it would even be written on his gravestone.

And so the Rabbi ruled, and the burial society agreed, that Sholem Yoyne Flask had justly earned his name.

THREE

BOREKH

There are several Borekhs in our town: Borekh Broder, Borekh
Hillel the deaf, Borekh the watchmaker, Borekh "*shokheyn od*" ("You
who dwell in eternity"), and many other Jews who have the name
Borekh with some kind of an addition attached to it. But there was
only one who was called Borekh and nothing more than Borekh. Indeed, nothing more was needed.

Everyone knew him, even a child, even a servant girl. And everyone had some business with him: he was a member of everyone's
household and everyone had an opinion about him.

Without Borekh, no proper housewife put in a pane of glass, or
put up pickles or sauerkraut for the winter, or rendered chicken fat,
or baked matzo. If there was a joyous event in the town—an engagement, a wedding, a circumcision—Borekh had already washed the
long tables from the study house of their usual greasy residue and had
carried those tables—alone or with a helper—to the celebrants' house
and toiled at setting them up and arranging them as long as he had
the energy to do so.

He also made it his business to assemble plates, spoons, forks, and knives for the celebration, and after the celebration to return each item to the person it was borrowed from with no losses or displacements. Borekh knew who owned each object and he never broke his word.

If it happened that someone in town was, God forbid, sick, Borekh spent his days and nights near the patient, or he ran for the doctor, the barber-surgeon, or to the pharmacy. On a hot summer's day he would not hesitate to go five miles outside of town to the beer brewery in order to bring back a bucket of ice to put on the patient's head if the doctor or barber prescribed it.

One did not even get a proper Jewish burial without Borekh. He brought the stretcher for the body, attended to the ritual washing, and busied himself with the funeral. It was also his mitzvah to bring bagels and hardboiled eggs to the mourners, and to help make the minyans for the entire shiva period. And Borekh led daily services and recited the Kaddish for any family who did not have a male capable of the duty. He read from the Torah, called upon whoever he wanted, and conducted the service with all the respect due among Jews.

He was at home everywhere, a member of everyone's household, and he sat down to each table without having to be asked. No housewife was afraid to have him; he was not picky about eating, and whatever was made, offered, or he found for himself in the kitchen, was acceptable to him. Even the cooks gave him food gladly. Borekh was not ashamed to carry water buckets and often set up the samovar himself while the cooks were busy with something else.

But Borekh was even more influential with the town's children. What couldn't Borekh think up and make for them! He could pick up a piece of paper and a pair of scissors and cut out all kinds of animals, human figures, soldiers, horses, goats, lions, bears, leopards and anything else you could think of. Whenever he came into a home where there were little children, boys or girls, the children brought him scissors and paper, and no matter how busy he was with anything else, for their sake, he would quickly cut out anything they asked for.

Borekh never permitted any boy in the town to be without a dreidel for Chanukah or a grogger for Purim to drown out Haman's name, or a bow and arrow and a little wooden sword for Lag b'Omer and Tishah b'Av.

Borekh's dreidels and groggers were especially famous. He had a special knife for woodcarving, which he always kept sharp as a razor, and which could shave the hair from a grown man's arm from the hand to the elbow in one stroke. With that knife and other tools of his own making, he carved a pair of goats that butted one another with their horns, a pair of roosters that fought one another, eagles with two heads that beat their wings, and the dreidels and groggers that took him months to carve.

As people listened to the Megillah, the Purim story, they would notice Borekh's new groggers and the artistic work and skill that went into them. "He seems like such a fool," people would say, "Such a simple mind. Yet he has the brains to spend months making such things!"

"That's why he has no head for learning," others explained, "because he puts his whole brain, his whole life's effort, into such foolishness!"

However, the children did not care about his inability to study, and they found Borekh very valuable. They may not have behaved properly for their parents, or for the rebbe at school, but they would do anything for Borekh with just a wink from him. And he loved the cheder boys and even smaller children more than anything else in the world. In an argument about the blade of an old knife, a fistfight over a brass button, or an old rusty pen, Borekh would become their court and judge. With great seriousness and fairness, he smoothed things over and made peace among them, just as one would do if he were handling an important matter.

Borekh was not only their court and judge, he was also their beloved friend, who played and joked with them, and who got the same enjoyment and fun from it as did the children, although he was three times bigger and two times their age.

"There's a child's soul in that big, poor, overgrown Borekh," people would say when they saw him in a group of cheder boys, earnestly handling some childish matter.

"A soul?" others joked. "He doesn't have a soul, just a child's intelligence. He will never be an adult!"

But mostly no one took Borekh's non-adult status seriously. Whatever he lacked in other departments, he was a free and useful attendant to everyone.

Whose obligation was it to look after him? Who did he belong to? He had no relative and no redeemer in the town. No one even knew where he came from. People only knew that he had always been in the yeshiva, the study house; that he had always called one of the benches "home," and that everyone in the yeshiva knew that bench as "Borekh's bench." Indeed, that had been his bench since he was a small child. He had grown bigger and taller each year on that bench and he still slept on it at night.

Underneath his bench, he kept a locked box, where he stored his few poor possessions consisting entirely of a couple of grimy shirts, a hat for Shabbes, a pair of cut-off bootlegs that he had bought a long time ago with the intention of buying feet to sew onto them, though he never managed to save enough money to complete the job.

In addition to these few possessions, the box was full of various blades and sharpened nails which he used as chisels, and all kinds of little springs and tops that were necessary for his carving. And so many pieces of wood—birch, oak, ash—that you couldn't count them all.

"That's just part of his foolishness," said the young men at the study house. "Borekh would sooner let something with God's name on it remain on the floor than pass up a nice piece of wood!"

Once he had seen a piece of wood he needed, he would spend his last kopeck or give up his last bite of food for it. And what was it good for? Didn't he already have plenty of wood for all his dreidels, groggers, and other clever things that he made and gave to the children? No amount of talk, ridicule, or joking would convince him.

Once he had seen a nice piece of wood, something like a *yetzer hore*, an evil inclination, would ignite in him and he would do almost anything to obtain the wood and lock it in his box.

Borekh got along well with the group in the study house; that is, the other poor youths who studied there. They ordered him around as though they were the proprietors, and Borekh obeyed them and did whatever he could do for them.

He always had a needle and thread, which to a poor boy is as necessary as life itself. Borekh would even repair a boot for a friend if he were allowed to do so. Sometimes he would sit at a distance, smiling to himself as he watched one of the yeshiva boys struggling unsuccessfully to patch his torn clothes. Borekh, knowing how to do it, would take the clothes and mend them himself, even if the boy was his worst enemy.

"Borekh's patches," the poor boys would say, "could be in the Paris exposition!"

"Where did he learn it?" the boys asked each other, surprised at Borekh's skill. "When did he learn it?"

One unfounded opinion was that Borekh's father had been a tailor, and that he had simply inherited it.

"But what about the woodcarving?" someone asked. "Perhaps his father was a woodcarver or a lathe-man."

"Not necessarily," said another. "Craft does not have to be for one thing only. If you are a craftsman, you can be a craftsman at everything!"

"And I say that it just depends on having a feeling for it!" someone else added. "All artistry and craftsmanship are things of the senses. Borekh has a feeling for it, that's all."

When Borekh came in they asked him, "Borekh, what was your father?"

"How would I know?" answered Borekh with a sigh.

"How can you not know what your own father was?" the boys wondered.

"I've been an orphan for so long I can't remember," Borekh said sadly. "I don't even remember saying Kaddish for my parents. I just remember being called 'orphan.'"

"But how do you know how to sew and carve? Everything you pick up comes out like something turned on a lathe?"

"How do I know?" answered Borekh like a simpleton. "You shouldn't make fun of me."

"Heaven forbid!" said one of the yeshiva boys.

"Heaven forbid!" said Borekh in return.

"What can I do then?" asked the boy.

"What can I do, either?" answered Borekh.

"You can make anything you want to," explained another boy. "If you want to make an eagle, you make it. You make such beautiful things that take you months to make. If I could make things like that, I would certainly know how I got the ability to do it."

"It's not ability!" said Borekh.

"What do you mean? What do *you* call ability?" asked a boy.

"To be able to learn like the boy from Brisk," answered Borekh enthusiastically. "That's what I call ability."

"The Brisker again, that little darling!" burst out one of the boys angrily, as though Borekh had said that only the Brisker could learn and no one else. But Borekh had no desire to get involved in a big dispute and went off to his bench.

The Brisker was Borekh's weak side. He took orders from everyone, but for the Brisker, no task was too difficult. Called "The Brisker" because he came from the town of Brisk, the Brisker was a youth of seventeen, a spirited boy, always happy, always joking. If an idea occurred to him about how to play a joke on someone he spent little time considering the consequences, he just did it.

Studying appeared to be like a game for the Brisker and he always asked the most difficult questions. And when he argued with the headmaster of the yeshiva about one of the commentaries, his eyes always sparkled with fire. Borekh loved such eyes and could never get his fill of looking at the Brisker.

And Borekh took pride when he saw the Brisker argue with the rabbi. Even the headmaster would come over as all the boys circled around the Brisker. Everyone sided with the rabbi—all the adults and all the shrewd thinkers—but the young Brisker was never daunted. He answered each of them as though the holy spirit was literally resting on his shoulders.

Of course, Borekh always sided with the Brisker. He did not get involved in the dispute—he rarely even understood what they were arguing about—but he always felt the Brisker was correct. His head was lighter and faster than their heavy old minds, and so Borekh wanted the Brisker to be victorious over the adult Jews, even though they were the biggest people in the town.

But Borekh also suffered plenty from the Brisker who mocked him more than anyone else and constantly teased him. Borekh would not have tolerated so much from any of the other boys. At some point, he would have answered back. But he let the Brisker do whatever he wanted.

"He doesn't do it from maliciousness or hatred," Borekh would say to the others, "but you do mean it maliciously!"

When someone laughed at him, Borekh remained silent, or asked what kind of idea it was that made the other boys laugh? But if the Brisker said something and everyone laughed, Borekh good-naturedly laughed along with them, even if the joke was on him.

"What are you laughing at Borekh?" the Brisker would sometimes ask, when Borekh laughed along at one of his witticisms, because the Brisker knew that Borekh did not understand the joke.

"What are *you* laughing at?" Borekh would ask him back.

"I laugh when I am enjoying myself," the Brisker answered.

"I am enjoying myself, too," answered Borekh and he meant that he was happy to see the Brisker enjoying himself.

Once the Brisker played a practical joke on Borekh, poor thing, which sent him off to his bench where he lay sick for an entire day. The jokester had not calculated that what he did would have such dire consequences when he put something into Borekh's food that made him very sick and caused him to throw up the entire night.

The Brisker soon expressed his regret and tore his hair out. He was especially afraid that the school authorities would find out and drive him from the study house. But Borekh calmed him and swore the other boys to secrecy.

"Are you mad at me, Borekh?" the Brisker asked later in the voice of a true penitent.

"No, you fool, I love you!" Borekh answered.

"Love me? For the misery I have caused you?"

"No, that's over; I'm already better," Borekh comforted his friend.

"Why then?"

"Because you can learn so well!" stammered Borekh as though ashamed by the truth he was telling his friend.

"What do you get from my being able to learn?" asked the Brisker.

"It just delights me when I see how you argue with the head of the yeshiva or even the rabbi," explained Borekh with genuine joy that he had the opportunity to so openly tell the Brisker what he felt in his heart.

"I don't understand your delight, Borekh," said the Brisker.

"Why don't you understand it? You can understand a complicated interpretation from the Talmud and yet you cannot understand such a simple thing?"

"I don't understand why my learning ability is such a concern of yours. I am not your brother or even a relative."

"And not being a brother, and not being a relative, is it not good that a small boy can spar with a great rabbi over a matter of Holy Scripture?" asked Borekh, explaining what was in his heart. "Brisker, what is fine is fine, whether it's yours or another's. I enjoy everything that is fine. Whether it's mine or not mine. Understand?"

"Then that is how it will be!" replied the Brisker, though he really did not understand what Borekh meant. "So just tell me, Borekh, if you think that learning is so fine, and you love it so much, why don't you do it yourself?"

"Because I can't!" answered Borekh with a heavy sigh.

"Then learn what you can!" said his friend with pity.

"I just can't!" Borekh said with a tone of disillusionment.

"Learn, I tell you, whatever you can!" the Brisker insisted. "If you want, I will study with you a few hours every day!"

"No, you don't understand me," Borekh struggled to explain to his friend. "I mean, that I can't learn, I can't sit still and study like you do. Do you understand?"

"You are a pretty sharp thinker," smiled the Brisker. "What comes first, learning or ability?"

"Ability is first!" answered Borekh with certainty as he would have answered a question in school.

The Brisker laughed at Borekh's response. "Fool! If you didn't know how to study, from where would you get the ability?"

"Maybe carving," Borekh offered as a proof for his answer.

"Carving? What kind of an answer is that?" laughed the Brisker, and began to get impatient with Borekh's excuses.

"And I say that it's a good example!" Borekh argued, defending his side. "I never learned carving but I can do it anyway, and because I can, I do, and if I had time, or rather, if people would let me, I would carve day and night. It's the same with learning: because you can learn, it's nothing for you to sit and study for six hours on end. Now do you understand what I mean?"

"Not in the least!" answered the Brisker impatiently as he walked away. "It's just something from a muddled mind!"

Borekh often sat down with the intention of studying earnestly and with all his powers, like all the other yeshiva boys, but other things always fought their way into his thoughts: A bird sat on the windowsill, a breeze tossed the branches of a tree against the window-pane, a soldier sounded a bugle call for a meal, children chased after a puppy on the street, and other such events. Borekh could not let these things go unnoticed and he quickly lost all track of studying.

He had to go to the window to consider the bird, amazed by its little face; he could not stop looking at the tree as it swayed from side to side, its leaves turning over and whispering to each other; or he had to enjoy the children, shouting and playing as he used to do, and that was the end of studying! His mind was already busy with something else that drew him more than the Talmud and its concerns.

Other times, when he had painstakingly gotten the issues into his head, he was horrified to turn the page and see two or three lines of type and a huge field with Rashi's and other commentaries in small print all around it. He felt suddenly powerless as though he had been thrown into the middle of the sea and would never be able to fight his way back to shore. A chill ran through his body, he trembled, and he was glad when someone interrupted him so that he had an excuse to close the book.

But Borekh loved the non-legal writings. He loved *Ayn Yankev* and other commentaries and books that told stories. He went into the desert with Rabbi bar Khana and set off for the place where the earth and the sky meet. He knew Rabbi Akive and was angry with him for the unmerciful way he dealt with his faithful wife, the daughter of Kalba Savua. His heart melted with pity for her when she had to go and knead bread for other people so that she would have a livelihood. And he forgot that this all took place a long time ago. He imagined that this was happening now and he wanted to help Kalba Savua's daughter by bringing her a pail of water, or chopping some wood, or helping her in any way that was within his power to keep her from feeling so lonely.

He felt a similar pity for Rabbi Akher, too, except that he was a heretic, a turncoat. "He had so much learning," Borekh thought to himself, "what happened to him was such a curse! That such a great scholar had to meet with such a curse to be a heretic and to lose his portion in the World to Come."

So Borekh lived his internal life in the stories of the Talmud and his exterior life in the house of study without a care in the world. He had no desire to get involved in the grownup business of the town. He was always happy, always satisfied. When he sighed, it was for someone else's loneliness, and when he wrung his hands, it was for other people's troubles.

He toiled, worked, and ran for others; he went to no trouble for himself. He was certain that he lacked nothing. He was happy. He had shoes and a shirt; what else did anyone need?

"Even Jacob Our Ancestor, who was no doubt reared better and more cultivated than I, only asked the Ruler of the Universe for bread to eat and clothes to wear," said Borekh to himself. "Where is it written in the Torah that bread necessarily means pot roast and fancy stews, and that clothes should be of silk and satin? Even Rashi the Holy who found warnings in every word, every letter of the Torah, did not warn that bread meant marzipan and clothes meant an expensive tapestry coat at four rubles a yard. Thank God, I do not suffer from cold and hunger. At least I can share with others."

And Borekh did indeed share everything. From every wedding or celebration for which he worked, he brought back cookies, cake, and often a goose leg to share with his hungry friends at the study house. When it happened that a boot got a hole in it, a seam tore in a pair of pants, a sleeve wore so thin that the underclothes showed through, Borekh said, "What did God make needle, thread, and patches for?"

Said and done! He set to work, filled the hole in the boot, repaired the seam in the pants, and covered the worn sleeve with a clever patch. Once done, Borekh was again whole and happy.

"If there is one person in town without a care," people used to say, "it is Borekh!"

And so it was. Always working with other people, he never thought to ask for anything for himself. Always in the company of small children and playing with them, it never entered his mind that he had already become a young man. Mostly what he thought about was the hard work that he did. If a thought presented itself, pushed its way into his mind, he would quickly rub his forehead with his hand to drive the vision away, and go back to being the usual unthinking, carefree Borekh.

Until one day, while he was serving the guests at a fancy wedding as he often did, Bunim the Matchmaker put a hand on Borekh's shoulder and out of the clear blue sky said, "Borekh, tell me, how old are you?"

"What does it matter?" Borekh replied, not understanding what Bunim meant by the question.

"It matters!" Bunim answered.

"But why does it matter?" Borekh asked again, not because he understood Bunim's question and wanted to know why he was asking, but because he was showing the clever style used by the yeshiva boys to let others know they belonged to the study house.

"Why does it matter?" answered Bunim in the same style. "So tell me Borekh, are you already twenty? Are you of legal age?"

Borekh looked at him innocently and did not know what to answer.

"Why are you silent, simpleton? I'm asking you a very important question!" Bunim did not back off.

"Do I know?" Borekh shrugged. "Leave me alone, I don't have time for this! Don't bother me."

"It's time, Borekh," Bunim shook his finger at him. "It's time for you to think about the fact that you are not a boy anymore. You already have a beard and you think that you will always be a child?" said Bunim, translating the lines from the Passover Haggadah.

They both knew the passage was from Ezekiel.

Borekh pulled away from Bunim and soon forgot all about him. He threw himself heart and soul into the wedding and when a band with a big bass drum began to play merrily and the men began to dance, Borekh put his hand on someone's shoulder and danced like everyone else for as long as his strength held out.

Bunim looked at Borekh from a distance and thought, "A childish soul. Go ask him to do something."

Going home at dawn, happy and with his pockets full of good things for his friends at the study house, Borekh spotted a group of men who had left the wedding a few minutes before him. He started running to catch up so they could walk together, but as he got closer, he recognized Bunim from behind and fell back, though he himself could not account for why he did so. But something occurred to him in that moment: better not to meet up with him again, and he felt his joy suddenly fade for no apparent reason.

When he saw from a distance that each had turned onto his own street and into his own home, Borekh continued on his way. He walked quickly and thought to himself that in the study house he would divide everything he was bringing for his friends. They would talk together, it would be merry as always, and he would forget all about Bunim the Matchmaker.

Why did he want to forget Bunim? What had he done to him? What could he do to him? He himself did not know, but he wanted to forget him.

"Feh, a nasty man!" he said to himself as he arrived at the study house.

It was already light outside, but all his friends were sound asleep on their benches, snoring like princes. Only Khaym, the old yeshiva caretaker, was awake, washing his hands and reciting the blessing after natural functions, pronouncing each word thoughtfully. He did not look up as Borekh entered.

Borekh wanted to wake up his friends. He needed them to laugh, even if they made fun of him. But a thought occurred to him: Don't make them commit a sin by causing them to stumble. Here he was, ready to wake them up at dawn and give them cake like a heathen before they had time to wash their hands, without a blessing and before reciting the morning prayers, and sooner or later someone would say, "On you, Borekh, the sin is on you! You are an evil inclination!"

It wasn't worth it. He knew that if he woke them it wouldn't matter what his intentions were, they would tease him. "Give yourself a piece of advice," Borekh thought to himself. "It's not worth it."

So Borekh went to his bench to stretch out and take a nap until everyone else was awake and gathered for prayers. But then he thought that it would be better to pray by himself and then go upstairs to the women's section to sleep. For some reason he was more weary today than ever before.

"Bunim, may his name be blotted out, has put a spell on me. If I can get some sleep, I will forget about him as though he didn't exist."

He began to pray as he put on his tefillin, but he prayed without zeal. His tongue got tangled and an incredible thing happened: instead of hearing the words he was praying, it seemed as though Bunim was standing behind him, whispering into his ear, "How old are you, Borekh?"

"A curse on you, Bunim!" thought Borekh, not holding back his anger even in the middle of his prayers. So he stopped, squinted his eyes, and began reciting his prayers word by word. He concentrated on the meanings, not so much out of piety, but to forget Bunim. But the tighter he closed his eyes, the clearer he saw Bunim standing before him, waging his finger and looking him straight in the eye: "It's about time, Borekh. It's time for you to think about the fact that you are not a boy anymore. You already have a beard!"

Borekh touched the hair that had just begun to appear on his cheeks. He was shocked and lost his place in the prayers. He began a few blessings before the place he knew he had been, rocked like a tree in a storm, and prayed with all his heart. But Bunim soon returned. "Ho, Borekh have I told you a lie? You already have a good beard. In half a year it will be something to grab onto."

It seemed that he heard Bunim's words even more clearly than the words of the prayers. Was he even praying? Suddenly his back hit the bench behind him and Borekh jumped as though waking from a difficult dream. He opened his eyes. No one was there. His friends were still sleeping like the dead.

"Fie on him!" Borekh said angrily. "He has really gotten to me, he's chewing away at me, and won't even let me finish praying! A libelous devil, a curse on him!"

He took off his tefillin, laid them aside, and looked around to see if any of his friends were awake yet. "Maybe if I ask them, they will tell Bunim not to pester me anymore with his stupid questions, or else they will do something to him. Some kind of little accident!" He laughed at his own silly wishes. "What has he done to me? So what if he asked how old I am? Anyway, can you hate a person for what he asks? What were you thinking, having them avenge you? For what? Because he asked my age? Won't they ask me themselves soon enough? 'Well, how old are you, Borekh?' Will they become your enemies, too? I need some protection from this! Why am I taking this to heart? The cure? Some sleep, a good sleep and to wake up refreshed and whole!"

Thus decided, he climbed up to the women's section, stretched out his big body on a bench, and closed his eyes to sleep. But before he could fall asleep, he felt that something was gnawing at his heart. "It's a strange thing. I've never hated anyone in my life, but I hate him, really hate him! And what has he done to me? It's a groundless hatred."

He thought about the sin of groundless hatred and tried not to hate Bunim. "He should know that I forgive him and am not his enemy. Tomorrow I'll go and tell him. But really, how old am I?" And he began to count his childhood years. He remembered very little about them.

They called him "orphan" in that other town where he must have been born. He did not remember any parents. Apparently he had been very small when his parents had died. His heart pained him that they had died so young. "If only they would come back to me in a dream sometime!" And he was almost angry at them for not coming in a dream. And if they did, how would he even know what their faces looked like?

"They brought a child into the world," he said to himself, "and then they up and died. Then they forgot about him and won't even come to show themselves in a dream! Anyway, they could not have known in advance that there would be some punishment for their sins. We know we have to pay for our sins on the other side, but what is the cost? Today they must be finished with any suffering and as free as birds in Paradise. Why don't they come flying from their holy rest and tell me in a dream, 'Borekh, I am your father. Borekh, I am your mother. We beseech God for you. Be a good Jew and be well!' It would be very nice and honest on their part. I would never demand anything else from them. Only if they came to me today in a dream, the first thing I would ask them is, 'How old am I?' They would certainly know."

The question of his age dug at his mind like a plow. He could not stop thinking about it. He reminded himself of everything he knew about his childhood. He wanted to remember his home, too. Did he have a home someplace, just a little house, a room where he used to have a bed or even where he lay on the floor like other poor children? But he could not remember it.

So he remembered every study house where he had lived as a small child. "They were all like the study house where I am now!" he thought to himself. "The same long tables and benches, the same bimah where the Torah is read, the same Jews praying in the mornings, the same voices and moaning during the prayers; only the two lions holding up the tablets of the Ten Commandments over the holy ark were different: stronger, meaner, and finer than these. These lions look more like goats! If only they would let me carve a pair of lions, I would carve real lions, kings over all the other animals in the forest, and frightening to look at. These are goats, but just try to milk them!"

He fell asleep with these visions and woke up an hour before afternoon prayers. When he opened his eyes and looked around him, he suddenly felt so lonely, so unhappy, as if he had lost everything in his domain, in his head and in his heart. He did not feel pain, but something clenched inside of him, as though he might cry like a little child. He did not want to get up from the bench and go downstairs. He was ashamed to appear before his friends, and he lay there with his eyes wide open, looking at the ceiling, and in his head everything was mixed up with the question: "How old am I really?"

"Could I really be twenty?" he asked himself. "Don't I remember my bris, my circumcision? Who remembers his own bris? But I do remember my own bar mitzvah."

He remembered Reb Gruns, an old study house Jew, who he had studied with for as long as he could remember, and who he had served, bringing him food, hand washing water, and going with him every Friday afternoon to the bathhouse. One day Reb Gruns offered him a pair of big tefillin with cracked, yellowed straps, and said, "Now, Borekh, you have a pair of tefillin. After Shabbes you will start to put on tefillin. It seems that it is time. You see how old you are!"

That same day Reb Gruns began teaching him the "Laws of Tefillin," and a lot of ethical teachings, which he did not remember, but there had been a lot of them.

"A precious Jew, that Reb Gruns, may he have a luminous Paradise! A shame he is no longer alive. I could ask him now how many years it was since he started the alphabet with me, then Khumesh, then Rashi, then Talmud. He also had to go off and die."

He tried to count his years by the Passovers, and the householders who had hosted him for Passover, but he got so mixed up that he could not arrive at any correct total. Yet Bunim was right about one thing: "I am certainly no longer a boy anymore and it is time to start thinking about becoming a mentsh. But how do I suddenly become a mentsh?" he asked himself and a cold sweat poured over him.

"What is a mentsh? A mentsh is his own person, a mentsh makes a living, a mentsh has a home, his own home, not the town study house that is a kind of a 'no-man's land' for everyone who lives here. Where will I get such a home and how can I make myself a mentsh?

"And if I say that I am no longer a boy anymore, who will have anything to do with me? It would be good if everyone who sends for me and asks me to do things for them—to run errands and drudge for them—would understand and stop sending me on errands and demanding things of me. But they won't, I know them. What concern is it of theirs if I am already an adult? I could be haughty and say, 'I won't obey you anymore; I'm not a little boy anymore!' But they would just laugh at me, and I would have to obey them anyway.

"Master of the Universe!" his heart cried out to God, "give the townspeople here the concept that they may understand this themselves, that I will not be their errand boy anymore. And don't let them forget that there is a Borekh in the world.

"But what will I be," he wondered? "A cheder teacher? The children won't obey me. And how could I hit them? What will I be? Answer me, Master of the Universe!"

Meanwhile, people had gathered downstairs for the afternoon prayers. Borekh went to the water basin, washed his hands, and went down to pray with the minyan.

"Where were you, Borekh?" the yeshiva boys asked him. "What happened to you?"

Borekh made an effort to put on his usual happy smile, but it would not cooperate. So he handed out the treats he had brought for them. But today their laughter and their jokes stabbed at his heart. He looked at them forlornly, while on his lips the words lay ready: "Boys, it's my turn now to laugh back." But he could not say it.

After prayers, someone asked him to do a task, but Borekh just looked at the man like a simpleton, as though he did not understand the request.

"What do you say, Borekh, will you come?" the man asked.

"I don't know," Borekh answered, not quite able to refuse.

"Look how he makes you beg!" the man said with some anger. "If someone says to you, come, you don't have to discuss it or whine and look at me as though you don't know who I am."

"I'll come," Borekh managed, but quickly added, "If I can. I'm not quite well, may it never happen to you."

After prayers, a group of cheder boys gathered at the study house with important business to discuss with Borekh. When he saw them, he promptly forgot all that was on his mind as he inquired about their innocent matter. But he soon remembered and his heart began to clench again at the thought that he would have to separate from his dear friends whom he loved and who loved him. In that moment he was angry at God who had created the world in such a way that living people must get older from year to year.

"How would it bother God if we were children our whole lives? Or at least to remain happy as children?" He was not angry just for himself now that he was no longer a child like those who stood before him. He knew that he was already lost, but he had pity on the young ones, for in just a few years Bunim, or someone like Bunim, would come and ask the same question: "Tell me, how old are you?"

And then they would feel what he felt and their hearts would also pain them as his did now. Tears sprang into his eyes as he looked at his little friends. He wanted to kiss them, to press them to his heart, to cry over them, and then to say goodbye.

The children, who had never seen Borekh so sad, looked at him wonderingly, but soon were tugging at his sleeve, urging him to discuss their trifles. It was very difficult for Borekh to free himself from the children. His heart clenched as he left, wiping his eyes with his coattails.

"Borekh," called one of the yeshiva boys, "where are you? Bunim the Matchmaker is looking for you."

"Please, tell him I'm not here," Borekh replied. "I am not his enemy. He has done nothing to me, but I do not want to see him." Then Borekh sadly left the study house and went off to be alone.

When he returned later that night, his friends were already asleep. He was very tired and he went to his box to get a piece of clothing for a pillow. But as his hand reached into the box, he found a little wooden animal that he had started carving a long time ago, yet never finished. He studied it, looking at it from all angles, and almost forgot his weariness and sadness.

He had never considered his own work in this way before. And as he began searching through the various tools and pieces of wood in his box, a curious thing happened: he forgot all about Bunim the Matchmaker, he forgot about his sadness. It felt as if a stone had been lifted from his heart.

"Why not a woodcarver?" his lips stammered, almost of their own free will. "Why not learn how to carve an entire holy ark? One like people have never seen before, with magnificent lions holding up the Ten Commandments!"

"But who will teach me? It doesn't matter. If you seek, you find. But not here. Here they will not let me be. I must find a place where people do not know Borekh. I'll have to go there, far, far away. And soon too, I cannot put it off any longer!"

Comforted and strengthened by his decision, Borekh felt like someone who had been drowning and suddenly felt the ground beneath his feet. He stretched out on his bench and soon fell into a deep and restful sleep.

Very early the next morning, before it was even light, Borekh got up, washed his hands, prayed quickly, and packed his few possessions. Standing before the holy ark, he kissed and wiped his tears on the curtains. Then, as he started down the steps, he saw his sleeping friend, the Brisker, and his heart clenched again. "How can I leave my beloved friend without even saying goodbye?

"Be a good person, Brisker," his lips muttered and tears stood in his eyes. "Be a great scholar and the whole world will resound with you! And one day, when I hear of your honor and greatness as a rabbi, I will send you a gift, something I have carved with my own hands. A present from your old friend, Borekh, may God help and protect me on my long journey!"

With that, he went to the door, and walking backwards, kissed the mezuzah three times, then left the study house forever. When his friends woke up and people started gathering for prayers, Borekh was already far, far from town.

FOUR

MOTL FARBER, PURIMSHPIELER

The folks in town said about Motl Farber that along with the additional soul that one receives in honor of Shabbes and the holidays, he also received an additional beard. During the week he was a Jew with just one beard like everyone else, but for Shabbes and the holidays, his beard divided itself in two, half to the right and half to the left, so it looked like two separate beards on the same person. And that's what people called it: "The extra-soul beard."

People would ask him, "Reb Motl, what do you do with your second beard during the week?"

And he would reply: "I salt it and pack it away in the same box where I pack away my stomach and half of my soul for the winter. When summer is over and the Master of the Universe takes away my trade by painting everyone's rooftops with fine white snow without a penny's cost, then I am out of business, no longer a painter or much of a person. What good is a person without a livelihood?"

And Motl was not exaggerating. When you saw him in summer, sitting on a roof and ordering his helpers around, he did not acknowledge winter.

In summer, he was a tall, happy Jew with big shoulders. He sang like a cantor with a sweet voice, and his helpers responded like his chorus. He was alive; his work was alive in his hands. Everything about his work had a gay tone. He was happy and God and people were happy with him.

On Shabbes in the study house, you might think that he was the elder of the month. He always provided a poor guest with a place for Shabbes and also invited a few for the afternoon meal. But when summer was over and snow covered the roofs and his business began to die off, Motl withdrew, and there was only half of him. No one heard his voice, and he was rarely seen in the study house even on Shabbes.

Until Chanukah he lived on whatever profit he had made during the summer. They had borscht and thanked God for it. But after Chanukah, when the big freezes came and no one thought about painting, and the expense of firewood and warm clothes for his sons in cheder grew ever greater, Motl lost all his courage. Then he just lay on the bench near the oven and waited for summer.

When people asked him: "How goes it, Motl?" he answered with jokes: "Going, it's not going, brother, it has stopped, frozen. A small thing, this frost! Better to ask, how lays it? The whole winter I kick back and lay around. The Master of the Universe is busy now painting people's roofs. It's His time now. No matter, my time will come again."

"But what are you eating in the meantime?"

"Meanwhile we are eating copper frying pans and brass candlesticks. If we had silver spoons, we would eat silver spoons. Have you heard that a person can relish a tin samovar? Any week my stomach could swallow that tin samovar of mine, and today I will eat it again. For Shabbes we put together a tasty dish: a pillow with feathers. How could you hurt your stomach with such digestible meals?"

He often addressed his hunger with such jokes and so bluffed his way through the entire winter. But his wife was not comforted by his humor and always yelled that it would be better if her husband was a shoemaker or a tailor or even a water carrier, anything but a painter who earned half the year and the other half had to store his teeth on a shelf in disuse.

"A painter," she said, "is a beast worse than a bear. A bear lives half the year and sleeps half the year. A painter doesn't live more than the summer either, but he can't sleep the whole winter. He wants to eat in the winter, too, because he's still awake!"

"Do you know why a bear sleeps the whole winter, Yente?" he called out in answer to her complaints.

"Why?"

"Because a bear has no wife! If he had a wife like a painter, he wouldn't be able to sleep the whole winter either, just like a man."

"Bitter is the lot of a woman!" his wife interrupted. "All your clever sayings are only about women. What would you do if you didn't have me?"

"If I didn't have you," he answered, "I would be free as a bird and would do what all free birds do. When summer was over, I would fly off to a warmer country where you can paint roofs, shutters, and fences the whole year 'round!"

"Fly, if you can! Why don't you fly? Who's holding you back?"

"It's hard to fly when your wings are clipped," he sighed. "Yente, another month, another week, it's already closer than farther. Soon it will be summer again, there will be work again, and our hearts will be happy and our stomachs will be full."

And soon the days were longer, the blessing was said for the month of Adar, and a warm sunlight shone on the streets. The sullen sun underwent a change, gradually throwing off her morose veil. She was charming and winked at her longing lovers to come outdoors.

"Please, forgive me," she says to them, "it will be good again, it will be peaceful again! I will comfort you, don't run away, don't hide from me!"

And little children pour out of basements and attic apartments into the street and rejoice and warm themselves under the loving sun. We hear happy childish voices outdoors and even the cranky old Jews who go around bundled up in ten layers of clothes begin to smile and toss off a layer or two.

Motl Farber always perceived the summer before anyone else did because he was waiting and counting the last minutes of winter. As soon as the blessings for the month of Adar had been recited, he sprang up from his bench, straightened himself out, and headed outside. By evening he was back home with a group of painters. They shook out their pockets and collected a few kopecks. Motl's wife ran to the market and brought back bread and herring, and with a pot of potatoes, they made a feast in honor of the New Moon of Adar. They ate bread, herring, potatoes, and drank a pot of tea as though they were kings. It was lively, and Motl divided his beard into two equal parts, stuck out his big chest and gave the command like a general, "Now, children, to our business!"

This meant that they should begin to organize their *purimshpiel*, the play they would produce for Purim. It was because of Purim that they would all have money for Pesach. And they only played in important places, in the homes of rich Jews who always paid for the play with a three-ruble piece or even a fiver.

This was Motl's claim for many years. Motl played Mordecai the Jew. Itsikl Glezer, a sturdy youth, played Haman. Itsikl's father, who had been a soldier in Nikolai's army, played King Akheshverus, the king of the Persian Empire. Two boys, Motl's young apprentices, played Queen Vashti and Queen Esther, a woman with a veil, a wig, and a golden crown on her head. Other younger and older helpers played other parts in the Megillah, the Purim story. Haman's sons were not absent, and there was even a horse.

In place of a real horse, Motl tied on a costume with a horse's tail on the back and a screen on the front, which was painted with big horse's eyes. There was a bridle and reins, and the whole animal was covered with a Turkish shawl so it looked as though the tall Mordecai was riding on a horse.

However, the point was not the costumes, but the style of the words and the tunes they sang. Motl was better with words and music than all the other Purim players. Motl had a wonderful voice and was well known for his leading of the prayers. He could have even led the afternoon service during the Days of Awe and earned a pretty penny for it, but Motl always had some opponents who would not let him up to lead. They maintained that a painter and a *purimshpieler* could not also lead the community in prayer.

Motl rehearsed the group for two solid weeks. Night after night they besieged his little house, going over the songs of Akhashverus, Vashti, and especially Motl's Mordecai the Jew, with his tenor voice that diffused through every limb.

On Purim eve, right after the reading of the Megillah, everyone gathered at Motl's house. They brought out the horse costume and Motl saddled up. He combed his beard into two parts, put on a fur hat with a rabbinic brim, and picked up the golden scepter. Haman put on the general's uniform, which was hung with medals, orders, and everything else that Itsikl Glezer had rented from Shmuel Epoletnik the pawnbroker. On his head, he placed a three-pointed hat that looked like a hamantasch. And in these clothes, no one can recognize Itsikl, a tall healthy fellow, for who he is. Strangers can really take him for a general.

The rabbi examines Vashti and Queen Esther to be certain that they are not real women but men dressed up like women, then tells them to present the *purimshpiel,* and enjoys the old merry custom very much. He blesses Mordecai, curses Haman, spits at Vashti and Zeresh, pats Queen Esther, and wishes the company to survive another year to present the play again.

After the rabbi, the company goes to the head of the community council. There the play flows a little more freely. The group is served cups of whisky, which soften their hearts and raise their voices, and no matter how stingy the council head is—may he come to no shame —his pleasure rises above his stinginess and he gives Motl a whole five rubles for himself and the company. The group moves on, playing for influential people, and if one is uncertain about what donation to make, they bargain first. Motl says, "My merchandise, your money. You have a choice: yes or no. You are not compelled and there are no grudges here. On Purim a Jew is not stingy." Motl also knows his way around things and both sides are satisfied.

So the business goes from year to year. Jews are Haman's downfall, that is, Itsikl Glezer's downfall, as his own father Yisroel, Nikolai's soldier, who is King Akhashverus, orders him to be hanged. Mordecai the Jew walks around with the big tin crown on his head and everyone bows to him. And Motl looks at the audience and thinks, "It will be Pesach, and I will have you all under my thumb."

So it always was and so it will certainly continue wherever people follow the customs. Every year there is Purim, every year we read the Megillah, beat Haman, and hang him. In truth, Haman remains Haman with his own torments, but Jews remain Jews, too. The folk is eternal.

Eternal, also, are day and night, summer and winter; maybe it has to be that way. And maybe our Motl Farber would have remained a painter in the summer, a merry pauper in the winter, and a *purimshpieler* on Purim and forever after, if it had not been for the incident with the police.

The story with the police goes like this. A few weeks before Purim a new police chief arrived in town from a distant Russian city. He had never heard of Jews or any of their customs. And just before he became acquainted with Jews and their customs, Purim slipped in.

He already knew something about what Purim meant, but he certainly had no concept of a *purimshpiel*. Leaving the police station, he chanced to encounter Motl and his Purim troupe and suddenly saw Itsikl in his Haman's uniform with the chest full of medals and orders. Thinking that this was an important general whom he did not know, the police chief was stunned. He stepped back, straightened up, and brought his hand up to his visor in a salute, as is the custom in such a situation. Haman—Itsikl, that is—realized the error, but pretended not to know. He also brought his hand up to his visor, but in the manner of a higher saluting a lower.

Seeing such a scene, the Jewish and Christian shopkeepers who were standing nearby, broke into laughter. The police chief went pale. He understood that what had happened was a serious error and was greatly embarrassed.

He looked around and saw Mordecai the Jew with his horse; the old king Akhashverus, Itsikl's father with the gold scepter in his hand; Vashti the queen with the boil on her forehead; and Queen Esther wearing a yellow wig, a long veil, and a paper crown on her head. Stringing along behind were remnants in various military uniforms.

Embarrassed and enraged, the police chief turned around and hurried back into the police station where he ordered several policemen out to apprehend "The General" and his group, and ordered the whole lot thrown into jail. And that's how the entire joy of Purim was destroyed for the town.

First of all, pity on Motl Farber and his troupe, who suffered in the cold, dark jail, and God only knew how the whole thing was going to end. And second, everyone was simply shocked: this was no small thing, embarrassing a police chief.

That same day a rumor spread throughout the town that the police chief had decreed an end to the entire *purimshpiel,* so the joyous party of Purim would not be so obvious to others. Jews were out of their heads. Boys and girls cried because their happiness was ruined. It was not a Purim but a Tishah b'Av.

But the Eternal One always sends the cure before the plague.

The police chief's wife had to go shopping that morning, and one of the town's shopkeepers, a modern woman with a glib tongue, recognized the police chief's wife as an old friend. The women kissed and hugged one another like two sisters. What friendship, you might ask, between a police chief's wife and a Jewish shopkeeper? But God, may He be blessed, turns the wheel so that things come out well.

The police chief's wife had once spent the summer in Marienbad where she met the shopkeeper who was also visiting there. While in Marienbad, the police chief's wife became very ill and the Jewish woman did everything under heaven to help her get better. She brought doctors, consulted with them because the police chief's wife did not know any German, and in general, protected her like the apple of her eye. It was natural that she, the sick one, felt a powerful connection to the Jewish woman. Later, though they parted emotionally, as often happens in such cases, they gradually forgot one another.

Now they had come together in different roles: one as a police chief's wife and the other as the proprietor of a store. They both hugged each other again and again and were very touched by it all. As they calmed down and talked of other things, they recalled their experiences in Marienbad and remembered that summer when their friendship had been so warm. The police chief's wife spent several hours at the store and then went home.

That same day in the evening, the Jewish woman dressed in her finest clothes and went to call upon the police chief to plead for the arrestees. The young woman was now transformed into Queen Esther, but not so naïve, and she shone and glowed like the morning star.

She was received very warmly at the police chief's house. The police chief already knew that this was the Jewish woman who had once saved his wife in her illness, need, and loneliness. After a long chat about other matters, as is necessary in such a case, the pretty young "Esther" said to the police chief, "I have something to request of you. No, I have a favor to ask of you."

The police chief was quite surprised. "A favor of me? I would do anything within my power to help you!" he said in his own language, but much as it is written in the Megillah.

So the Jewish woman told him the entire story of Purim, about giving little gifts of food, and about the Purim play in which the Megillah story is acted out. And that today, probably because he did not know about this custom, he had arrested the entire company of poor and innocent Jewish *purimshpielers,* who had been anticipating this day as though it were an annual fair. With their earnings from their performances today, they would be able to buy provisions for the holiday of Passover, and to settle their debts from the past winter.

The police chief laughed good-naturedly, and asked that all the Jewish arrestees be brought before him. He asked their intercessor to remain seated beside him. He wanted to see their presentation and she would translate the entire story into Russian.

Motl and his troupe were brought in and they were honored with glasses of cognac and snacks. Then they were asked to perform. The audience warmed to them and it was a lively evening. The jailbirds played out the story merrily and the police chief laughed, even though he did not understand it. The police chief freed all the players and the whole town was as though restored.

Everyone rejoiced and from that time on, the lovely young shopkeeper was known throughout the town as "Queen Esther."

FIVE

YOSL ALGEBRENIK AND HIS STUDENT

(In honor of my colleague and friend I. L. Peretz)

Yosl was a middle-sized Jew who was hardly distinguishable from other Jewish teachers by his height or by his face. The rabbi, the slaughterer, and many others had high, half-round foreheads like Yosl's, but no one had eyes like his. Whoever looked into his eyes could never forget them.

Some said, "They are wise, trusting eyes. When they look at you, they press into your heart and make it light and secure. Unwillingly, and even without understanding what he is saying, you must believe and love him."

Others said, "He has sharp, cutting eyes. With one look they can obliterate the most haughty man, who would no longer have any desire to argue or mock him."

But everyone agreed that there was a quiet fire like an eternal lamp that burned in Yosl's eyes, illuminated his face, and distinguished him from other Jews like him, so that it was hard to forget his face.

It was his nature to listen calmly and to be silent. It was hard to get a word out of him. But when he did speak, pearls literally poured from his mouth, assembled and strung out on a thread.

He generally spoke in terms of algebra. "One must learn algebra, one must think and live in algebra! Only algebra and algebraic logic teaches the human mind to think properly and to properly understand a thing. Without algebra," he insisted, "a person could be acquainted with everything, but know nothing."

And he taught, "The difference between knowledge and comprehension is as vast as that between blind faith and reason, or between talk and action, or just beginning to approach a thing and having it!" So he wanted all Jews, all people, even little children in cheder, to learn the principles of algebra as the very first thing, so they could accustom their minds from childhood to think and understand everything through algebraic weights and measures. Through algebra they would conceive of ideas differently and understand the world and its purposes differently.

But people ridiculed him: "He wants to bring *Meshiekh* through algebra; it's a kind of sickness." And that is why they called him "*Algebrenik*," "the Algebra-man."

Whether this was a curse put on him by some rebbe, or whether it was a kind of madness—may heaven preserve us—no one knew, but people said that it simply had to be one or the other. The town's older householders who remembered by-gone times, said that Yosl had studied Talmud until he was thirty years old. It was thought that he might become the greatest genius in the world, and the most important Jewish communities were already encouraging him to take the position as their chief rabbi. There was not a scholar of comparable depth and intelligence, but suddenly—and no one remembers the reason for it or what brought him to it—Yosl tossed aside the Talmud and the commentaries, and took up mathematics.

It was because of mathematics that he studied languages until he reached algebra, and here he dug his grave. From then on, he was absorbed only in algebra. He wrote down numbers and letters from the Latin alphabet. He drew squares with his quill and large and small circles that were intricately tangled together with one another. He added letters—some kind of code—spending days and years at it and never picking up a holy book.

But can you say that Yosl got anything from it? That anything came out of all his labor? "May the enemies of Zion find the same limitations that he has found in his algebra!" wished the townspeople.

And even when he encountered some strange little prince of a student who was preparing for his exams—who came to him for a few hours to learn algebra—did he take any great happiness from it? If someone paid him, that was good, but if they did not, it was all right, too. The favor that someone did for him in letting him explain his algebra was payment enough, and he did not need to add a kopeck into the deal. His own wife said that it was fine that her husband had nothing, because if he had, he would probably pay people to come learn algebra from him.

Nevertheless, the townspeople considered Yosl a smart man, and they used him for arbitration and mediation, and told stories of his tremendous good sense and essential comprehension of every matter. Even the finest householders sent their children to him to spend a few hours a day teaching them Talmud, a little arithmetic, or some languages, as is the custom these days. And that is how he earned his living.

He did not want to organize a cheder like most simple elementary school teachers. He had no time for it. He needed to study algebra for himself. He needed time. Sometimes he would spend three years working on the same thing.

And it was not easy for him to get even the two or three students that studied with him. Each time he was given a student to teach, it was on the condition—on which he had to take an oath—that algebra would not be taught. It was clear that this pained Yosl a good deal. It was his hope, and you could see it in his face, that *this* boy would be the one to whom he could teach algebra. His persuasions, pleading, and promising did not help. The fathers and mothers of the town's children feared algebra as they did some evil spirit, may heaven protect us.

"This must be a very difficult subject," they said, "that can divert the sharpest mind from the correct path. Yosl himself is the evidence of this. Is there a better head or a sharper mind than his? And what became of that good head and that sharp mind? A poor man. A pauper who can barely get through each day. If his children did not send him a few rubles from America, he would starve on what he makes as a teacher!" And what argument did he bring to counter this attitude? Algebra!

Only one single time was he lucky and permitted to teach a student algebra. The story goes like this: Reb Mayer Goldman, the town's wealthiest man and main contractor, was looking for a teacher for his only son, Neykhele, a boy who had just become bar mitzvah. The boy was reputed to be a prodigy and the greatest teachers in town were not good enough for him.

Of course, Mayer was a little "Enlightened" himself, and was kindly disposed to algebra, and he became convinced that there was no better teacher in the world for his only son than Yosl. So he sent for Yosl, who interviewed Neykhele, and was very pleased with the boy.

"Let me teach him as I see fit," Yosl said happily, "and I will draw out of your son the person that he can and must become!"

The rich man was thrilled, but he made it a special condition that Neykhele's mother must never know what Yosl was teaching their child. "A woman is a woman," the rich man said about his wife. "I cannot ask her to be more clever than the other men in our town. If she should, heaven forbid, hear that her only son is studying algebra with you, I would have to run away from her or even get a divorce. Fear clutches her if she even hears the word 'algebra.' Probably even God Himself could not explain to her that there is no danger in algebra. She cannot understand it with her own sense, and even the Master of the

Universe cannot convince her that anyone could study algebra and—don't be put off by this—remain in his right mind. So it's no wonder that she doesn't believe in it.

"So what did I do to make her agree to bring Neykhele to you to teach? I told her that I had even more fear of algebra than she does and that I am certain that algebra will not be part of his studies. But I am telling you that you may teach Neykhele a little algebra if his mind seems to comprehend it. But be sure that no one knows, not even Neykhele himself, that what you are teaching him is algebra."

Yosl agreed and Neykhele became his pupil. He was not to take on any additional pupils and Mayer paid him a tuition for one student that he might not have gotten from another ten.

It soon became clear that Neykhele was the very pupil that Yosl had been searching for all his life. Whatever he taught him, Neykhele's sharp mind took it in. Yosl gradually acquainted him with the methods of algebra and composed a little book for his student. He called it, "The Best Logic," and with the book, he taught Neykhele proper thinking and proper comprehension of a thing. Yosl called the study of algebra, "Logic," and he kept the name "algebra" a secret from the boy until Neykhele had already gotten a substantial knowledge of it.

Yosl loved his student as he did his own life, and Neykhele looked upon Yosl as his rebbe. Yosl paid so much attention to his student that he hardly made a step without him. And it was said that Neykhele did not eat a bite unless his rebbe was eating with him. The world had probably never seen such love of a rebbe for a student or of a student for his rebbe.

Even Neykhele's mother soon saw the advantage of a teacher such as Yosl. Her Neykhele, who had always been a spoiled only son with his own wild whims, had become another child entirely: so smart and steady, speaking with such understanding like a grownup. So she showered Yosl's wife with gifts, and Yosl became her most beloved guest.

Yosl himself remarked that he was happier during that time when he was teaching Neykhele than at any other time in his life. "God has surely sent me an angel," he said, "who has made my heart lighter. And the angel is my pupil who has already begun to understand me, and who will with time, understand me completely!" Yosl had never wanted or wished for more.

But his beloved student had one flaw: he often, out of the clear blue sky, became lost in thought. When Yosl would ask him, "What are you thinking, Neykhele?" he would be like one awakened from a deep sleep and not know what to answer.

Another time he would gaze into the sky, literally unable to tear his eyes from the golden clouds under which the sun glowed in the evening. He would look at the clouds until they had melted away or until they had lost their golden borders and were ordinary clouds again like any others.

Sometimes it happened that Yosl went out walking in the open field outside the town and Neykhele was elated by everything he saw. "Over here, over here!" he shouted enthusiastically, pulling his rebbe by the hand to go with him into the forest, although it was some distance away and hard for Yosl to keep up with him.

"What do you see there, child?" the rebbe asked him, having no idea what drew Neykhele towards the forest.

"Oh, it is so beautiful!" Neykhele shouted, his eyes beaming with enthusiasm. And Yosl wondered what kind of beauty he saw there.

If Neykhele found a flower along the path, he bent down and kissed it, as though it were a normal thing to do. But if Yosl stepped on a flower, Neykhele cried out as though he had felt the pain himself. He picked the flower up, pressed it to his heart, and tears formed in his eyes.

"A child, but such a child!" mused Yosl consoling himself. "It's no wonder that a rich child, reared with all kinds of ornaments and toys, thinks that the flowers in the field, the clouds in the sky, the forest, and everything that his eye sees is a child's game. As if nature created them all for him to play with. Once he gets older, he will learn that clouds are just vapor, the gold on them is just a reflection of the sun, and the point of the flowers is the fruit that grows out of them, and so it is with everything."

But over time, both the rebbe and the student became so accustomed to one another that they no longer looked for any flaws or found any flaws in the other. It seemed to them that they would study together this way forever; that they would never be parted.

Until one day, when Neykhele arrived home and his mother fell on him with tears in her eyes and told him that she knew that he was studying algebra. How did she find out? The doctor had told her and she asked if the doctor was trying to make her ill? Rather, said the doctor, he had told her the truth in order to share her pride, to praise her only son, who was able to solve the most difficult algebraic problems.

She did not need to hear any more than that. She was already sick from horror and worry for her poor child and what his father—the thief—had done with him! She feared, even though Neykhele protested, that he might already be, heaven forbid, losing his mind.

Neykhele comforted her, swore that, on the contrary, algebra helped him to understand every subject more deeply and more clearly. But talking to her was like talking to a wall.

It was like Yom Kipper in the house. She did not eat, she did not drink, and she never took her reddened eyes off her child. Let the world turn upside down, she screamed, she would not allow her only child to go back to Yosl. She would not allow Neykhele to completely lose his mind, heaven forbid, studying Yosl's cursed algebra. She would not allow Neykhele to become a failure like Yosl *Algebrenik!*

It was a real catastrophe that night in the rich man's house. The father and son fought against the mother. They struggled the whole night and she triumphed. She might not have won had her terrible nerves and spasms not come to her aid. In order to calm her so that she would not lose her mind and go running to Yosl and tear out his beard and break his windows—as she swore she would do—father and son conceded and made peace. The peace cost Neykhele half his life.

In the morning, instead of Neykhele, it was Mayer Goldman who arrived at Yosl's cheder. He explained the entire episode, apologized a thousand times, promised to pay the tuition until Neykhele's wedding, but Neykhele could no longer be Yosl's student.

"I don't need your tuition," Yosl began to answer calmly, but suddenly his fiery eyes flamed, and he shouted, "I will get another pupil who will pay tuition! But you, you thief, give me back my friend, that unique pure soul who understands me! I will be so lonely, so alone!"

Mayer was so shocked by Yosl's eyes and by his tormented shouting that he soon took his leave. Coming home, Mayer told his wife that he now realized that she was right.

Neykhele, however, was not so quickly calmed. He did not want to study with any other rebbe. He did not talk, did not eat, did not drink, and would not be comforted in any way. They called the doctor for help and it was decided that the rich woman would take him away to another country and show him the world. The trip would distract him and he would forget about his rebbe.

The prospect of traveling abroad with his mother to see beautiful mountains, valleys, and large cities as was described to him, pleased Neykhele, and he said, "So let's travel, let's not stay here!"

Before he left, Neykhele sent his rebbe a note asking him not to be angry with him. He would come to ask forgiveness himself, he wrote, but they would not let him go. He was as though in a prison; they never let him out of their sight. But he did ask the rebbe to take the trouble to come to the train station at nine o'clock to say goodbye to him. Otherwise he could never rest.

At nine o'clock Yosl walked to the train station and looked for his student. There were several relatives traveling together, people who served Mayer Goldman, and domestics that hang around a rich provider. There were even religious functionaries from the town. Yosl saw the crowd and saw Neykhele's father and mother from a distance, but he did not see Neykhele himself. He did not want to go to the crowd and ask, and his eyes searched from afar for a chance to see his student alone for a moment.

It appeared that the parents had encircled their child with their own people on purpose, so that Neykhele would not see his rebbe. But suddenly Neykhele tore away from the crowd, ran to Yosl, threw himself on him, and began kissing his hands. Yosl stroked the boy's head and soothed him, the father and mother and friends came running, amazed that the brilliant child clung so tightly to the old, wizened, shabbily dressed Jew. But no one had the heart to separate them.

Mayer was embarrassed at that moment that his only son clung to this strange Jew with a love that was greater than anything the father had seen from his own child. The mother quietly spit three times and whispered a protective prayer for her child, and maybe she also called all kinds of curses onto the *Algebrenik's* head. Yet she was afraid to approach, take her child by the hand and tear him away from this crazy old man.

Finally a bell sounded. Neykhele kissed his rebbe once more and the rebbe gave him a kiss in return. Then Yosl told him to go into the train car with his mother. At the third bell, Yosl shouted into the car, "Don't forget, Neykhele, what you studied with me!"

"I will remember, Rebbe! And I will not forget you either!"

Yosl did not wait for the train to move. He started to walk back home. It was already late and he had a long way to go.

Soon, however, Mayer Goldman's coach drove up with a pair of horses in harness. When Mayer saw Yosl and how dejectedly he was dragging along, the rich man told his coachman to stop, and he himself got out to ask Yosl to get into the coach.

"Why should you have to go by foot?" Mayer asked. "Come, I will drive you home. And perhaps you would allow me to have you over for dinner? Why not? My Alte is traveling, in good health. Who do you have to be afraid of?"

"Afraid?" Yosl repeated and looked at the rich man.

In that moment, the rich man felt poorer and lower than the poor little Jew who so piteously dragged himself home by foot. He was unable to find an answer to Yosl's question.

Yosl did not wait for an answer and continued on his way.

*   *   *   *   *

Since that day, several years have gone by and Neykhele has still not come home. People said that he was studying somewhere abroad where there were no *algebreniks,* and where the rich woman, Mayer Goldman's wife, was certain that her only child would not be tempted anymore with the dangers of algebra.

And as it turned out, not only did the student forget the rebbe, the rebbe forgot the student. Because from that time on no one heard Yosl talk about Neykhele or even mention his name. He soon found another couple of boys that he taught Khumesh with Rashi's commentaries. Algebra was not mentioned.

There were several Jewish book peddlers in town and three or four Christian book dealers. When Yosl could scrape together a ruble, he was off to one of the book dealers. He knew the book dealers well, and all the people in their shops. Often he would stand and look at the thousands of books, reading the names on their spines, and not finding anything he needed, he would say softly to himself, "Why so much chaff and so little wheat?"

Yosl could come ten or twenty times and go away not having found a book in the great mass of books for which to exchange his ruble. But when he found what he was looking for, he did not go away until he bought it. He did not bargain. He paid what was asked. If he did not have the whole amount, they let him have it on his word. They knew that he would not owe it for long.

And what did he buy? Just what no other customer would pick up. The book dealers knew what the poor Jew wanted for his sweated ruble. Even an outsider not from the Jewish neighborhood knew they called him *Algebrenik.*

Arriving at the study house early one morning, as was his habit, Yosl found the group gathered in a circle talking about the dowry some bridegroom would bring. Yosl heard the chatter from a distance, but it did not interest him, until he heard the names: "Mayer Goldman," "Neykhl," and the words, "He is a great author, he writes and gets printed in the newspapers." But why should he listen to such babble from people who had no more to do than talk about each other and wish for things they would never get?

But the group was curious to hear Yosl's opinion on the topic. "What do you say, Reb Yosl, about your former student?" one of them asked.

"About Neykhele? Has he come home?" Yosl asked, just as though he had never had any other student in his life.

"And who do you think we are talking about?" asked someone in response to his question. "Of course he has come home!"

"A shame," said Yosl with a sigh. "I had such high hopes for him."

"How does he fall short then?" asked Goldman's houseman, who was, it appeared, very interested in assuring that his boss's son's name be famous in the town. "I can tell you that Neykhele is now a finer person than you ever thought."

"I wish him well," said Yosl, "but I doubt very much that he went further with the things we used to study and pursue."

"Of course, you mean algebra!" Goldman's houseman laughed. "He thinks he can bring the Messiah with algebra!"

Yosl did not answer again. He just gave a piteous look at the jokester. The look had an effect on the rest of the group and everyone fell silent with nothing left to say. Yosl noticed it and it vexed him, as he had not meant to disrupt the group from talking about something that gave them pleasure. He said, "I am sure that my Neykhele continued to study algebra and I am sure I can welcome him back."

The group felt better after these words and went back to betting on the dowry and talking about the kind of bride a rich man's accomplished only son was likely to take.

After praying, no one stays long in the shul unless someone calls out announcements or the cantor goes to the pulpit. And the cantor never wasted any time going to the pulpit if people wanted to talk. The cantor was a Jew, too, and had a knack for talking. And what does a Jew enjoy talking about most? About someone else's luck or someone else's children and whether or not they are successful!

But Yosl wanted to get home quickly to tell his wife that Neykhele had come home and that they should get the house in order and prepare to welcome their guest. He had no doubt that Neykhele would come. How could he not come? He had to come!

Yosl was busy the whole day and in a holiday mood. He helped to put the house in order and arranged his books and papers. A white cloth was spread on the table and three clean glasses with spoons were set out, along with an old silver sugar box. In the kitchen, there was a brightly polished little samovar and near it coals lay prepared so that when the guest arrived everything would be ready to heat up the tea.

Finally in the evening, the door opened and a tall, handsome young man of eighteen or nineteen walked into the house. He was carrying a package.

Yosl quickly recognized his student, perhaps because he was expecting him. The student knew the rebbe even more quickly. Yosl had gotten a little older, but his appearance had changed little. Yosl began to get up, to take a few steps towards his dear guest, but in a moment, the guest had run to him and kissed his rebbe.

They stood still for a few minutes as they both lacked words to say to each other. Finally, Yosl began, "You are the same as you were in your enthusiasm. I cannot deny that you are taller and broader. It makes me so happy to see you like this. Sit down and tell me, my son, how have you been? What have you seen? I don't need to ask about your studies; your wisdom shows on your face."

The guest sat at the table across from his rebbe, telling him about his life abroad and about the cities he had visited. "And Rebbe," he said, remembering the gift that he had brought, "I did not forget you completely, and whenever I found a book that I thought would be useful to you, I bought it for you!"

While saying this, he untied the package he had placed on the table, which was full of mathematics books in German and French. Yosl took the package eagerly and pulled it over to the edge of the table near the window. Out of curiosity, and so as not to embarrass his guest by not looking at them, Yosl began leafing through the books. He was always ready to read about algebra, and his head bent lower and lower over the pages. Eventually he was so engrossed in the books that he completely forgot his guest.

It was a good thing that his wife came in with a little tray of glasses filled with tea and told the guest a little about herself. She did not have much time to talk, however. She excused herself and went back to the kitchen. Because of this dear guest, she wanted to run to the marketplace to buy sugar cookies to go with the tea. She had not bought them earlier, because if Neykhele had not come, it would have been a waste of money.

Yosl sank deeper and deeper into the new books that lay before him and the guest had time to look at his former teacher and think about him. "Heaven and earth," thought Neykhl, "he does not talk. Instead he listens as the white pages with silent black letters and numbers talk to him. He finds more life and harmony in these books than in bright, free nature. He has immersed his whole life in them—his whole world—so why should I be vexed or surprised that he is drinking in the joy from the books I brought him? People are not alive for him so much as people's ideas. I cannot imagine such a life. I shudder to see my beloved rebbe like this, almost dead, so dead to the world, so cold and dry towards life!"

When the rebbetzin returned from the marketplace with her sugar cookies, she found both men deeply absorbed: her husband in the open book and his guest in his own thoughts. "Yosl!" she scolded, taking her husband by the sleeve as though she were waking him from a deep sleep. "Yosl, is this how you treat your beloved guest? The tea is already ice-cold! Oy, men, men, they don't know which end is up! So, that's enough!" she went on. "You will have plenty of time to dream day and night over your books!"

Yosl lifted his head and looked around as though he had just arrived from another world. With one look at his guest, he noticed that his earlier natural happiness had left his face. "Akh, that's my old illness, my son! I'm beginning to think that I am not suitable for company," he said, almost to himself. "You know yourself that these dead books are like my living friends, and I cannot humiliate them by not hearing out their theories, or understanding their proofs."

The guest's heart clenched hearing the rebbe answer a question that he himself had not wanted to ask.

"What are you thinking, my son?" said Yosl, attempting to cheer him up.

"Nothing, nothing!" Neykhl answered, as though lost in thought.

"Is that just your old habit," asked Yosl, "of suddenly falling into deep thought—like you used to do—and not knowing what to answer when someone asked you what you were thinking?"

"No, Rebbe," the guest replied, feeling a little more cheerful. "Now I know what I am thinking. If you will allow me, I will say openly what I was thinking about you just now."

"Of course, please do Neykhele, tell me. It is very important at our first meeting to know what you are thinking about me."

"Yes, Rebbe," said the student, openheartedly expressing his concern that his teacher seemed to expect so little from the world and from life.

"No, my son," Yosl answered. "Perhaps you are right in some details, but in general you've mistaken me. Don't think that I do not know that there is other wisdom beyond algebra and higher mathematics, that there are other sciences and ideas that must occupy the human mind. I also know that learning alone is not the point, but the *doing*. But my belief is that the learning will bring about the *doing!* And one can only do that through algebra and algebraic logic. One employs algebra for mathematics because with large numbers and spaces it is impossible to do without it.

"However, I want algebraic logic to be the foundation for all those human thoughts for which we often cannot find the right solution. I want the human mind to become as accustomed to that logic as feet are to walking, hands are to doing, or the fingers of a good musician are to playing an instrument. We will comprehend the sciences differently, will think about them differently, and our lives in the world will be quite different!

"I do not see *tikkun olam,* the repair of the world, in the new machines of which there are so many. These have created their own problems without improving the character of humankind. I see it in the course of study that the new generations must pursue. In that course of study, the young mind must be accustomed from the very beginning to properly understand things, to properly conceive of things. Even before you show a child the letter *alef,* he should be accustomed to algebraic logic. Step-by-step the child should be taught how to measure by the scale of algebraic logic, until he is naturally accustomed to it. Only then may you teach him what you want. Then the teacher can be a teacher, and the pupil a pupil, and the learning will result in action."

"Will humankind be made happy through this?" asked Neykhl, having heard something quite unexpected from his rebbe.

"If there is happiness for mortal man," Yosl answered, "then humankind will be happy! In any case, life itself will be a happier life than it is now."

"How would that be?" asked the student, and in his voice there was another question: "Why is your own life, Rebbe, so sad, so unhappy? You are certainly thinking with algebraic logic."

"How, you ask?" answered Yosl. "Very simply. All doubts will be eliminated with such study. Once everyone knows that whatever cannot be figured out with logic is not true, then practically all obstacles and forces that keep people from being happy will disappear. People will not do what is not right and will not allow others to do it either. That is my algebra, my thinking, and my wish for the world," said Yosl, almost as though he were talking to himself. "I found the truth in algebraic logic and I see the repair of the world in that truth."

The student looked at his rebbe in amazement and thought seriously about his words. Yosl sighed heavily and began to speak from his heart as though he were talking to himself. "Perhaps, the question of why I am not happy bothers you. Why don't I live according to the truth I have found? I came to the idea too late, my son! For thirty years in a row, I studied and adapted my mind to Rebbe Ishmael's *Thirteen Principles* by which the Torah is expounded. The algebraic logic that I became acquainted with in that thirty-first year demanded that I remake my mind so that I would now think only with logic! A person sits in a cellar for thirty years and accustoms his eyes to the darkness. Then people want him to live outdoors and be happy with the sunlight."

Yosl fell silent, deep in thought. His eyes had no expression, not for his guest who sat opposite him, or for the world, or for the times in which he had lived his sixty-odd years.

Neykhl also sat thinking, but his eyes rested on his pensive rebbe. And what wonder and sympathy his eyes expressed!

"And that's not even all," Yosl quietly began again to pour out his heart. "It is not one person, not one algebraic head that can construct the new building for repairing the world. An entire generation must be educated, must grow up in the light and purity of logic, knowing that he can comprehend the world and the truth. I am only one, one in a town of thirty thousand Jews, brothers who have always been frightened of me.

"You alone, Neykhele, are the only pure soul in my entire life who loved me with his whole heart, even though you were a child who did not understand very much. And do you know what hopes I put in you, and do you know what pain it caused me when you were torn away from me so suddenly?"

Yosl shook his head. "No, I don't want to talk about that, I will just tell you that I was so lonely in my own town with thirty thousand Jewish brothers who made me ill from their ignorance and with their ignorance.

"If I had been born an eagle," he went on, "an eagle who was supposed to fly high up to the sun, the first thirty years of my life plucked me feather by feather. My entire strength of spirit and strength of heart died in me and I feel as weak as a little chick for disputing the world and waging war against falsehood. Akh, there are plenty of excuses I can make so I don't have to be disgusted with myself or hate myself. And why am I telling you all this now, my student? If I tell you, you will be disgusted with me and hate me too!"

"Akh, Rebbe, Rebbe!" Neykhl finally found the words to say. "As a child, how little I knew you! How well I understand you now!"

The next day, Yosl went to visit his student as Neykhele had so urgently asked him to promise. He was so engrossed in his own thoughts that he barely noticed the many changes in the rich man's house, where he had once been such a frequent guest. Goldman had gotten much richer in the intervening six years, and had made his house larger and decorated it in the richest style. Neykhele's parents welcomed Yosl with joy and he greeted them with a demeanor of peace. A conversation began between the rebbe and his student, which the parents did not interfere with, but listened from a distance to their only son's intelligent conversation.

The student told his rebbe what was going on in the wide world. He explained many new ideas and new currents in human thought that had inspired him and hoped that his wise teacher would be inspired by them, too. Yosl listened intently to Neykhele's explanations. It clearly gave him pleasure to hear all this.

"Not all these ideas are right or possible to carry out," Yosl remarked, "and I am not happy with all of them, but since we search for new ideas, it is good to know that there are so many that have the audacity to express themselves. But I tell you, my son, that another hundred of such new ideas will be born and be abandoned, and the human condition will come to the truth that the repair of the world can only be accomplished through a new course of study that includes algebraic logic, as I explained to you yesterday."

Going with Neykhele into his study, the rebbe said, "Until now all we have talked about is what the world is thinking and doing. Tell me, what are you yourself thinking?"

The student was perplexed and did not know how to answer. "Should I tell him which things I agree with?" he wondered. "Did he ask which of the ideas that I have explained in such detail are the ones I like?"

Yosl quickly comprehended his student's embarrassment and to help him out of it said, "People say that you have written books and that what you write is printed in newspapers. Read me one of your pieces, Neykhele. I would like to hear which of the new ideas you accept."

"I write poetry, Rebbe, or what we Jews call 'psalms.' I also write observations and mood pieces," Neykhl answered with a note of satisfaction."

"Read me something you've written, I want to hear," asked the rebbe.

The student read aloud in an inspired voice a sketch about an early spring morning in the countryside and his feelings when his eyes beheld the beauty of nature. Yosl listened quietly, considering the student's movements, his voice, his happiness, and shrugged his shoulders, unable to understand what use this was, why someone would write it, or what there was to be so enthused about.

"Is it an accurate picture, Rebbe?" Neykhl asked, awaiting his teacher's agreement.

"And if it is accurate?" asked Yosl in return. "What use is it? Are you God's bookkeeper, that you must describe His own things for Him? Who does not know this, and who would fail to know it if you had not taken the trouble to write about it? Wasn't it like that years ago and won't it still be like that a year from now as it is today?"

"No, Rebbe, nature is always beautiful," the student answered, "but her beauty is not always the same. Her image changes every minute, every moment, and so the pictures of her change. What my eye missed seeing a moment ago, I can see now, and in another moment later, there will be another beautiful thing! So people describe it, try to capture the beautiful picture in words on paper, because in a moment nature will change the picture again. The poet is not God's bookkeeper, but his own bookkeeper, whose own eye sees to record the moment, just so that he might see it again in his mind and feel his spirit moved by it again."

"But what use is it?" asked Yosl. "What good for the world comes out of it?"

"It will be difficult for me to explain it to you, Rebbe, if you lack the eyes and feeling for God's beauty!" said Neykhl with respect, but also with annoyance. "Allow me to quickly say that besides reason, logic, and algebra—which I value and honor in you very much—a person also has *senses*. The world offers other ways to feel life and to appreciate the good in life. The senses awaken and inspire the poet and artist in us to record and create!"

While speaking, he took the rebbe by the hand, and led him into a lavishly furnished room, where he showed him item after item: beautiful vessels, paintings, woodcarvings, and drawings, and he explained the artistic work that went into creating each one of them. Then he sat Yosl in a soft chair and went to the piano, where he began to play a Jewish melody that he was sure Yosl would know. Gradually he went from that melody into others, touching, melancholy melodies that his dear listener would appreciate.

At first Yosl was a little angry with his student. Why did he want to show off his ability to play the piano? But gradually the sounds entered his heart, and there they soothed and warmed him until he began to feel his stony heart soften somewhat and began to rock himself as though in a sweet dream. He felt something deep inside that he had never felt before.

The student played more touchingly, more emotionally, and more comfortingly. Yosl listened as though intoxicated. Sighs escaped from his heart. He was reminded of something more lovely, better, and more light-filled, but he did not know what it was.

Meanwhile, the sun began to set and its last rays began to reflect and change colors in the crystal chandelier, throwing a fiery, bewitching light on the inspired pianist and on his swaying, pensive listener. Neykhl stopped playing, went over to his rebbe, took him by the hand, and led him to the window to show him the setting sun. In a moving voice, he said, "Rebbe, don't you see how beautifully the colors change, how everything is alive, moving and soaking in the beauty of the surrounding glory? Don't you feel the joy in your heart to see all this with your own eyes, to grasp this with your consciousness, and at the same time to feel a part of it all; that the world is for you, too, Rebbe? Perhaps everything can be figured out with algebra but you can only feel with your heart!"

Yosl did not answer. Lost in thought, he sat back down, but now his thinking was different. His student had never seen him like this before. A kind of weariness from despair lay in Yosl's expression. His bearing was different somehow and his eyes expressed trouble and loneliness, as for something long lost, vanished, that could never be recovered again.

The student stepped away from the old rebbe, who sat deep in thought. Neykhl did not have the courage to disturb or comfort him. He waited with sympathy and love until Yosl could settle the war going on inside himself.

The father and mother stood far off, regarding their fine son with awe and pride, listening to his inspiring talk, and looking with wonder at the old bent-over Jew who sat conquered and stunned by their child, who had once been his student.

Suddenly Yosl got up from his chair. He straightened himself up so that it looked as though he had become taller, fresher, and stronger. The sparkle returned to his eyes and with a firm and sure voice he said, "The world is made new every day, say our sages. I had not understood that concept until you showed me how the world is made new every hour, every moment. You have taught me a chapter of the praise-songs that I have never known. Nevertheless I will still say again and again that I found the truth in algebraic logic and in that truth I see the repair of the world!"

Saying these words, Yosl's eyes wandered again to the setting sun. The rays shone on his face and his eyes followed the golden clouds to take in the entire glory and enormity of the moment far away. And as he stood there with the sun reflecting on his face, a deep sigh tore from his heart that said more than words could ever say: "Your world is beautiful, O God, and my eyes have just seen it for the very first time!"

SIX

NONSENSE: THE COMMUNITY GOAT

A *narishkayt,* a foolishness, is remembered says the world, and this indeed is true. Foolishness is the opposite of wisdom, just as darkness is the opposite of light. We are pleased by the light of dawn because it sweeps away the discomfort of night's darkness. By not dwelling on our childhood follies, we improve our chances of becoming sensible and wise. Yet recalling some childhood follies has been useful in my life.

I have encountered many difficult questions for which I have desired an expert opinion. There are questions about human dealings that have tormented me to find an answer. Yet no amount of reasoning can help in understanding something that goes completely against reason. But a childish foolishness—unsearched for and unconsidered—has often helped me solve a difficult question which no sage with all his wisdom could answer.

The Dreyfus Lawsuit—the Dreyfus Affair—for example, awakened many questions in me that gave me no rest; questions that may not have touched others as deeply as they touched me. My heart has pained me as much for the innocent victim as for his innocent family, but at least that pain has helped me find an explanation: I know as well as I am a Jew, that the body, no matter how far its limbs are spread out in the wide world, is so bound together, that if any part of the body is wounded, the farthest limb still feels the pain.

This has always been the best indictor to me that the Jewish body, however hurt or broken, remains forever fresh and young, still filled with blood and life and with hardly a paralyzed limb on it despite enduring so much wrong and torment for so many years.

Our enemies, I suppose, know this better than we do, so they seek out a limb to strike in their attempt to cause pain in the whole Jewish body. And that was the main intention of the whole noise and commotion that became known as "The Dreyfus Trial." I was able to calm myself by knowing how a sick person can be comforted when it is clear that his present difficulties are not from a new illness but from an old fever that was never quite cured.

In truth, even a child can make the same mistake when he has had his first taste of a raging fever and then thinks, in the time between one bout and the next, that the fever is past and he is well again. The Jew, however, does not forget, rarely resting, never forgetting, that the enemy is for him a kind of fever, may heaven preserve us. It may let up for awhile, but will certainly return, and it is fomenting even now in France between one bout and the next. Even though the doctors may give it a new name, it is nothing more than the old fever. Long known and as bitter as it is, it is still not the kind of illness one dies from, although it is certainly rattling our bones right now.

I remember a scene in cheder. The rebbe was striking a boy. One of the stricken boy's friends approached the rebbe, kissed the sleeve of his coat, and tearfully begged the rebbe to let his friend go.

For his good heart, this boy received several hard blows from the rebbe's elbow. Then, when the stricken boy got up from the bench, he let loose his anger and pain on his faithful friend, grabbing him by the hair, throwing him to the ground, and stomping him with his feet.

It seems to me that during the French-German war, no people or nation prayed to God for France in a manner to match our Jews. Are we not now seeing in France the same justice, or perhaps the same psychological attitude, as that cheder boy who took out his anger at the rebbe on his loyal friend? The rod is guilty of everything, and only the rod!

And "The honor of the Army," which we hear shouted so often in the streets of Paris and which, by merely pronouncing it, turns night to day and day to night. What kind of incantation is this? I confess that I do not believe in the supernatural power of an incantation, whether from a Baal Shem, a regular Jew, or even a Tartar. The power of such a formula is inconceivable to me. And yet, because of this incantation, a known bandit and swindler, Esterhazy, whose guilt no one doubts, was released from a lawsuit and accompanied by a parade as he left the courtroom. A royal prince kissed him and half of Paris shouted, "Long live Esterhazy!"

Because of this incantation, people scorned the world-famous Zola, who more than any other man, rescued France's honor. People treated him like a common criminal, forbidding him to say one true word. And half of Paris followed suit, throwing mud at him, while the entire educated world marveled at this great writer who had the courage to demonstrate that his love for truth and justice was greater than his talent!

Because of this incantation, Zola's badge from the Legion of Honor was taken from him; an award that was given to him by all of educated humanity. Because of this incantation, five ministers swore falsely; openly and solemnly swore falsely.

When it seemed that the sky was clear and fair with the truth shining out like the brilliant sun, a voice was heard: "The honor of the Army!" and the once-bright sky covered over with heavy black clouds and the sunshine disappeared.

And what about the honor of the Army? And who is the Army? Is the Army not the people itself? Is the Army's honor of a different kind? For what people in the world are law and judgment, truth and justice, not an honor? Why should the honor of France's Army be offended through law and judgment, truth and justice?

And even when that honor might suffer due to a few representatives of the Army, what kind of violation is that? Is the Army not made up of thousands of different individuals just like the French people? Does one incident show that the entire French people have no honesty and no conscience because Esterhazy is French? Esterhazy and his like are just individuals whose crimes can no more stain a people of some thirty-thousand than a few drops of muddy water can dirty the entire ocean. One asks these questions when one is convinced that all this trouble has come about because of the formula, "The honor of the Army."

*   *   *   *   *

I recall another folly from my childhood. It is one of those silly things that one remembers just because it is so silly.

We were already old enough to study Torah and we had studied up to *parsha Vayishlach*.

"Say it," commanded the rebbe, "*Izim*, goats, *matayim*, two hundred. Two hundred goats!" he marveled. "I don't know that there are that many goats in the whole town. Perele!" he called out to his wife, the rebbetzin, who was sitting in a corner of the cheder knitting a sock. "How many goats do you think there are in our town?"

"How should I know?" she answered.

"How many do you think?" he asked again.

"Including the non-Jewish goats?"

"Let's say with the non-Jewish goats. About how many?"

"Maybe a hundred. I haven't counted them. But why do you ask?"

"I ask it because Jacob our ancestor sent his brother Esau a gift of two hundred goats. Understand?"

"I don't begrudge him!" the rebbetzin interrupted. "How did he get them? If I had two hundred goats I would sell them and buy us a little house of our own."

"Silly woman!" exclaimed the rebbe. "She would buy a little house! You could buy three big houses with a big garden for such a sum of money. Think of how much you would get for two hundred goats!"

"You'd have to have the mind of a statesman to figure that out."

"A statesman?" laughed the rebbe. "I'm no statesman, but maybe I can figure it out. How much did you pay for our goat yesterday at the market?"

"Six rubles! I should live six years of pleasure before I'd have to pay six rubles! He didn't leave me with a single kopeck," complained the rebbetzin.

"Nu," said the rebbe, "it's just simple arithmetic: six times two hundred is a total of . . . Yes, it's twelve hundred, get it Perele? It's a thousand rubles and another two hundred rubles! Today, children, you mustn't forget: back in those days, those goats were not just any goats, not like our kind of goats. Those were *izim*, honest-to-goodness goats of *Erets Yisroel*, the Land of Israel. Do you have any idea what *Erets Yis-roel* goats are? Do you know that this is everything? *Izim*. Say it children, '*Izim!*'

"*Eylim*, rams, *esrim*, twenty. Do you know what *eylim* are?"

"We know!" a few boys called out. "When Avrom was going to sacrifice Itsik, there was an *ayil*, a ram, with his horns caught in the branches, and because he served as the sacrifice instead of Itsik, *eylim*, rams, are honored by making the shofar out of their horns."

"Good, you remember!" the rebbe praised us, happy that we remembered the ram and the whole story around it.

"*Gemalim*, camels, *meynikot uvneyhem*, suckling their children, that is, the little camels; *shloshim*, thirty, remember it well, thirty!" He told us about camels, that they were a kind of horse that you ride on in *Erets Yisroel*. They have two humps on their backs and you sit between them to ride. If the camel gets angry with the rider, he can press the two humps together and suffocate you. He did not explain things like asses and mules.

Going out to the courtyard to play a little after our lessons, and seeing for the first time the goat that the rebbetzin had bought yesterday at the fair for six whole rubles, we greeted it with the verse we had just learned in cheder: "*Izim*, goats, *matayim*, two hundred!" And the goat promptly answered us in its language: "Meeeeeh!"

A few days later, when some of us arrived early at cheder while the rebbe was still at the study house praying, we saw another kind of animal in the yard. This goat was very similar to the rebbe's goat, but much bigger and wilder, with a pair of bigger and stronger horns, a long tail, a broad beard as bushy as Esau's, and such a pair of eyes: scary!

"That must be an *Erets Yisroel* goat," one of the boys called out, remembering that the rebbe had said that the *Erets Yisroel* goats were bigger than the goats in the Exile. One boy wanted to get a greeting from *Erets Yisroel* and so he approached the animal, getting close enough to shake its hand. But the animal got angry for some reason, we didn't know why, and charged us with its terrible horns.

Luckily for us, there was a woodpile in the courtyard that belonged to the nearby bakery. We climbed up on the woodpile and started bombarding the wild beast with chunks of wood.

Suddenly the rebbe spotted us and shouted, "Hoodlums! Rascals! You could, God forbid, kill him! What are you doing to the *bekhor*?"

"Ho? What kind of thing is this?" we asked one another with our eyes, not daring to say a word. "What does the word *bekhor* mean here?"

A *bekhor*, we knew, had to do with firstborn sons. There were two or three boys in cheder who bragged that they were firstborn sons and that they had to fast on the day before Passover. When *Meshiekh*, the Messiah, comes, and God reestablishes the Priesthood among the Temple Priests, the Temple will be given back to the firstborn sons as described in the Torah. But if a wild animal, even one with a beard, could also have such a pedigree and be called a *bekhor*, we, with our childish reasoning, could not comprehend it.

And if he really was a *bekhor,* why would we be forbidden to hit him? If a firstborn son was really such a holy thing that no one could lay a finger on him, then why did the rebbe hit the firstborn boys in cheder just like everyone else?

Indoors, the rebbe explained everything to us. "At one time, the Jews had their own land, and to this day we still call it *Erets Yisroel,* the land of the Jews. There we had our Temple where the Priests offered sacrifices on the altar, and all the firstborns belonged to the Priests. One could redeem a firstborn male of a human being with five shekels, but the firstborn male of an animal had to be given to the Priests. In those days, the Priests slaughtered it and ate the flesh in sanctity and purity in Jerusalem.

"So a firstborn son is considered holy and you must not cause a blemish on anything holy. It is because holy things were allowed to be violated that the Temple in Jerusalem was destroyed and we Jews are still in Exile today!

"So now can you understand, children, how great a sin it is to cause a blemish on a firstborn? Remember, the goat is sacred, and no one may gain from it, not even a Priest. Outside of our Temple, even a Priest cannot eat a sacrifice. What do we do with him then? We feed him and protect him from harm. He belongs to no one, but everyone takes care of him, and because of that merit of caring and protecting, and not beating him even if he does us harm, we may merit the coming of *Meshiekh* who will lead us back to our Holy Land, and we will once again have our Temple where Priests can eat sacrifices in purity. Do you understand what I am saying, children?"

We did more than understand. In one moment the wild beast that we had bombarded with firewood had become sacred to us, perhaps more holy than the rebbe himself.

One boy asked innocently, "Rebbe, after a hundred and twenty years when the holy firstborn dies, what happens then?"

"When he lives out his years and dies without a blemish, he will be wrapped in white, but not a burial shroud, and he will be buried in a prepared place."

"Rebbe," asked another student, "will this firstborn son also be in the World to Come and sit in Paradise with the saints?"

The rebbe, as I recall, was silent, probably not knowing how to answer. Maybe he himself would be worthy of sitting in Paradise after a hundred and twenty years and did not like the idea of sitting at the table of the Feast of the Leviathan with a firstborn ram with horns. But he said nothing.

We took the rebbe's answer as a clear response that this firstborn goat with his big pointed horns and long, wide beard would certainly sit among the important people, as would be fitting for something so holy that you could not even beat him if he did you harm.

Gradually we began to look upon the *bekhor* with respect and awe. We all believed that on the merit of this goat we would return to our precious land where the worms do not eat the bodies of the dead and where people sit and eat carob all year round as we can only do once in a blue moon.

From that morning on, we shared our breakfasts and our lunches with the sacred goat. We offered him contributions and tithes, and some of us wanted to gain favor in his eyes to be influential with him, so that he would let us pet him.

And he was good to us, too. He accepted our bagels with butter, our bread, he sniffed our pockets, and he would become angry if we did not give him something to eat. And he had a point. For suddenly his sacredness increased and established him in our childhood fantasies as some kind of hidden saint who knew all secrets, who even knew when *Meshiekh* would come.

One day, one of my friends came to cheder crying. He told us that his little brother was very sick. His mother had been crying the whole night and his father was reciting psalms. He was sent to cheder with instructions that while he was praying he should ask God for a cure.

With these words, he broke into such sobbing that we all took him into our hearts. We all wanted to help him ask God for a cure for his little brother, and in our childish reasoning, there was no closer advocate than the goat—the holy firstborn male—who could direct our prayers to God and plead for the necessary cure.

Although we did not know the power of a ransom, we had enough sense to understand that we would have to compensate the goat in some way, and we gave away almost all our breakfast. And he, although just a goat with horns, had the good sense not to refuse such a ransom and ate up the bagels and other foods with quite an appetite. And he was so kindly disposed to us that he licked the crumbs from our hands. For us this was a certain sign that a cure would come and the child would soon be well again.

Later when we saw the goat standing and chewing his cud, it was clear to us that he was praying in his language, with great intention and secrecy, and we comforted our friend, telling him he should not cry, his brother would recover and live because the sacred goat was pleading for him. His prayer would surely be accepted in heaven.

The goat became even more holy to us when the sick child suddenly recovered. I heard my friend's sister explaining how the doctor had saved the boy from death, but we knew for certain that it was not the doctor who was a Gentile who brought the cure, but the holy firstborn goat who had eaten our breakfast as a sacrifice so the sick boy would live!

Thus the goat gradually became for us children a kind of idol, and any of us who was heavy-hearted or worried went to talk with the goat, quietly telling him all our secrets, confessing to him, and seeking help and comfort. We had no doubt that he could understand what we told him and would help us.

He was so holy! If *Meshiekh* would come because of him, then he could certainly understand and help us with our troubles.

But we began to have some difficulties trying to understand his ways and his customs. We began to perceive that he did not comport himself in the manner of a saint—like a true holy one—especially when we discovered him dancing around with the goats that belonged to the village priest—those unkosher, wanton she-goats—and actually became an in-law with the priest!

Once we saw with our own eyes how the priest's maid, a coarse peasant girl who wore a cross over her heart, brought out a slop bucket with peelings and all kinds of unkosher scraps from the priest's kitchen. And the holy goat without a moment's hesitation, stuck his kosher snout and his thick kosher beard right into the unkosher slop and ate and drank as though he wanted to forget that he was a firstborn Jewish male and had no regret and no shame in the face of his heritage or his acquaintances.

This slovenly behavior caused us a lot of grief. How could a saint do such a thing? Didn't he know about the Law? How could he ever atone for his actions?

We told the rebbe about this and swore that this was not slander, that we had seen it with our own eyes. How could we not hold the firstborn responsible?

"Fools that you are," said the rebbe, "he is holy, but he is not required to fulfill the six hundred and thirteen mitzvahs. Don't forget that he is just a goat with horns; a do-nothing. He eats, drinks, and doesn't hurt anyone. You must not hate him; he is really sacred. He is ours and not the priest's, and if we lived in our own land he would, of course, have nothing to do with the priest's goats. In the Exile, no one can observe all the mitzvahs, especially a goat with horns, even though he is a firstborn!"

That excuse was enough for us, and we felt pity for the goat for having to wander around in the Exile like us and for being unable to be as pious and as holy as a firstborn male should be.

And it was not only we, the young ones, who so innocently believed in the goat's holiness. So did our mothers and fathers. Even the rebbe and all the other pious Jews who waited and hoped for *Meshiekh* and for the Redemption, they also had great respect for the goat, the firstborn male, and never said a bad word about him or his friendship with the priest or the priest's goats. They would never harm a hair on his head, even when he did them harm.

For years I saw that same goat wandering through the markets and streets, snatching treats from the poor women's stalls: a bagel from one, a potato or a carrot from another. From one he trotted off with her entire package of food that she had brought from home to sustain herself for the long day in the marketplace. The poor woman sprang up, grabbed a piece of wood and ran after the goat with a wail and a curse. But another woman shouted at her, "Yentl, Yentl, don't make a mistake, that's the *bekhor*, the community goat!"

The words had the effect of a kind of charm on the angry Yentl. She let the stick drop from her hand, she gave herself a little slap on the face, and stammered, "Kind God, don't count it against me that I got mad at your holy *bekhor*!"

After awhile I realized that he was called "*der kahalisher bok*," "the community goat," because he belonged to the whole community; all the Jews in the village. Everyone recognized him, everyone knew his pedigree, and though he did injury to everyone, no one raised their voice to him.

His usual station was at the entryway to the women's synagogue. He rambled through the streets all day long, and even when he stayed at the priest's or with the shepherd during the day, he spent the night at his station. In the summer, he lived out in the fields with the other goats, where he could do no damage and where there was no one to complain or judge his idleness.

But as the years went by, he seemed to fulfill his noble descent. Every year he got bigger and stronger from pleasure and freedom, and the bigger and stronger he got, the wilder and more proud he became, until no one was safe on the street.

One day we heard that he had tossed a child with his horns. Then came an even worse report about him: A young wife, who went to pray in the middle of the week, surprised the goat, who got angry at her for disturbing his rest, and butted her. She fell down the steps and miscarried a child in the sixth month!

The woman's husband made a big stir in the study house and demanded to know why the community maintained such a town menace and had even turned over the women's synagogue to it? But Arye the Judge paid off the young man for his damages. And he also gave him to understand that he, the young man, was marked to be punished at some future date for such angry words against the holy goat that all the Jews in the community had seen fit to protect so that no hair on its head would be touched! Whether or not the young man understood that he had committed a sin by speaking against the goat, he did not say another word against him.

Whenever anyone lost their temper with the goat or had complaints against him, there was Arye the Judge or some other pious Jew to say just a few words: "The sacred goat, the sacrifice!" and it worked like a magic charm to keep the complainer silent so that no one would —or could—express anything bad about the goat.

Until the day when Avner the Teacher had the courage and impudence to speak the truth: That it was not the goat that was wild, but all the town's Jews who had become some kind of wild creatures.

"It's true that he's a firstborn male," Avner protested, "but does that make him as holy as a person? How come you can ransom a firstborn human with a five-shekel contribution, but not a firstborn goat? And what kind of noble birth does he have that we have to indulge his every whim? May he go to the devil! What is he good for? How much trouble do we have to go through to take care of him? There aren't any Priests, there is no Jerusalem, no Temple, and until the *Meshiekh* comes and gives us back Jerusalem, you can slaughter and eat his great-grandchildren's grandchildren or sell them to the peasants. Who ever heard of a whole town full of Jews paying such respect to a goat with horns, accepting whatever damage he does, and no one is even allowed to say a word against him? I must tell you, gentlemen, your holy goat is nothing but a big fool! You would assign any other goat in his situation to the ewes. You would milk them and take the milk out to the villages to sell."

Do you think that Avner convinced anyone with his mockery? Not a bit! Rather, he received an ugly punishment in a big way. Arye the Judge openly announced in shul that Avner was an *apikoyres,* a heretic, and shouted, "Don't you believe in *Meshiekh* either? If you don't want to believe, don't believe, but scoundrel, why are you impeding the Redemption with your mockery?"

And sure enough from that day on Avner was known as "Avner the *Apikoyres."* He was not called up to the Torah for a full year, and he was never included in a minyan. Young boys ran after him in the street shouting, "There goes Avner the *Apikoyres,* who doesn't believe in *Meshiekh!"* And pious housewives used all their worst curses on him.

Someone else in his position would probably have spit on the town and moved away. But luckily, Avner was a stubborn little Jew and accepted everything for the best. He continued to speak slander against the goat and continued to suffer abuses because of it. And who knows how long the war over the goat's honor would have gone on between Avner the *Apikoyres* and Arye the Judge had it not been for an incident that stirred up the whole town.

It happened like this: Small children began dying in the town. Arye and his people went around the town looking for sins and offenses, because when little children die, it is a sure sign that there must be some wrongdoing going on.

The Russian superintendent of the district arrived with a whole commission to inspect for garbage and mud in the Jewish homes and courtyards. He did not overlook a single house. He was everywhere with his commission and gave the householders plenty of headaches.

In the middle of the summer he demanded that the Jews make their houses as clean as for Passover, including the cellars and attics. And as if that weren't enough, he told them that they must clean the courtyards and the stables, and seal the bathhouse and the mikvah. He also concerned himself with the study houses and the synagogues.

But when he went up the steps and opened the door to the women's synagogue, the superintendent came face-to-face with the *bekhor*. The furious goat rushed at him, apparently intending to knock out the superintendent with his horns.

As luck would have it, the superintendent had the good sense not to go alone, because one-against-one the goat would surely have been the victor. But the superintendent's constables interceded for their chief and rescued him.

But that was not enough for the superintendent. He could not just go away and let the goat live in peace. No! The superintendent was burning with anger at the impudence of this Jewish goat that aimed to injure him, the head of the district! He directed his constables to catch the goat, take him to the slaughterhouse, and give him what he deserved.

Naturally there was a great hue and cry in the town that was even louder than for the crazy decree to scour and clean in the middle of the summer as if it were Passover. Arye the Judge threw himself at the superintendent to defend the goat. But Arye was not adept at speaking Russian; he spoke half Russian, half German with a little Hebrew thrown in. He explained to the superintendent that he, the goat, was a firstborn male of noble descent and a sacrificial animal, and therefore no one must harm him. The superintendent and his constables laughed in his face, and he went away humiliated.

But Arye did not give up. He hurried through the town collecting a sizeable contribution, which he took to the superintendent as a gift for a "reconciliation."

Some say that it was not Arye's ransom money that released the goat from his appointment at the slaughterhouse, but the village priest's intervention that saved the day. And that it was not the holiness of the firstborn, but the fact that the goat was useful to the priest. He had a lot of female goats and he was simply afraid that without a billy goat, his goats would stop giving milk.

However it happened, the goat was saved and let loose again to turn the town upside down. He roamed through the streets and not even the superintendent tried to control him. Until a certain shepherd came along who swore that he would supervise the goat, not take his eye off him, and not spare the whip.

And so that is how it ended. The shepherd took the goat in hand, kept him, and it became much easier to live in the town. From then on, the market women sat at their tables of fruit and herbs without fear and terror. They could even grab a quick nap. No one would take their merchandise for free or without reason. Boys going to cheder could ramble freely through the streets without a guard, and their mothers were not afraid that their dear ones would encounter the goat and be trampled. Even pregnant women were not afraid to go to the early minyan on Shabbes. They knew that the goat was with the shepherd and that the synagogue was just for them.

And one other thing happened: Avner was no longer a heretic anymore. The bad things that Arye had said about him had long been forgotten. In fact, one wondered now, why it took so long to comprehend how right Avner had been. His worst enemies from before were now his best friends, and pious wives who had hurled their worst curses on him, now wished to have children and grandchildren as smart and kind as Avner.

Later, when I was older and traveled to various towns and villages, I encountered that same goat time and time again, although with a different color of coat or with a different beard; and sometimes without a beard at all. What of it? The horns were always exactly the same. Everywhere people suffer from such goats and everywhere people are silent. The suffering is accepted with love because there is a community goat to whom one must not raise a finger.

* * * * *

Apparently, just a silly little story about a goat. But as stated, folly perpetuates itself, perhaps just because foolishness repeats itself so often in life. However it is, this story may help us comprehend today what others may not understand about the power of the incantation, "The honor of the Army," which has made the people of Paris so foolish, so laughable, and so dishonest.

It is not hooligans in the streets who are shouting, "The honor of the Army," but their own Arye the Judge who runs around Paris with his walking stick in hand. And whether or not he is shouting, "The honor of the Army," you can still hear his original words: "The sacredness of our *bekhor* has been profaned! Anyone who says a bad word about our goat does not believe in *Meshiekh* and is impeding the Redemption!"

France has suffered and bled for twenty-eight years maintaining and supporting its sacred goat. For twenty-eight years that goat has trampled around freely without a care, never doing any work except raiding the tables of the market women, knocking things over, and making trouble whenever the spirit moves him. No one except the village priest and his goats ever gets any pleasure or use from him. Even though everyone saw how wild the goat was, and how he was turning the whole town upside-down, they still shouted "Avner the *Apikoyres!* You don't believe in *Meshiekh!* You are a traitor and anyone may attack you in the streets!"

The poor Avners in Paris are still crying out that a country does not need a goat to make it strong, but it is of no use to remind France of the verse, "Zion will be redeemed through judgment and resettled in righteousness." No shouting and no reminding will help.

"Avner and his people are heretics!" shout the Parisian Aryes. "They don't believe in *Meshiekh* and they don't want us to be strong!" And schoolboys and wags run after the Avners and throw mud on them. Housewives hurl curses at their heads.

Old sinners are buying up the World to Come in Paris, even while they shed hot tears over the sinfulness of David, because the same heresies were born in Avner and his people. As I read the newspapers that bring fresh reports every day about what is happening in Paris, I am reminded of the community goat, and I say: "All this already happened long ago!"

My old *bobe*, my grandmother, seems to stand before me and says with her sweet smile, "Listen, children, the whole world is one town and all people have the same way of thinking. Little children, little problems; big children, big problems."

Because of that, I do believe that one day a superintendent will come to France and take her big-horned goat and put him into the hands of a good shepherd who will teach him respect and not allow him to run wild and do injury to everyone.

And then the light will shine in everyone's eyes again. Avner will go back to being a smart, respectable Jew, and in Paris important people will laud him and pious housewives will wish to have children and grandchildren like him.

But what is happening instead? The priest is still dominating Paris, he is clever and he is strong, and he and his people believe in the goat with all their might. Of course, it is better for them not to have a wise shepherd over him and to allow him to make a lot of trouble in the town. Trouble makes the world more pious, and if the world is pious, the goats can be milked in the Exile, and his people will never lack for milk and cheese and butter!

SEVEN

APOCALYPSE

Several idlers sat in the Chassidic *shtibl*, the house of prayer. They were not poor young bachelors who had come from some place else to study in a yeshiva or with some purpose of their own, but Jewish elders without money or worries. No one cared that they sat all day in the *shtibl* and frittered away the time.

Reb Fishl Beyle-Menukhe's was a Chassid, a gentle, sickly Jew of about fifty, who depended entirely on his wife, Beyle-Menukhe. This is why he was called "Beyle-Menukhe's." He did not get involved in her business at the shop where she sold herring, salt, soap, and other every-day items to the peasants. He let her have as many children as she wanted, let her raise them and marry them off to their chosen mates, and allowed himself to be called to the wedding canopy: "Reb Fishl, the father of the bride will bless the bride!" He collected his "mazl tovs" from the guests and was finished.

On Shabbes and the holidays, he was at home from the Friday night meal through the Saturday evening ritual. During the week, he ate at home and studied Zohar in the *shtibl*. And in the winter when it was too cold to go outside, he had his food brought to him in the *shtibl.*

Reb Yisroel the Slaughterer, an old man of seventy, was a tall, thin Jew with a little white beard. Just a few years earlier, he had turned over his slaughtering business to his young son-in-law, who in turn gave him whatever he needed for his meager expenses. He ate his meals at his oldest daughter's home and slept in the *shtibl.*

Reb Meshulem the Teacher, left a widower by two wives, had only one son, who was in America; a president or some such important person, judging from what he wrote in his letters. Once a year he sent his father a draft for ten dollars, which Meshulem used to supplement his meager wages as a teacher.

Meshulem was a Chassid who was always immersed in Kabbalah, and who knew for certain that the whole world was created for the sake of the Rebbe of Vinogrodke, may he live and be well. But the Rebbe did not want to profit from anything more than what his Chassidim gave him.

Meshulem was waiting for his third wife, but until she came along, he was at a loss for his monthly rent of three rubles. Anyway it was not suitable for him, an old widower, to sit alone in an apartment, so he packed up his few belongings, gave them to a relative to hold on to, and moved himself into the *shtibl.*

It was just three days since he had returned from Vinogrodke, where he had gone by foot to confer with the Rebbe about his third wife. Now he was very enthusiastically telling Fishl and Yisroel about the trip.

"I enjoyed it very much," said Meshulem. "I went there, thirty, maybe forty years ago, and I never enjoyed it so much as this time."

"In what way?" asked Fishl.

"Everything. First of all, there was a rich man there who came from Kiev. They said he was very rich, worth several million. And besides giving charity to all the poor people, he also had a table set for all the guests, even for the rich, and provided a complete meal for everyone at his own expense. There was lots of grape wine and brandy. I don't care much for such things, but the Chassidim drank plenty of it and got pretty tipsy. Secondly, I saw with my own eyes how the rich man, right during the feast, took out a marvelous little velvet box. He pressed a hidden little spring and the top cleverly opened by itself, and he took out a precious gold snuffbox—a wonderful thing—and gave it to the Rebbe. All the Chassidim tried to get a look at the little snuffbox.

"I got pushed aside a little, but I still got a good look. Experts estimated that it was worth several thousand rubles, but in my estimation, it was worth much more. I have never in my life seen such an exquisite snuffbox. Thirdly, as a matter-of-fact, the Rebbe, may he enjoy long life, later offered snuff to several of the Chassidim at the table. I took some with three fingers, which for me was enough to last for a whole day. And meanwhile, the Rebbe's face shone like the face of the sun. We realized that the Rebbe took extraordinary pleasure from this gift and that this was a favorable time. The Chassidim talked amongst themselves about a great salvation for all Jews.

"I myself felt full of joy and happiness. I felt a kind of elevation of spirit. Then later, when I was going to the Rebbe to discuss the matter that I had come to see him about, they did not let me in. I saw through the keyhole that the Rebbe, may he live a long life, was sitting with that same rich man. But how do you think he was sitting? Just like I am sitting with you now! And for hours. I felt as though I might fall into the sin of coveting. I felt jealous of that rich man from Kiev and I wanted to be as rich as he was so that I could give the Rebbe a gift like the gold snuffbox, and could sit for a whole hour in a room and talk with him alone. I wanted it so badly that I felt that I was becoming melancholy. It was a good thing that I still had some snuff from the Rebbe's precious snuffbox, and I took a sniff. But it was also good that there was a miracle and that I brightened up and felt remorse, and was able to forget about my jealousy. You can say what you want, but to see such glory and the greatness of such a rich man with your own eyes, it is a great miracle not to fall into the sin of coveting!"

"Why were you so surprised?" asked Fishl. "I wouldn't give five kopecks for your rich Kiever and his wealth! I also know about wealth in the world! Since I heard talk of Rothschild's wealth, none of the local millionaires—or rather 'paupers'—have anything on him. For example, which of them has his own source of quicksilver? Only Rothschild! He can take out a thousand bucketfuls and in an hour, another thousand has appeared. Do you have any idea how much a bucket of quicksilver is worth? Ask my Beyle-Menukhe, she will tell you. I was in the shop one day when a Gentile man came in with a drop of quicksilver in a tiny bottle. It was smaller than a pinch of snuff. He sold it to the apothecary and was paid five rubles for it. So I reckon that Rothschild's wealth is really beyond calculation; it cannot be measured. Today, just imagine his lands, his possessions, his household goods, and his cash money. And you, Meshulem, are so excited about some rich man from Kiev who gave the Rebbe a golden snuffbox? Let's say that the snuffbox did cost several thousand rubles. Let's say that the rich man really does have millions. But against Rothschild he is still a pauper, a beggar. I feel sorry for him!"

"What are you talking about, Fishl?" asked Meshulem. "Is there really such a Rothschild anyplace on earth?"

"What do you mean?"

"I mean that in reality there really is no Rothschild. It is just an exaggeration, an illustration of great riches. As it says in the Talmud, Job did not exist, it is just an illustration, an example."

"A fine illustration!" laughed Fishl. "A source of quicksilver is an illustration! And the governments in the east and in the west that borrow money from him for their wars, are they also an illustration?"

"And what is your proof that he exists?" sparred Meshulem. "I say that the rich man from Kiev is the most wealthy. You say Rothschild. Does Rothschild exist or is he just an illustration of a rich man? I will believe that Rothschild is not just an illustration and is a man born of a woman when you have actually seen him and sat at the Rebbe's table with him as I have with the rich man from Kiev!"

"I just hate it when Jews fight like this, not knowing the facts," Yisroel stepped into the conversation. "I have not seen Rothschild and not eaten at the same table with him like Meshulem, but I have a vision that there really is a Rothschild, that he really is fabulously wealthy as Fishl says, and that we will live to see him take us back to our land of *Yisroel!*

"Listen to this story, how I arrived at this vision. My son-in-law —you both know him—he is not a liar, he is a quiet fellow, but he knows a lot about the ways of the world, about how things work; he understands politics. About a month ago, he went to Kiev. He had to take care of something about his conscription notice. And listen to this: he went there with a petition that he had written himself! I want you to know that he is an intelligent, mature man, versed in the law. When he arrived back from Kiev, he gave me a gift. What do you think it was? A gift that is worth all the wealth in the world to me: a bottle of wine whose value, I think, is not possible to estimate! A bottle of wine from Mount Carmel! I saw it with my own eyes. Even the seal on the bottle was written in Hebrew letters, actual block letters! There was a kind of label glued onto the bottle that was painted with an image of the 'Spies' carrying a huge cluster of grapes. I don't remember the entire thing, but I remember that the wine was from Rothschild's vineyards in the land of *Yisroel,* probably from Mount Carmel. I tasted the wine and I can tell you that I felt like I was tasting real *Erets Yisroel* wine. Delicious! Where does one ever see such wine outside of the land of *Yisroel?*

"And over a glass of this wine, my son-in-law tells me that in the big cities it is no secret that Rothschild, may God help him, intends to buy up the whole land of *Yisroel* from the Turks! Every year he buys more fields, more vineyards, settles more Jews there, and each one sits beneath his own vine and his own fig tree in perfect peace. And eventually he will have purchased all of the land of *Yisroel!*

"So you see, Reb Meshulem, that Rothschild is not just an illustration, since we can taste the flavor of his wine on our own tongues."

"So? And that same Rothschild is also a Jew?" asked Meshulem.

"He has just heard that I drank his wine," Yisroel said to Fishl. "Would I drink wine, heaven forbid, that was not kosher?"

"And just as extraordinarily rich as Reb Fishl says?" asked Meshulem.

"Probably that rich and maybe even richer. People say that he will buy up the entire land of *Yisroel,* and for such a purchase, it seems to me, one would have to be as rich as Koyrekh."

"And how much would you suppose that golden snuffbox cost that your Rothschild brought to the Rebbe, may he live and be well, when he made his pilgrimage to see him?" asked Meshulem.

"I don't know what you are talking about!" answered Yisroel. "Rothschild did not go to visit the Rebbe!"

"What do you mean?" Meshulem said in amusement. "Didn't you just say that he was a rich Jew and that you had drunk his wine yourself?"

"There's something else I can tell you, gentlemen," Fishl called out. "According to what I have heard, Rothschild is a German with a homburg. And there are those who say that he is also a Catholic priest!"

"Eh!" Meshulem stood up and made a dismissing sweep with his hand. "So what is his breeding, his family? I am not jealous of his wealth or his wells of quicksilver! What does that have to do with me? I beg your pardon, but there is nothing to be jealous about and I do not want to hear anything more about him!" With this Meshulem walked to another part of the room, but Yisroel objected and found something else he needed to say about Rothschild.

"Don't be angry, Meshulem," Yisroel said. "One may not judge a Jew until one has been tested by the same temptations as he."

"Do I know what you are talking about? Are you trying to convince me that if I were as rich as Rothschild I would no longer go to the Rebbe? On the contrary, if I had Rothschild's wealth, the snuffbox that I would take to the Rebbe on my pilgrimage would have no comparison in the whole wide world. And secondly, how could anyone accept such foolishness as a German in a homburg? What Fishl is saying, that he is also a priest, I flatly do not believe. It is not believable. No, it's a disgrace, honestly, not nice of Rothschild, why would he be a German? What would he do with a homburg? Feh, he has fallen in my estimation."

"But you're not letting anyone talk!" Yisroel shouted hoarsely. "First of all, Rothschild has influence with the powers that be and is permitted by law to do things that we may not do. Do you understand what I'm telling you, Meshulem? Secondly, you don't know if Rothschild even knows our Rebbe. You know, as my son-in-law says, there are whole countries of Jews who don't know the Rebbe at all. It could be for that reason alone that *Meshiekh* hasn't come yet. But they are still Jews anyway, sinning unintentionally, not even knowing it, and Rothschild doesn't know it either."

"Do you think that's news to me?" Meshulem called out, his anger subsiding a little. "But tell me, if Rothschild, for example, knew that there was a village called Vinogrodke and that there was a saint there such as our Rebbe, would he come to visit him just once a year?"

"Without a doubt!" answered Yisroel. "People already discuss it. If Rothschild only knew, he would have come to the Rebbe long ago and would have become one of us. The whole problem with Rothschild is that he does not know."

"Why then couldn't we find someone who could inform him?" asked Meshulem.

"Oh, now it starts," answered Fishl. "Do you think that all these idlers like you have anything on their minds except trying to make a living? What should a Jew worry about first: the rent, the store, shoes, clothes for the wife and children, a wedding for a son or daughter, and other such worries that leave no space to breathe, let alone go to the ends of the earth inquiring where Rothschild lives so that he could tell him a story about Vinogrodke where the Rebbe lives? Donkey, he wouldn't believe you!"

"And how easy do you think it is to get to him?" offered Yisroel. "He has plenty of attendants and servants who stand by his door day and night and won't let anyone in without a ticket. If only I could get in to see him, I would explain to him that it is a waste of his money to just give it away to the Turks. I don't begrudge the savage Ishmael such a sum of money for *Erets Yisroel!* On the contrary, it would be just and right for the Turks to pay us to lease *Erets Yisroel.* No one denies that *Erets Yisroel* is our land! Even the Turk himself knows it, as is seen in the name they still call it to this day, *'Erets Yisroel,'* which means 'the Jewish land.' So why is the Turk getting such a huge amount of money for it now?

"And it is a wonder to me why Rothschild is pressing so much money on the savage, since it is common knowledge that a man like Rothschild is certain to be a man of intelligence and must have some knowledge of business as well. He knows that gold is not scrap iron, so why is he shoving off such a fortune on Ishmael without any dispute! Does he have any idea how much that could cost him?"

"Do I have any information about it?" Fishl interrupted.

"Come here and I will total it up for you. Even when I was a little boy, the whole world was talking about how Montefiore was going to buy *Erets Yisroel* and pay the rulers of the lands in the east and the west three ducats for each Jew living in their states. At one time the ducat was a big coin; today they are not worth much; now you'd be talking about Imperials that cost twice as much as the ducat used to cost. You must not forget that between Montefiore's and Rothschild's times, the Jews have increased in number many times over. Today who could begin to calculate what treasuries of money it would take to pay off the Turks and then all the other states! And so I say it's a waste of Jewish money and it would only be right for someone to tell Rothschild that he should not try to do this alone! Who knows what can happen? Maybe if he could be informed about the presence of a Rebbe of whom one can ask advice, the Rebbe, may he live and be well, could advise him of a way to get *Erets Yisroel* back without spending so much money."

"And I think," added Yisroel, "that if Rothschild could only know about the Rebbe the way that we know him, he would certainly come to him. There would be a meeting of the Higher Worlds, a stir and a sensation, and there would be such a pinnacle of faith as a man with the wealth of Rothschild stands in awe and quaking before the Rebbe. And perhaps just from that meeting alone, *Meshiekh* would come and Rothschild could save his money and bring us all over for free."

"And truly," said Meshulem, "Rothschild could find much better things to do with his money. Jews today are so depressed about making a living, may God have pity on them! Jews have stopped taking gifts to the Rebbe. Just poor people are going, former well-heeled householders, fallen on hard times. In Vinogrodke you can see it plainly. Once a Chassid went to the Rebbe to ask for children or good matches in marriage, important businessmen slogged through the rain and snow. This time I saw so many requests being written and they were all about livelihood, about bread, about poverty, may God preserve us.

"And do you think that I myself, although I am one single person and my son in America sends me a few dollars once in awhile, could I not find a use for a million rubles? I would, first of all, give up teaching; I've already lost the heart and the lungs for it. Second, I would be able to go to the Rebbe with a fine present for him, may he be well, and offer him a gift for his advice, a proper sum! How the Rebbe would indulge me! Today, after all my efforts, I still have to go back and forth nine times on foot, and perhaps on the fifth day I will merit having the Rebbe take my request slip and speak a few words to me. There is no time to tell him the real issue that I wanted to ask his advice about before the doorkeeper is already showing me the door, and that's it!"

"I could put to good use even half a million rubles," said Yisroel. "The enemies of the Jews should have to turn to their children in their old age! My son-in-law is a good-hearted fellow and he gives me the few kopecks a week that he has pledged to give, but he is still my son-in-law, my own pauper. And my heart pains me enough for each kopeck that I take from him, because I know that he falls short of meeting his own expenses."

"Since you're talking about the good use you could make of the rubles," said Fishl with a sigh, "here's what I can say: I have three daughters to make weddings for and I'm not as young as I used to be. It used to be good to have your own shop, your own business, but the prince isn't what he used to be, and the Gentiles are also quite different these days. Today it's difficult to put together a dowry for a child, and today's dowries are not the old ones! Once three hundred was quite a hoard and that used to be written into the engagement agreement. But it never goes back, and today three hundred rubles is not much money at all. And what about writing the agreement? Today you practically have to put cash on the table. Today promises and even guarantees don't help. Besides that, my Beyle-Menukhe is not what she used to be in her younger years. She's tired from having children, tired from raising them, and is not so young anymore. So it would be doing a great justice if, before Ishmael gets it, that I could have the benefit of a couple of million rubles. Anyway, he has enough, that Rothschild; he can just scoop up another thousand buckets of quicksilver. He wouldn't even notice it!"

"What is coming out in this talk," said Yisroel, "is that there is no person who will take the mitzvah upon himself to go and explain it all to Rothschild, and I am afraid that before someone will chance to do it, Rothschild will force such a fortune on the Turk and be sorry for it later! If I were just ten years younger, I would set out to do it my-self. I would go by foot, I would not eat or drink until I had fought my way in to see Rothschild and explained to him about the Rebbe and about the advice that the Rebbe could give him about returning to *Erets Yisroel* without spending a kopeck."

"What kind of advice?" asked Meshulem.

"Whatever the Rebbe can do!" answered Yisroel. "The Rebbe just needs to talk it through with Rothschild. Rothschild is no youngster. He will comprehend the Rebbe's advice immediately and the result will be a great salvation."

"This talk is a waste of time," sighed Fishl, who very much wanted the couple of million rubles that Rothschild would certainly not spare him after Rothschild came to visit the Rebbe and the Rebbe explained to him that he could get *Erets Yisroel* without paying the Turk anything. And that it would be better for Rothschild to distribute his money to needy Jews for dowries for their daughters and to spruce up their shops with a little merchandise.

Reb Fishl had only now realized what a pauper he really was and how much he and his Beyle-Menukhe needed the couple of million rubles. He began to speak with fire: "Don't you think that if there were a Rothschild in times past, that Jews would have found someone who would have risked his life to go see him? Today, because of our many sins, we do not have such fervent Jews. Every one thinks only about himself and the good of the whole community of Jews does not enter his mind.

"Everyone has an excuse. I tell you myself I am too old and weak, I'm barely alive, and if I did want to consider it, do you think Beyle-Menukhe would let me go? A woman! How could she understand how great a mitzvah it would be and how great a salvation would come for the whole community? Good if Meshulem, a man still in his strength, a man who still has legs strong enough to cross the whole world, a man who has no wife and no children who would hold him by the coattails and cry, 'Meshulem, don't go!' As the devil would have it, the very one who has the ability to be the emissary, is absorbed in his own thoughts, has a cold soul, is not for us, and is not concerned for the community. It's warm and light in the *shtibl*, he can sleep here, study and think, and what else does Meshulem need?"

"What should I do?" asked Meshulem with his eyes lowered.

"You need to know two things, Meshulem," Fishl explained. "One is, that study is a very fine thing, but it is not the point; a Jew studies so that it leads him into action. And second, that a Jew who has a true desire to do a good deed does not need to ask, 'What should I do?' Just have the true desire, and the Master of the Universe will show you the way! Don't fall down just because you are not of a practical mind. Sometimes it is the impractical man who carries off the greatest mission, a mission that even a great sage may not undertake. It's worth giving it a thought, Meshulem, and perhaps to come to the realization that life is not for one's self alone, and some Jews are obligated to sacrifice their life for the good of the whole community."

Meshulem looked at Fishl in amazement. It seemed to him that Fishl knew what was going on in his heart. He had already felt a strong desire to visit Rothschild, and in his head, he had already started to plan how he would carry out the mission. But just then, Jews started coming into the *shtibl* to pray the afternoon prayers and so the conversation ended.

*   *   *   *   *

After such a long discussion, Meshulem could not close his eyes for the whole night. He could not get Rothschild, *Erets Yisroel,* and the Rebbe out of his mind.

"The more one lives, the more one learns!" he said to himself. "I had always thought that Rothschild was non-existent, but now it is clear that he lives and wants to purchase *Erets Yisroel.* Reb Yisroel is no liar! If he says that he himself has drunk Rothschild's wine from Mount Carmel, I believe him. Why would he tell a lie? But what Fishl said about Rothschild being a German with a homburg and that there are whole countries full of Jews who do not know any rebbe is very hard for me to believe! What use has Rothschild for a homburg? If he is a Jew whom God has helped to become so rich that he can buy up all of *Erets Yisroel,* what does he need to be a German for? Foo! That reduces him in my eyes!

"And what if it might happen that *Meshiekh* does not come because of this, because not all Jews have faith in holy men yet, and not all travel to see such a holy man as the Rebbe? Who knows what the world can do? So it would be right to open Rothschild's eyes so that he would know about the Rebbe of Vinogrodke. No matter how clever Rothschild may be, he still needs to know that the saint of Vinogrodke has more wisdom in his little finger than he, Rothschild, has in his entire being. And if someone could tell him, he would understand quickly, and would travel immediately to Vinogrodke."

Meshulem went around with such thoughts all week, asking himself questions about Rothschild, about the Rebbe, and about *Meshiekh,* and answering all the questions himself. Rothschild became like a brother to him. Once in a dream, Rothschild came to him in the *shtibl.* In another dream, Meshulem traveled to the ends of the earth to visit Rothschild's palace.

He kept getting closer and closer to Rothschild in his nightly dreams, so much so that when he was awake he started seeing him on the street. And Rothschild became so close to Meshulem in his dreams that he was not ashamed to pour out his heart to Meshulem, and admit that since he had heard about the Vinogrodke Rebbe, he had become very eager to meet him. But what could he do, as the devil stood in his way on the road and would not let him move on? And Meshulem saw in the dream how the devil blocked all of Rothschild's paths with hordes of little demons who would not allow him to bring *Meshiekh.* Rothschild begged Meshulem to tell the Rebbe so the Rebbe would do what he could to move the devil out of his way.

Meshulem believed completely that the dream was a prophecy, though it bothered him that he did not have the good sense to ask Rothschild for a few million rubles in the meantime, for himself and for a gift for the Rebbe, as was appropriate. And Meshulem began thinking about carrying out his mission. Each day his desire became stronger. He studied many works of Kabbalah in order to understand the secret of *Meshiekh,* searching all the passages in the entire Talmud that mentioned *Meshiekh,* and finding that *Meshiekh* could only come in a generation in which everyone was a saint or everyone was a sinner.

"Everyone a saint," he said, "will never be. Let's suppose that the evil inclination came to me and promised me mountains of gold if I would be a German with a homburg. Would I listen to it? I think I would sooner be buried a living person than I would bear the shame of being a German, may God have mercy, and go around in the street with a homburg and look like a fool. But one must not say about himself that he is the most clever person in the world. Perhaps the evil inclination would be successful, may the time never come! But what would happen with the Rebbe, may he live and be well? Could it be that the Rebbe would also become a German? Heaven forbid! How could the evil inclination even approach him? But what if it got to him and talked to him until the end of time, would the Rebbe let himself be talked into such a sin? So I see that if a generation of all sinners is not possible, then neither is a generation of all saints possible, so long as there are whole countries of Jews who live like the savages, poor souls, without faith in the holy men, without knowledge of a rebbe in the world."

He carried that question around with him all week and was in doubt whether it would be of any help for Rothschild to buy up *Erets Yisroel* so long as there were Jews who still did not know about a rebbe. When all at once, while studying a book of Kabbalah, he read that the virtue of a saint may be enough. That through prayers and ransom, a saint could reclaim an entire generation. Meshulem felt light pouring into his mind. He had found an answer to his question.

"I searched and I found it!" he shouted. "Heaven has shown me how it can be that a generation can be unwitting and the Messiah will still be obliged to come. Rothschild only needs to give eighteen ducats of ransom money for a few Jews—for children and adults, for

Germans, and for heretics who don't believe in a rebbe—and in that moment, when the Rebbe receives the ransom money for the whole community of Jews, he can reclaim everyone, and the entire generation will be acquitted. *Meshiekh* will come and when he comes, the Turk will have to give up *Erets Yisroel* without a kopeck. In fact, the Turk will have to pay rent money to the Jews, since for so long he kept the land for free. Rothschild is a Jewish businessman and will understand this accounting and see that this is more worthwhile than paying three rubles for every Jew!"

Meshulem figured it out with ink on paper, and decided that from the money that Rothschild would save with this plan, he, Meshulem, should get half at least! And he began preparing to take to the road to go see Rothschild. But first he had to speak with the Rebbe. The Rebbe would bless him and give him an amulet for the road, so the devil could not do anything against him.

So one fine morning, Meshulem performed ninety-five immersions in the mikvah. He finished the morning prayers, put his prayer shawl and phylacteries under his arm, and set out on his way to visit the Rebbe. Yet one problem still bothered him. He was going without a kopeck in his pocket. He needed nothing for himself, but he would have to provide some monetary gift to the Rebbe. The attendant who stood by the door would require something slipped into his hand or he could keep you waiting for weeks before you could get in to see the Rebbe, and time was wasting already!

That is when it occurred to Meshulem that he could offer the Rebbe half of his portion in the World to Come as his gift. Why did he need to be sparing of it now? He knew that once his plan was carried out, there would be no limit to his reward in the World to Come. It would not be "nothing" to end the Exile and bring on *Meshiekh!* Half was enough for him. The other half he could not begrudge the Rebbe for his blessing and for an amulet for the trip.

The attendant may not listen to him, but he would have to believe that in a future time Meshulem would pay him a thousand times over for the missing ruble. And if not, Meshulem would use force to push his way in to see the Rebbe. And so Meshulem set out for Vinogrodke.

He heard the trees in the forest talking to him, sharing secrets, and it seemed they were telling him secrets about himself. He saw how they bent and bowed to him, they sang a song because they knew what kind of a mission he was on, and they showed him plainly that it was *Meshiekh's* time already, when all the trees in the world would sing. He forgave them. He wanted to ask them not to show their joy, so that Satan would not know just yet what he was up to. But he enjoyed it nonetheless and went on, not getting tired, not feeling any hunger, walking and reciting songs from the psalms and incantations from the Zohar until it was night.

He arrived at a sort of inn along the road, washed his hands, recited the evening prayers, read the night prayers, lay down to sleep, rose at the crack of dawn, prayed the morning prayers, and went on, until finally on the third day he arrived in Vinogrodke. Although he did not feel tired, he had become so thin and pale from his fasts, his immersions, and his journey by foot that no one recognized him. His face was white and his lips blue like a corpse. Only his eyes burned with an unnatural light.

He spent an entire day preparing and arranging his speech to the Rebbe, and in the morning, he began pushing his way towards the door where the attendant stood holding a key and letting each guest in and out of the Rebbe's room. Meshulem tried talking with the attendant, telling him that he had come about a very important matter. He promised to soon pay him in thousands for the single ruble that he owed him now, but the attendant was hard as a stone and would not let him into the room. Meshulem would not move one step, although the attendant treated him to a poke in the side every minute.

Suddenly, possessed with an unnatural power, Meshulem grabbed the key from the attendant's hand, turned the lock, pushed open the door, and was there in the Rebbe's room. The attendant raced after him to grab his collar and throw him out, but Meshulem began to scream, "Rebbe, don't let this Satan do me harm! I am here as a messenger for the whole community of Jews!"

Though the Rebbe did not hear him, it was enough for the Rebbe to look at Meshulem's darkened face to understand that this unexpected visitor had put his last hopes in him. The Rebbe waved the attendant away and Meshulem was finally alone with the Rebbe.

In all the years he had been coming to see the Rebbe, Meshulem had never had the honor of being alone with him. He saw this as a sign in itself that this was a favorable time and so he courageously announced, "Rebbe, the first thing I want to say is that I offer you half of my share in the World to Come as a gift so that you will accept me and listen to my speech from beginning to end."

But the Rebbe answered, "I do not want your World to Come. If you have some coins, eighteen gold pieces or eighteen kopecks for me to take as a ransom gift, and if not, I don't need it."

"Rebbe, is my World to Come worth less than eighteen gold pieces?"

"Heavens," answered the Rebbe, "however small a person's portion in the True World, it cannot be valued in terms belonging to this world. If you want some kind of resolution, you will have to give me some donation, because this generation has done wrong with money, and so the resolution must come with money!"

"Rebbe," Meshulem said, speaking faster and more heatedly, "for the time being just take my World to Come, because after my meeting with Rothschild where I will get a few million rubles, I will pay you back for your gift."

"What are you talking about? What Rothschild? Are you completely mad?" said the Rebbe angrily, and he began to be alarmed at Meshulem and at his eyes, which were burning with such a wild fire.

"Rebbe, you know that I am not crazy!" yelled Meshulem with his last ounce of energy. "You know already that I have come to you to discuss the Redemption and *Meshiekh*, but you don't want to urge me on, you want to test me, to see how strong I am in my resolve. Don't think that I will go away! You must give me your blessing and a talisman for my trip to see Rothschild!"

"Khatskl!" yelled the Rebbe to the attendant. "Come quickly and get this crazy man away from me! He's going to hurt me!"

The door opened and Khatskl came in, but before he had time to grab Meshulem, Meshulem, his eyes flaming, grabbed the Rebbe with both arms, wrapped himself around the Rebbe with all his strength, and started yelling, "I am holding the horns of the altar! Get away from me, Khatskl, agent of the devil! You have no power over me since I am holding the holy Rebbe!"

"Save me, Khatskl! He's a madman, a lunatic, may God save us! Why did you let a lunatic in to see me?" screamed the Rebbe in a strange voice.

"Rebbe," pleaded Meshulem, "I swear by *Meshiekh* himself and by the community of Jews that I will not leave you until you hear me out! Cut me up right here, beat me up right here, I am not afraid! The Redemption that I will bring for the Jews is stronger than a thousand Khatskls!"

Khatskl saw that he could do nothing by himself, so he opened the door wide and shouted, "Jews, save the Rebbe! He's being attacked by a lunatic!"

A few dozen Jews raced into the room and threw themselves on Meshulem. They bit his hands, beat him, and tore him away from the Rebbe. Meshulem fought like a hero, felt no pain, and would not let himself be dragged away from the Rebbe's room. His pale face was aflame, big drops of sweat poured from his forehead, and his eyes blazed with fire.

The Rebbe shouted, "Jews, take him to the well and pour cold water on his head until this frenzy leaves him! It's some kind of seizure, a possession, may God save us. Cold water quickly so that he doesn't hurt anyone!"

Meshulem received plenty of slaps and blows on the way to the well where the crowd dragged him and began to pour cold water on him. Ten Chassidim drew up the water and another ten took on the mitzvah of pouring it over him. They doused him with cold water for so long that he no longer had any strength to resist and he was left lying chilled and frozen in the river of water that surrounded him. His teeth chattered from the cold.

Nevertheless, in their over-enthusiasm, they tied his hands and feet and threw him into the makeshift infirmary among the sick, the epileptic, the psychotic, and those possessed, who awaited the Rebbe's healing. Meshulem lay there a day and a night on the muddy floor of the shed, beaten, wet, soaked through, until someone looked in and realized that his ravings were not those of a lunatic but caused by a terrible fever.

The Chassidim were fearful of a libel. If he died, there would be a legal investigation, so they untied him and put him in a bed, and the Rebbe's own doctor gave him medicines. Meshulem did not know how long he lay unconscious, but when he opened his eyes and realized what had happened to him, he thought to himself, "I am to be a sacrifice for our sins. I couldn't have planned it any better myself! It's true, I have a lot more pains this way, but suffering can be a solution to my plans, and now I am certain that my plans will be carried out."

Once he was able to stand on his own and walk around in the courtyard, he still saw how the Chassidim ran away from him as from a madman. He called after them, "Don't be afraid! The Rebbe has healed me, I am healthy now!"

Finally, Meshulem asked to see the Rebbe. He wanted to thank him for the miracle he had brought about. He wanted to say that he was well again and would continue on his journey.

The Rebbe was told that the lunatic had recovered and that he requested an interview to ask his forgiveness, but the Rebbe answered, "I forgive him, he is forgiven, may God send him healing, but I do not want to see him anymore. He made me sick. He is an evil spirit of some sort, may you not know of it!"

Meshulem was very sorry about the Rebbe's response. He thought hard about how this had happened to him. Didn't the holy spirit know of his intention and the holy mission that had brought him here?

No, he had to know why the Rebbe was so aggrieved with him? If the Rebbe had perceived that he was not competent to bring *Meshiekh,* he would simply have said, "Meshulem, your desire is a very good one, but you are not competent enough for this great mitzvah." Then he would have believed him and spared himself all this pain and suffering.

But since the Rebbe had not said this, he probably knew that Meshulem was indeed able. So then why wouldn't he see him now? Was he afraid of him? Had he ever in his whole life harmed anyone?

Maybe something had happened to the Rebbe? Who knew what the agents of the devil were capable of doing to a person? Meshulem was reminded of the story of King Solomon, of how the devil once swallowed him and spit him out four hundred miles away, and then put himself on Solomon's throne and fooled the whole wide world. Everyone thought that it was King Solomon, while the real king was going from town to town like a beggar and crying out, "I am Solomon!"

"Why could it not be that the same thing has happened here," Meshulem wondered? He began to pray to God for each Chassid who went in to see the Rebbe, that the Rebbe would not get angry and that the Chassid would come out peacefully.

He wanted very much to get in to see the Rebbe and take off one of his shoes to see if he had feet like people, or if he had chicken's feet as a devil would have. But he was still too weak. They might take him to the well again and pour cold water on him. Cold water has the power to douse the strongest flame that Kabbalah can ignite. Still, he doubted that he had made an error.

Finally, Khatskl said to him, "Meshulem, go home. The Rebbe told me that your foot may never cross his doorstep again. And if you don't leave Vinogrodke soon, they will pour cold water on your head again, and this time you may die, because no one will look after you."

Now it was clear to Meshulem that some devil was sitting in the Rebbe's chair, and that the real Rebbe was wandering around a four hundred mile perimeter, shouting, "I am Solomon!" But no one believes him! So Meshulem left Vinogrodke.

Back in the *shtibl,* people knew that Meshulem had been very ill in Vinogrodke and they took him back with joy. But he did not respond to any of the questions that they asked him. He engaged with more determination and more fire than ever in the study of Kabbalah, in secret letter combinations, and in fasting.

Soon people began to consider him a lunatic. He was no longer interested in teaching, did not need much from life, and to supply himself with the bit of bread and salt with which he broke his constant fasts, he gradually sold off all his possessions. When he had nothing left to sell, he set off on his long journey.

Before he left, he disclosed to Yisroel the Slaughterer that he was going to search for the ousted Rebbe in an area four hundred miles wide in every direction from Vinogrodke. Perhaps he would find him and together they could bring about the Redemption of the world.

"I swear to you, Reb Yisroel," said Meshulem, raising his hand as his eyes glowed with fire, "you should go to Vinogrodke yourself and examine that Satan who is sitting in the Rebbe's chair, and on the day that you reveal to the world that there is a devil sitting beneath the Rebbe's fur hat, *Meshiekh* will come and I will not need to be a wanderer anymore!"

After hearing such a devout Chassid as Meshulem speak in such a way, Yisroel wanted to tear his clothes in mourning. But later, when he went to Vinogrodke, it seemed to him, too, that the breath of pitch and sulfur surrounded the Rebbe and his assembly. Nevertheless, Yisroel had no desire to look at the Rebbe's feet or to examine him for the other signs that the sages had once used to test and recognize the devil on King Solomon's throne.

As time passed, Meshulem went farther and farther from town to town and house to house, searching for that saint who was worthy of bringing about the Redemption of the Jews. He had long since forgotten Rothschild. He no longer even looked for the Vinogrodke Rebbe.

His long journey opened his eyes, and he saw that the Redemption did not depend on a Vinogrodke Rebbe or on a Rothschild. The real Redemption depends on the real deliverer—the true Jew—who will bring the Redemption without miracles from rebbes or fortunes from Rothschilds, but by how he lives his life.

The farther Meshulem traveled, the closer he got to finding such a Jew. And it would not even bother him if instead of finding one he found another. If only he could be sure that the one he sought was really out there and that if you seek, you will find him.

EIGHT

MY FIRST LITERARY ACCOMPLISHMENT

Before I begin relating my memoirs from that time when I had already written an entire story or novel, and even dared to read what I had written to those older and more experienced than myself, or to listen to their advice about whether it was worth getting printed, I cannot ignore the influence of two events in my life that made an enormous impression on me at the time. Two events that it seems were the main reasons that I dared to take my pen in hand and try to write.

The first event happened just to me in those years when I was a little boy in cheder and the rebbe attempted to place me in the class with the Talmud students even though I was younger and smaller than they were. I recall that I did not feel any greater status that I was now supposedly studying Talmud than when I was studying Khumesh with Rashi, but other people—especially my good mother and my eldest sister—took this to mean that I was many years older than I was, practically an adult. So then, even though just a few days earlier I had done things that were completely unremarkable for a Torah boy, things that no one would have considered reprimanding me for since a Torah boy was just a child and did not have much sense; now, because of my Talmud study, I had to watch my every step.

The first time that I realized that I was, because of my Talmud study, no longer a child was by accident. My rebbe had asked me to come to cheder the next day with a volume of the Talmud called *Bava Msetsie* so that I would not have to share a book with one of the older boys. They used to pick on me while we were studying, and so if I had my own book I could keep away from them.

Our bookcase at home held a big set of the Vilna edition of the Talmud with wide page margins and leather covers, an edition that must have cost an arm and a leg. My father was rarely at home in those days as he was always traveling around to the various fairs. If he had been at home then, he would not have allowed such a treasure off his bookshelf for this little bit of Talmud study I was doing. He would have known that he could buy an inexpensive child's Talmud and would not have sent his big Talmud to cheder with me.

My mother, however, was in seventh heaven with happiness that she had lived to see the day when her beloved child had begun Talmud study, and could make use of the great Talmud that had, until now, stood on the shelf almost as an ornament or decoration. So she allowed me to take the *Bava Metsie* to cheder. She made me promise to protect the book, not to tear it or get it dirty, and not to leave it at cheder, but to bring it home every evening when the rebbe let us go.

And I remember how happy I was to carry it to and from cheder every day, even though it was almost bigger and wider than I was myself. I could barely reach around it with both arms and it was heavy. I used to sweat from the load and I can say that I really felt the heavy "yoke of the Law."

Coming home from cheder one warm summer evening holding the Talmud in both hands, I saw that there was a pile of fresh sand in our courtyard. Some neighbor was having his oven rebuilt and I loved to play in the sand, digging caves, building fortresses, piling up ramparts, and other such work at which I was a master and for which no one had ever said a cross word to me.

I did not stop to think. I laid the big Talmud volume there on the sandpile, rolled up both sleeves of my jacket, and started to dig a tunnel. Deeply involved in my work, I did not notice that my older sister and a group of other girls had come to the window and were watching what I was doing. Then I heard a peal of laughter and one of my sisters yelled, "Just look at the Talmud student, he's playing in the sand like a little boy!"

Then one of her friends called out, "Bravo! Bravo! A Talmud student who still plays in the sand!"

I was very embarrassed and quickly realized that it was not appropriate for a Talmud student to be playing in the sand. And although the inclination to misbehavior was strong in me, I conquered it, and from then on I never played in the sand again.

But I was not able to overcome a second impulse in me: the inclination that pulled me to listen to the lovely storybooks that my three older sisters read aloud in Yiddish every Shabbes afternoon with a big group of friends, some already of marriageable age. For those storybooks, I gave up all my boyish games and jokes during Shabbes and would sit quietly in a corner in the women's section and happily listen to the beautiful stories they read.

As long as I was not more than a Torah boy, my sisters and their friends did not say a word to me about it being inappropriate for a boy to sit in a group of women and listen to Yiddish stories. Rather, they liked the fact that I could occasionally translate a Hebrew term, and I always remembered where we had stopped and just what had been happening the previous Shabbes when it had gotten too late to keep reading. There were even some girls in the group who loved me and who hugged me to them, and sometimes I told them that I loved one of them better than the others.

But all that was before I started studying Talmud. Once I became a Talmud student, I could not understand what was going on with me, or with them. As far as I was concerned, I was the same boy I had always been, not a hair had changed. The girls were also exactly the same: not prettier, not uglier, not more dear or more pious than before, yet they drove me out of the room. "You are a Talmud student already," they said. "Feh, you should be ashamed to sit in the same room with us and listen to these stories."

It was in that state of despair that the thought came to me that it would be better if there was no Talmud in the world and that instead of being born a boy and having to say the blessing every day, "Who has not made me a woman," if I had been born a girl I could read storybooks the whole day and no one would say a word to me.

Even my dear mother never seemed to scold my sisters for spending so much time—all Shabbes afternoon—with the storybooks, in which things were all mixed up and improbable things happened. She might have told them that they would do better to read the weekly Torah portion and additional readings in the Yiddish translation of the Torah. But my pious mother used to forget her speech, get caught up in the story being read, and sit for hours with the girls listening to the story to the end. I was jealous of the girls who did not know about the rebbe, and about studying Talmud in cheder, and who were allowed to read such beautiful stories that were so marvelous to listen to.

Yes, I became ever more convinced in the belief that instead of being born a boy and reciting, "Who has not made me a woman" every morning, and going to cheder to study Talmud, and not being allowed to have fun anymore, it would have been easier to be born a girl, long on hair and short on learning, but at least one could read the most beautiful stories and no one would say a word of reprimand. But all the doubt and pondering did not help me. With the beginning of Talmud study, not only was I no longer a Torah boy, I was no longer a boy anymore. I was a man like all Jewish men and whatever was inappropriate for a man was inappropriate for me. And like all Jewish men, I had to carry that heavy yoke of *Yiddishkayt*, of Jewishness: go to shul, pray three times a day, listen to a preacher, recite psalms, and certainly not laugh and joke.

Often, when the preacher gave a funeral oration and I was obligated to listen, I did not understand what he was complaining about. But it was at just such an oration that something happened to me that was the first push along the path that I would later follow.

Under the bimah in shul, there was a little room where they kept the boxes of sand for the Yom Kippur candles and two big barrels filled with all kinds of torn books and pages that were called *"sheymos."* Today there may be young people, and not necessarily boors and ignoramuses, who do not understand the meaning of the word *sheymos.* But in those days, even little cheder boys knew that they were pages from old books that had God's holy name written on them. So I knew why they collected the *sheymos* in the barrels.

It was said that once in a blue moon when the barrels were filled to overflowing, all the pious householders in town would gather at the shul with kosher clay pots from their kitchens. They would take the *sheymos* from the barrels and place them into the clay pots. Then the local wagon drivers would donate their horses and wagons and all the clay pots would be put onto the wagons. The rabbi, judges, circumciser, slaughterers, and all the religious functionaries came, and there was a grand funeral.

But this was not a funeral with the wailing and weeping of widows and orphans, not a funeral with "May righteousness go before you" and the din of "Charity delivers from death," and alms boxes that scare you so. No, this was a funeral with singing by the town cantor with all his assistants, and music by the town musicians, who sang and played even better than for the most wealthy bride and groom under the chuppah. That is how they accompanied the holy *sheymos* in their kosher clay shrouds to the cemetery, where they were buried in a proper place of honor among the great holy men and people of the best families. After that, Kaddish was said, and everyone happily went home.

In the evening, there was a feast sponsored by the trustees of the Talmud-Torah. The rabbi gave a speech and the cantor recited a prayer for the well-being of all who had given donations to buy new books for those who studied the holy Law.

So once when the preacher gave a funeral oration for a great scholar and I did not understand a word of it, my friends and I dug around in the boxes under the bimah. Most of them were looking for the odd bit of wax from the Yom Kippur candles; others were looking for what the *moyhel* brought here in a dish of sand after each circumcision. I did not have any interest in either of those things, so I climbed up the hoops of one of the barrels, and holding on with one hand so that I would not fall in, began pulling out dusty and moldy pages, one after another, until I had collected a big tangle of them.

I wanted to look at all these pages, so I took them to the window where there was more light and arranged them before my eyes. I saw that it was a storybook in Yiddish and that it was so easy to read, it was marvelous! I could understand every word without a commentary and without having to ask anyone for a translation. Although I had already heard plenty of storybooks read aloud, until that day I had never read a page of Yiddish. The books were so dear to the people who bought or borrowed them that they would never let them out of their hands and I had to be satisfied with just listening to them read.

At home I separated the tangled mass of pages and laid them out in order, page by page, and realized that this was a whole book of several hundred pages. It was missing only the covers and the title page. At first, I, a Talmud student, was a little embarrassed with the storybook in Yiddish and only looked at it when no one else would notice. But as soon as I could steal through ten or twelve pages, I became so interested in the story that I entirely forgot my shame and the rest of the world!

Seeing that I was so entranced, life and limb, in the withered pages of a storybook, my mother wrung her hands and started shouting, "It must be a spell that has been put on him! He won't let that book out of his hands! Imagine, a Talmud student, whoever heard of such a thing!"

But this time her complaints did not help. I would never let go of the book. I remember that once in the early morning, while I was completely immersed in the book, a criminal was being taken to be hanged. The entire town followed after the wagon to the place where the gallows had been set up. At such a moment, I managed to close the book, put it in my coat against my chest, and headed out to join my friends and run after the wagon.

There at the gallows, however, very lengthy preparations were taking place. Since it was boring for me to wait, I took out the book and right there among the thousands of fidgety spectators, began to read again. Then as I lifted my eyes from the words on the page, I discovered that I was the only one left: the arrestee was already hanging and the soldiers and the band had left the gallows. That's how I missed the entire ceremony of the execution. Later my friends were all boasting that they had seen everything, but I had to keep silent because I had seen nothing.

And so the storybook ended, but the impression it made left me so distraught that I went around for weeks as in a fog. I did not know the name of the book as I said: it did not have a title page or any other name. But its contents were deeply etched on my soul.

It told the story of a person, a boy of fifteen or sixteen, named Alter Leb, who was very dear to his parents because he was the only child remaining out of four. But that same Alter Leb did not love his parents. He did not want to go to cheder or obey his parents. He was very spoiled and even went traveling in a ship on the high seas to see the world.

But the ship was sunk in a storm and all the people on board were drowned. Alter Leb would probably have had the same fate if not for his pious mother, who day and night had prayed to God for the life of her disobedient son. The Creator of the World heard the prayers of Alter Leb's mother and the sea spit him out. Half dead, he washed up on the shore of an island.

He lay there unconscious for a day and a night. Later he came to and looked around him. Yes, he was rescued from the sea, but what would he do on this empty shore where there was not a house to be seen, or people, or any sign of settlement? It was an empty, dead shore, a lonely land, a sad island. So it was described in the book, and Alter Leb spent eighteen years on that very island.

He regretted disobeying his parents, beat his chest in pain and anguish, and intended to live a kosher and pious life. God had pity on him and a ship passed by the island and took him home safely. He found his parents and everyone was very happy. It was a glorious end. Alter Leb was married, taking the daughter of a very wealthy man, and lives with her in wealth and glory until this very day.

Some time later, when I could also read books in Hebrew, I read this same story under the title, *Khor Oni.* The author of that book was ashamed of nothing and announced his secret on the title page, that he had translated the famous *Robinson Crusoe.* That was when I learned that the other dear book that I had found among the *sheymos* was nothing more than a faked *Robinson Crusoe,* and I was very vexed by it.

First of all, the author took Robinson Crusoe, a goy from the streets, and without asking him if he wanted to be converted to Judaism, gave him the name, "Alter Leb," told him to pray three times a day, to bless the New Moon, light Chanukah lights, and all the rest, and he obeyed the author of the book. There was only one thing he could not do by himself: go to shul and hear the Megillah read on Purim. There was no shul on the dead island. Alter Leb even tried to teach his parrot a few lines from the Megillah: "It was in the days of Akhashverus" and "Cursed be Haman, blessed be Mordecai." But he knew that hearing the Megillah from such a reader was not suitable and he suffered great agony of spirit.

Despite that, the author of that Alter Leb story told a lot of lies of which there is no trace in the real *Robinson Crusoe*. But only much later was I informed of the many errors in my Yiddish book.

At the time when I read it, I believed it, almost seeing everything with my own eyes and sympathizing with everything that happened to Alter Leb as though I were following in his every footstep. Alter Leb was never out of my mind and I liked to think about myself as someone like him. For example, I began to practice for such an adventure by letting myself go wandering all over the town or getting lost in the forest. I would collect myself under a tree somewhere and make up a plan of how to build some kind of shelter just like Alter Leb did on his island.

In truth, I was not so foolish as to believe that I would really be an Alter Leb as in the book. I wanted to be in Alter Leb's situation on the island for just one hour, but I never succeeded in doing it. I was afraid to wander too deeply into the forest, and at the edge where the forest began I could still see the vanes of the town windmill and even the steeple of the church. So those attempts did not satisfy me, and the impression of Alter Leb was never put to rest.

I might have gone crazy if I had not had the happy thought: instead of being an Alter Leb myself, something I could in no way realize, I could write a fresh, new Alter Leb. And why necessarily Alter Leb, when it could be called Zelig, Berl, or Shmerl?

But why such an ugly name? I could choose a nicer name. He could be Yoysef and he could be handsome like Yoysef in the Bible and have a story that was even better than what happened to Alter Leb in the storybook.

I liked that plan very much, and when I got a kopeck of my own, I bought a sheet of paper and began to write. I wrote with great passion, probably no less passion and enthusiasm than I had while reading the book. And I wrote for months, not once forgetting where I had stopped and what I wanted to say next until the new Alter Leb—or

Yoysef Leb—was completed. Only then was my spirit, so stirred by that storybook, finally quieted.

I do not remember now the composition or the content of my new friend, but if someone would bring me that manuscript today, I would quickly recognize it, and no reward would be too great.

One of my brothers-in-law, who at that time was considered a grammarian and an expert in language, took one of my manuscripts and read it to friends and acquaintances, and I received quite a few pinches on the cheek and kisses on the head for being able to write such a fine story, worthy of being printed, they said, seriously or as a joke, I do not know.

I left home when I was very young and the manuscript remained with my brother-in-law. If it has not been lost, and if the scribbling of a child can be called, "work," I would call that little friend, "my first work."

NINE

SHOLEM YANKEV ABRAMOVITSH
AND MENDELE MOYKHER SFORIM

I had thought for a long time that Sholem Yankev Abramovitsh and Mendele Moykher Sforim were two completely separate people who had no relationship to each other and probably didn't even know each other. I imagined that Sholem Yankev Abramovitsh was a middle-aged Jew, a great scholar and very knowledgeable, who did not write Hebrew in a purely yeshiva style like Mapu or Kalmen Shulman, but rather, in a manner that was easy to read and very palatable. His writing was both witty and biting, and he spoke audaciously against famous writers older than he, though always in a wise and judicious way. He wrote what he knew about and he knew a great deal. I had respect for him, but before I became acquainted with him through a letter, I thought that he was a little too proud.

I perceived Reb Mendele quite differently. I pictured Mendele Moykher Sforim as an older Jew in his sixties, may he live to be one hundred and twenty, tall, thin, with deep furrows in his forehead, and with kindly and wise eyes that looked at everyone with love and pity. Meanwhile, those same eyes dreamt and looked into the far distance from where he hopes a greeting will come or the good tidings of a salvation and avengement for all Jews. I never encountered Mendele in an altercation or argument with anyone; he always spoke quietly and calmly, and always had a charming sweet smile on his lips.

In the world at large, as well as in the Jewish world, he had seen and heard a great deal, and he related this mostly with a sigh and an encouraging tone, though at other times with a devilish and ostensibly merry tone. Mendele himself, it seemed, was not a writer. What I read in his stories was what he had narrated to someone else who had written it down for him.

I loved him with my whole heart. I wanted to meet him and tell him how much I loved him, not only for the things he wrote about, but also for what he was: Mendele Moykher Sforim, Mendele the Book Peddler, the one thing that I most earnestly wished to be.

I remember that once a book peddler came into the study house where I prayed and spread out his wares on the long, waxy study table. He was a tall, bony Jew with a gray beard, a stooped back, and almost the same physiognomy that I had imagined Mendele would have. From the distance when I saw him, I thought: "It's him! It's the wise and loving Mendele!" I was ready to run to him with a big greeting: "Reb Mendele! How are you? Where are you coming from? Where are you staying in town so that I may come and spend a few hours listening to your latest story not even printed yet? And if you like, I can listen and write down the story as you tell it."

But since I was standing by the window looking out on the courtyard, I wanted to see his wagon and his horse, that patient and humble beast, who, though he toiled so hard and was exhausted and ragged from dragging the wagon so heavy with Jewish books and Jewish sorrows, was still the envy of other more respectable horses, because he had such a wise master who understood him with just a wink, and sympathized with his pain, and always found a kind word to comfort him in his difficult situation. But as usual, the study house window had not been washed for some time, and it was impossible to see through the accumulated dust and smoke on the panes, what was on the other side. I could not see if the wagon and horse were there or not.

Anyway, I thought, better to get acquainted with Reb Mendele first, then to see his wagon, and finally, to meet his horse, to whom I would be able to speak Mendele's language. But just as I was going to put out my hand to him—Reb Mendele that is, not the horse—to give my friendly hello, he began scolding the caretaker of the study house, complaining about how he had spread his books out over the entire length of the table without even asking him. He burst out angrily at the caretaker and spit out several curses against him. They were pretty ordinary curses that you could hear any day even in a holy place from Jews wearing tallis and tefillin, but they did not have a good effect on me, and inside me a voice shouted out, "No, this is not him! This is not Reb Mendele, not his voice, not his words, not even a shadow of him!"

I did not even want to look at this book peddler anymore. I was ashamed for having made such a bad mistake of seeing, even for a moment, my wise and loving Mendele in such an ordinary person with such a voice and way of speaking.

Of course, in those early years before Mendele was anyone's grand-father and any of his readers had figured out who he was or would eventually become, I was certain that Sholem Yankev Abramovitsh was not Mendele Moykher Sforim and Mendele Moykher Sforim was not Sholem Yankev Abramovitsh. Those were the years when Sholem Yankev Abramovitsh was already nobility and the old aristo-crats were still a little ashamed of Mendele Moykher Sforim, as they are of a person in the family who is of lowly origins.

I was just a boy, a little bit of a *maskil*, an Enlightened one, a be-ginner just brushing up against the old aristocrats, but I could in no way consider Mendele a person of lowly status. Rather, if Mendele ever came our way and I was the overseer of the study house, I would give him the honor of the third or sixth aliyah like a noble person, despite the fact that he was not a wealthy man and drove his own wagon to all the fairs, and concerned himself with supplying Jews with Hebrew and Yiddish religious books, moldy merchandise long rejected by the aristocrats, and that he was a bit of a wagon driver and tooted his own horn.

I had thought about all this for a while and had not come to a different way of thinking. Even later when someone told me that Mendele Moykher Sforim was the great, honored, and famous writer Sholem Yankev Abramovitsh, I considered it an unfounded opinion. Only later did I realize that Sholem Yankev Abramovitsh and Mendele Moykher Sforim were really one and the same person and that it was a name invented by the first as an ordinary name for the second.

It happened while I was living in Moscow, on the very same day and in the very same hour as I merited seeing with my own eyes my own first work in the form of a whole book, a fat one at that, printed in black and white letters on dark bible paper, and published by The Widow Romm and Brothers in Vilna. At the time, I worked in the Moscow office of a well-known tea firm for a relative of mine. Not a soul there knew that I had some connection to the Jewish Enlightenment and to creative writing, and I did everything so that no one would know, though this is not the place to explain why I did so. Perhaps I will have another opportunity to tell about it. But since none of my relatives or acquaintances in Moscow knew about my writing, I could not let them know that there in Vilna, in fact in the famous Romm printing house, several of my manuscripts were being printed and one of them had already been released into the wide world. The more I thought about it, the more I thought that no one should know.

But one night, a Chanukah evening, I arrived at a friend's house, a fine family. Instead of finding the family around the table eating latkes for which they had invited me, or at the green tables with cards in their hands as was the custom in Moscow even during Chanukah, or involved in a discussion about Tolstoy's new novel, *Ana Karenina*, which had just been published that year in the journal *Ruski Viestnik*, everyone was sitting around the big dining room table listening to some guest read a story in plain Yiddish from a Jewish book. All the listeners were so involved that they did not notice me come in and once they did notice me, they invited me to take a place at the table and to listen too, as it was very interesting and they just could not interrupt the story in the middle.

I thought that they were probably reading Mendele's *Di Kliatshe*, *The Mare*, which those in the know had already told me about, but which I had not yet read myself. So I found a place at the table, but instead of hearing something by Mendele, what I heard sounded very familiar. I could swear that I was hearing myself!

My heart trembled; I could feel myself going red in the face, then pale. Thank God that everyone's noses and ears were turned to the reader and no one noticed what was going on with me. I sat at the table on hot coals for half an hour, supposedly listening to the reader, but really shuddering from surprise and excitement as though I had a fever until God sent me help and the reader came to the end of the chapter, and the audience breathed a little freer. Then they noticed my agitation and asked me why I was so pale, did I have a chill?

I leapt at their questions like a drowning man clutches at a straw that happens to float by. I quickly answered that, in fact, I did not feel very well, and I apologized and asked if I might take my leave and go home. I was offered various things to do, to take, or to rub on to my-self to make me sweat, but I had already sweated enough from the joy that I was finally free of the danger of being exposed as the guilty one whose work had been received with such intense interest by this family.

But the fact that I could hide my secret from this family and from other families did not mean that I could hide it from myself. It would be difficult to be in the same place with my work and have no one else know about it, to have people talk about it and ask if I liked it, and to hear them discuss how they liked it. But how could I be identified with my work when no one knew or suspected? I was told to read the work by people who had read it and told me enthusiastically how many tears they had shed while reading it. I was afraid that people would notice how interested I was in it, and that this would lead them to suspect that the author, Dinezon, whose name was printed on the first page, was not some distant relative that I did not know, but was, in fact, me.

Writing to the printer in Vilna, I requested that they send me one copy to Moscow by general delivery, but they were apparently in no rush to fulfill my request. What was the rush? Was Moscow burning down? They seemed to laugh at my request and answered my letter with "Thus we are sending one copy by regular mail."

And so in the space of a few weeks, every Jewish household in Moscow was reading my novel, while I myself had never had the luck to encounter it when no one else was around. Until one day I realized that in another part of town, there was a Jewish bookseller named Lidski—in fact, the father of the Warsaw Lidski—who was the local distributor of Mendele Moykher Sforim's works, and where you could get all kinds of Jewish supplies and books, including many non-religious books. So one morning on a Russian holiday when my office was closed, I took myself out to find the bookseller Lidski.

I fumbled around for a good ten minutes in a dark apartment building, feeling around with my hands to locate a doorway that would let me into the place where Lidski lived and kept my heart's desire, before I finally knocked on a door and asked in Russian, of course, if this was where Lidski lived. The answer was that Lidski lived in number 134 and this was 142. "But don't stand in the open doorway!" scolded the old Muscovite woman in Russian with an accent from Shklov. "This is Moscow, not Shklov and not Warsaw. It's thirty degrees and firewood is more expensive here than cakes are there!"

"But how can I ever find number 134 where Lidski lives when it is so dark out here?" I tried to wedge a word in so that if the person was friendly they might lead me to Lidski's number.

"Here we go with the provincials!" she scolded. "A Muscovite has the sense to bring along matches in his pocket. If it's dark he's all right, he strikes a match and makes a light and doesn't make these mistakes."

I did not smoke cigarettes at that time and so did not carry any matches, but the woman's words taught me how important matches can be to an author when he goes searching for his friends, even though he doesn't smoke. At that moment I made a vow never to leave home without a packet of matches in my pocket. Meanwhile, to get rid of me quickly, the women gave me a little box with a few matches in it. I asked her to excuse me, warmly thanked her for her hospitality, struck a match, and soon found Lidski's door.

I found the elder Lidski in prayer shawl and phylacteries. He had been praying and apparently was right in the middle, because to my, "Good morning," he just nodded his head; and instead of asking me who I was and what I wanted, he focused his questioning eyes on me and uttered, "Nu?" so as not to interrupt his prayers before he had finished. I answered his silent question by saying I had come to buy some books from him. With the edge of his prayer shawl he wiped the thick dust off a bench, gestured with his hand to indicate that I should sit, and hurriedly said, "Nu, nu," a sign that he would not be long in finishing his prayers and that I should sit and wait and then everything would be done properly.

I calmed him by saying that I could sit for awhile; he should not cut his prayers short because of me. He seemed to take it as a courtesy from my side, but not very seriously, as he went back to his praying, and in barely five minutes, he turned back to me. He welcomed me and asked where was this young man from, how long had I been in Moscow, where was I staying, and so on. I hardly had time to answer one question before he asked the main question: "What kind of book did I need, traditional or Enlightenment?"

"Do you have *The Mare*?" I asked.

"Abramovitsh's *Mare*?" he asked me.

"Mendele Moykher Sforim's *Mare!*" I answered.

"One and the same!" he answered in Talmudic jargon. He was an old-fashioned Jew and still knew the language of the Talmud.

"I've heard people say that several times, but it never sounded right to me," I pardoned myself, saying that I did not understand how the twinning of the two separate names, the two different characters, could exist in the same person, judging by everything I knew about the two writers.

"What don't you understand?" asked the elder Lidski. "It seems very simple to me, nothing could be simpler. Don't you know that one does not wear the silk coat that one wears to shul on Shabbes or a holiday to the mill or to the shop on a weekday?"

"What does that mean?" I asked, not grasping the meaning of his example.

"I just mean that the name Sholem Yankev Abramovitsh has long been renowned for his books in Hebrew. Was he playing around in his Hebrew works? So then, if he feels like having a little fun, or dashing off a joke like "The Tax" for example, or even *The Mare* in Yiddish, is he obligated to use his famous name, Sholem Yankev Abramovitsh? Would it bring him any special honor? Of course in *The Mare* for one example, there is so much mystical information that his followers interpret it as a Yiddish story about everyday topics. Wouldn't putting his name on such a book be like putting the same cloth over the borscht in the kitchen that should be reserved for the challah on Shabbes?"

I still did not really believe him, but I held on to the man's words and thought about them later.

"And do you think that's news to his friends, the Hebrew writers? Everyone is doing it!" said this man who I had just met for the first time and who seemed to want to prove what an expert he was and how much he knew about such things. "You don't have to look far. Just a few weeks ago a Yiddish book was published under the name *Ha-Ne'ehavim veha-ne'imim, The Beloved and the Pleasant,* supposedly in

Hebrew, but with a Yiddish subtitle in explanation: *Der shvartser yunger-mantshik, The Dark Young Man*. And what a grab there was for that book. The first hundred copies I got were snatched up in less than three days. I sent a telegram to Vilna. They sent me, in the baggage car as I had requested, another three hundred copies and before the week was out I had only one left. I sent another telegram asking them to send me another one hundred copies and was informed that there weren't any more left in Vilna either. A Yiddish book, you hear! Heaven and earth and *The Dark Young Man!* I never saw anything like it. If God would grant that there be such a rush just three times a year, I would have nothing to worry about.

"But why was I telling you this? Right, because each customer wants me to tell him who is the author of *The Dark Young Man*. Is the name really Dinezon as it says, and, the real point, do I know him? How in blue blazes would I know who the author is! But it is clear as day to me that the name Dinezon is not his real family name. Maybe the name Dinezon is a code for something else or a reworking of his real name, or maybe it is an invented name. You want to know who the author of this book is? I say: 'Dinezon,' now go look for him!"

"And why couldn't it be that the author's real name is Dinezon as it is on the book?" I wanted to know how he could be so certain that the name Dinezon was a code or an invention.

"First of all, I would know about such an author. I have, thank God may He be blessed, been dealing in all these books for more than thirty years, so how come I have never heard this name mentioned before among authors or by anyone who knows them? And second, as I can see from this kind of rush to get the book, he must be one of the big experts in that circle of writers, and if his is also a known name in the Enlightenment world, he is not going to go around in his silk Shabbes coat to the mill or the shop, and so he has invented a weekday name, Dinezon, for his Yiddish books, just like Sholem Yankev Abramovitsh made up Mendele Moykher Sforim as a weekday coat to go to his mill, shop, or to the marketplace."

The man's close scrutiny interested me, but I saw that for every new question I posed and every remark I made, he would give me longer and longer explanations. He loved to talk and there would be no end to it, so I asked him, "And where is your warehouse?" Here in the room where he had given me his long speech, I did not see a single book except for his prayer book.

"My book warehouse, you ask? What a question! Apparently you forget, young man, that this is Moscow, not Vilna, not Berditshev, not even Shklov. In Moscow, the Jew himself is contraband. Do you think we are all jammed in here for nothing? There is no alternative. Here you can buy your way out with a ruble; in another place the rubles won't help. Are you asking where my merchandise is? That's the secret. Small items you can stuff into the holes under the oven, under the bed, in the clothes closet. Larger things can be stored with the janitor and you pay him a monthly rent to keep an eye on them. You could make a bigger package of things, but you can't go running to the janitor every minute, so you move things around among the neighbors. Right here there are only Jews. Here in this neighborhood you can't find a non-Jew anywhere."

"And do you have a copy of *The Mare* here with you?" I asked, ready to be on my way.

"I am not such a coward not to have a few copies of my books with me! You can even get three copies of *The Mare* if you want them," he boasted proudly.

"Then please give me one *Mare*, and give me a copy of *The Dark Young Man*, too, if you have one here."

I did not have to ask him twice, he bent over, rummaged under the bed a moment, took out a *Mare* and a *Dark Young Man*, handed them to me and said, "I must tell you up front, young man, that this is Moscow, which means not Vilna, not Berditshev, and if you aren't in those places you can't get the same merchandise someplace else for a cheaper price. Understand?"

I understood and was prepared for anything. Did I have a choice? Nevertheless, when he said three rubles for *The Dark Young Man,* I was surprised. "How does a Jew have the heart to charge three rubles for one book, and a Yiddish book at that?" I asked him.

"Do you have any idea what kind of book this is?" he exclaimed. "No less than Madame Poliakova sent me after that book especially. Do you know who she is? Probably the biggest millionaire in all of Moscow. I sent her *The Dark Young Man* with an invoice that it cost three rubles; she should send no more than three rubles. If I sent it without a price, I am sure that she would have sent me a whole ten-ruble note. Why not a twenty-fiver? As a rule I don't bargain, young man. I only have five of them left, and I have letters all over to get even twenty more, and in Vilna, you have already heard, they are already out of them."

I paid him what he asked for, and from a five-ruble piece he gave me barely half a ruble change in big copper ten-groschen coins: a ruble and fifty for Mendele's *The Mare,* and an entire three rubles for my own *Dark Young Man.* I left quickly for home, driven by my impatience to finally get to know my own child, and to look at all its merits and flaws, for my own curiosity and because I had handed over the first manuscript from my pen to the printer and had published a book into the world.

I began reading Mendele's *The Mare* with more calmness and seriousness than I used in looking at my own work. I read and read, searching here and there for the significance, and finally had the impression that I had stumbled into an old abandoned castle, where at every step, I encountered some wonder or supernatural sight and sound. Although there was a bright world outdoors, the twisted pathways, tangled byways, and bizarre events that I had just seen were still shimmering before my eyes; their secret sounds still rang in my ears.

The first question that demanded an answer was: Is this really my old familiar Mendele who I knew from before and with whom I felt almost as one and had loved so well? Had I not been so naïve, I would have realized that a very educated Jew was hiding behind that same Mendele Moykher Sforim, and that—as the old man had said—Mendele Moykher Sforim was just the weekday outfit of the celebrated Hebrew writer Sholem Yankev Abramovitsh, who, using that weekday coat, had shown me an entirely different face in *The Mare*; a face in a fine silk coat worthy of shul on Shabbes and the holidays.

In *The Mare*, Mendele Moykher Sforim grew from an ordinary book peddler who told ordinary stories, no more than he saw and heard, into a scholar, a shrewd speculative thinker, who took in the whole world, whose every word must be attended to with its sense considered for the meaning he had put into it.

In the Mendele Moykher Sforim of *The Mare*, I no longer recognized the dear old, almost reticent Mendele Moykher Sforim from all his other books that I had read before, and it seemed to me that the writer himself had changed his Mendele into another one, a more significant, more knowledgeable one than the first Mendele. And to be honest, that change did not bother me, because I could still find in the new Mendele the tenderness, the simplicity, and the modesty of the old Mendele. He harbored no pretensions that great minds or rich people or aristocrats would listen to him. He moved only in an ordinary world, among Jews like himself, and he did not wish that his readers would be of a noble strain. Therefore, his language was also simple and not particularly polished, as though already processed a little for those who only understood Yiddish.

The simple Jews would hardly recognize the new Mendele, especially the one in *The Mare*, I thought. He related not only what he had seen and heard, but what he knew and thought himself, and he told it for a more sophisticated audience, for those educated enough to properly understand him and wring out every meaning and subtle interpretation.

And then I wanted to understand why he had written *The Mare* in Yiddish and not in Hebrew. Among those who understood Hebrew at that time, I could hardly find anyone who understood *The Mare* or appreciated it. Among those readers that I questioned who only read Yiddish, I found only one or two who understood the new Mendele of *The Mare* and were enthusiastic about what he had written, but fifty percent less than those who had understood the old Mendele.

TEN

ILLUSION

One time on a New Moon when the rebbe had let us cheder boys
go home earlier than on any other day of the year, a friend of mine
took me to the "*komedia*." The *komedia* was a kind of booth or sukkah
without the *skhakh*, the roof covering, assembled from new and old
boards in the middle of the market square.

My friend's father had an inn—there were no such things as ho-
tels in little Jewish towns in those days—and the "*komediant,*" as every
juggler and sleight-of-hand artist was called, was staying at the inn.
Because of this, my friend was acquainted with the performer, and
because of my friend, I was also allowed to see the show for free.

This showman performed many tricks in ways that were not very
interesting and I could not begin to understand why the audience was
so enthusiastic and applauding so loudly. But since I saw that the
grownups were surprised and applauding, I clapped my hands, too,
although not for what I had seen of the show.

Anyway, I thought that it had not cost me any money, and when
my friend said, "Clap hard!" I clapped until my hands hurt. My friend
did not seem impressed by the card tricks any more than I was, be-

cause he consoled me: "This is nothing, just silly stuff. But soon you will see a real trick that will really surprise you!"

And soon I did see something that was more of a wonder than all the wonders that Pharaoh the King of Egypt's magicians had once done in the Torah. From a small bottle like the one you get from the apothecary with drops for a toothache, that trickster poured—continually for perhaps an hour—big glasses of beer, whisky, wine, and any kind of spirits you wanted. All from the same little bottle, which remained full, like a spring that never runs dry.

I saw how people tried the drinks with the tip of their tongues, and others went further and drank the glasses to the end and enjoyed it. I heard people talking, saying what a fool the performer was; he would do better to own a tavern and sell the spirits by the glass and by the quart and make a lot of money, instead of charging five kopecks a show in a *komedia* and having to live like a gypsy, here today, someplace else tomorrow.

I agreed with them but that was not the point for me. I wanted to know whether he did this kind of trick with the holy name of God, or—may they not be mentioned in the same breath—with magic? I did not know of any other way that anyone could continue to pour all kinds of spirits from such a small bottle, and I could not figure out how he did it.

So in the morning I asked the rebbe: "Is the sleight-of-hand man a wizard or a great saint who has hidden the secret name of God in the calves of his legs?"

The rebbe gave a little laugh and said that the showman did not know the difference between a section of the Talmud and the secret name of God. With God's secret name, he said, you could even make a golem. At that time everyone believed that you could not make a golem without the secret name of God, while today most everyone knows that you can do it without God's secret name; that's why you see so many golems in Jewish towns these days.

"He is no wizard," said the rebbe, "although he is a Jew. That showman had a yahrzeit, an anniversary of a death, today. He said Kaddish in the study house and gave a ruble for whisky after the prayers."

"Then how does he do it?" I asked.

"Hmm, a tough question to know what kind of power he uses to make the tricks that you and the rest of the audience describe. But the answer is simple! Nothing could be simpler! He does it through illusion. Understand?"

I did not understand and asked, "What's illusion?"

The rebbe strained to explain it. "Illusion is— How should I say it? An illusion is simply a kind of trick in which one person knows and the other person does not know. Even in your case with the showman, if this is some kind of power that is available to anyone, it would no longer be a trick and there would be no surprise. Remember, children."

Then the rebbe tried to illustrate illusion with examples, asking several times if we understood as was his habit with any difficult question that he himself did not understand. "Once again, illusion is what one person knows and the others do not, and that is the trick, and that is the surprise in the trick! Do you understand?"

"We understand!" we all answered, although we did not understand it any better than the rebbe did.

"Rebbe," one boy, a simple child, jumped in with a question. "If one boy can learn and another boy cannot, is that an illusion, too?"

"You're a little dope," answered the rebbe. "Illusion is not about learning. Illusion is only about what you see. One does not see the ability to learn, one listens as best he can! Understand?"

Probably at that time, everyone thought that you could not show how one learned with illusion. Today you can see illusion in learning in shul and everywhere else; illusions as good as any you can see from the great sleight-of-hand artists on the boards in the middle of the marketplace. In those days, we only knew about sleight-of-hand, while today we see illusions of hands and feet, too. But I believed my teacher and did not think about it anymore.

Many years have gone by since that time. I left cheder and moved around a lot, and saw things that others knew and I did not. There were many things I did not understand: how a person knew something, for instance, or what another person did that I did not know. But my rebbe's explanation always came back to me: "Illusion! Just illusion!" And everything was clear. I had an answer. I was not surprised by too many things.

Then not long ago, a doubt occurred to me. I heard a new word that was strange and incomprehensible to me. And there was no rebbe who could explain the difference between illusion and the new word.

It happened like this: I was a neighbor of Reb Leybl Vaynshenker, an observant Jew who blessed God and people with his learning and his praying. Yet nevertheless, I felt that Reb Leybl knew the art of illusion even better than that magician in the *komedia* of my childhood. Reb Leybl had several barrels in his cellar, large and small, but he drew wine from only one of them. A strange barrel, I thought.

When someone came in on the eve of Pesach and asked for Pontak wine, sweet Pontak, Leybl drew real sweet Pontak from the barrel. When Hershl Vokhernik came in and said, "Reb Leybl, give me half a pail of Bordeaux, real Bordeaux from Bordeaux-land, and not too expensive!" Leybl drew Bordeaux from Bordeaux-land from the same barrel and figured it out with chalk as one ruble and eighteen kopecks more expensive than Pontak, and swore that he was not making more than the eighteen kopecks. At which point Hershl would give up bargaining about the eighteen kopecks—that is Leybl's entire earnings—because he was so happy and satisfied that he had gotten the real taste of Bordeaux from Bordeaux-land.

If a minute later, Shleyme Vayntraub came in, a rich Jew but a little haughty mean tongues say, and said, "Leybl, give me half a pail of good Madeira. I have grown accustomed to that wine. I get it every Pesach, and during the year I don't put any other wine in my mouth either." Leybl would put a finger to his forehead, wince a little, think a moment, and reply, "I have some good Madeira, but very little, maybe a fifth of a pail altogether. It will be hard to part with such wine. You must be a real connoisseur for it, and for such a connoisseur my price is not too high."

Shleyme would swear that he is a true connoisseur and that they would settle on a price without going to the rabbi. Leybl would again draw from the same barrel, wrap the filled bottles in thin, pink paper, and send them home with Shleyme with his greetings to the family. Shleyme would drink the proper Madeira for the seders, experience a taste of Paradise, and keep on proclaiming, "Ay, a rare gem! Only you have to be a real connoisseur!"

If someone is dangerously ill and the doctor, uncertain if the patient will make it, recommends that the family spare no expense to get the very best Tokay, at least fifty years old and no less, then Leybl— nothing against him and may he live to be a hundred and twenty— finds that he has just such a Tokay wine as an inheritance from his father, Reb Avrom Vaynshenker, of blessed memory. He is paid very well for it and he draws that, too, from the same barrel to save the patient and get him through the crisis.

To me it was clear as day that Reb Leybl was practicing the art of illusion. For me this art was no art at all. Illusion can indicate even greater tricks. The surprise for me was how such a simple and pious Jew with a beard and side-curls like Reb Leybl had gotten mixed up in illusion? To me illusion was the monopoly of people who might be nominally Jews, but were licentious Jews. Jews who would not wear a beard and side curls and who were only known as Jews because they had a yahrzeit and had to say Kaddish like that showman from the days of my first illusion. But Leybl, who never missed a minyan even during the week, how did he get into illusion?

I finally asked the question of Pinye Kuper, who had worked in Leybl's cellar for thirty solid years. I knew that Pinye had some resentment against Leybl because he would not raise his salary, even though his work was seven times more than it used to be. But Pinye denied it vehemently.

"There is no illusion!" said Pinye. "Reb Leybele is no sleight-of-hand trickster! There are no secrets here, there is just faith and nothing more!"

"What do you call faith?" I asked. "What relevance does faith have to do with Pontak, Bordeaux, and Madeira wine?"

"There is a relevance!" said Pinye. "Do you think that it is necessary for every customer to be a connoisseur? No, it is enough for him to be a believer and to believe with complete faith that Reb Leybl is drawing whatever he thinks he is drawing from the barrel. Reb Leybl is certainly such a connoisseur and so he is very successful. He built up his father's business, except for his children's weddings, which set him back a good bit."

"But I don't understand," I said to Pinye. "How can you say that he believes that he is drawing from one little barrel Pontak, Bordeaux, and Madeira wine? Doesn't he know what is in the barrel?"

"He knows perfectly well what is in the barrel. Nothing more than some cheap Bessarabian wine seasoned with all sorts of things: caramelized sugar, dried berries, and licorice. He also knows that he spends a lot on river water, and to that I also say with no joke intended, he believes that he can get any wine from that barrel that anyone can name or think up!"

"Do you think that he imagines it and says that he believes it, but really does not?"

"I tell you," said Pinye, "you don't know him. Let me try to sell Bordeaux at the same price as Pontak, even though the Bordeaux and the Pontak originate in the same barrel, he will shout that I will make him go broke, that I have an idiot's brain. He will figure it out to show me that the Bordeaux cost him more than what I sold it for."

"I don't understand any of it, Pinye," I shouted at him. "How can you say, 'He believes!' Let's believe that the walking stick here in my hand is gold! How can you believe when you know for certain that it is not so? And why don't you believe it?"

"That is the art, indeed," said Pinye Kuper. "What one can believe and another cannot! That's just what I'm talking about here: that it is not an illusion, but faith, faith, and faith! Faith in oneself, faith in the barrel, and faith that the whole world that drinks wine does not know what wine is. You only need to tell him in faith that this is Pontak, this is Bordeaux."

As he walked away, Pinye said with a sigh, "If God would send me a bit of the kind of faith that Reb Leybl has, I would not just get Pontak, Bordeaux, Tokay, and Madeira from that barrel, but also real *Erets Yisroel* wine, Carmel from Rishon LeZion. And I would not even need to know that there was an *Erets Yisroel* on the face of the earth where the Carmel wines come from!"

These explanations from such a simple person as Pinye Kuper set my mind in turmoil. Until then I had thought that only with illusion could one make such a trick and that only illusionists knew such secrets that could confuse most people. But now I began to believe that it is not necessarily an illusion. It was just the truth: a firm faith in oneself, in the barrel, and in the ignorance of others.

Until that moment, I had even suspected that my compatriots, the writers, wrote everything with illusion. One moment earlier, they did not need to know or to think about what and how they would write, but they just said, "Write and get honoraria!" Then they did the trick of illusion to create something with pen and ink that someone could read and think about. Suddenly, I saw that there was no secret to that either. It was just faith! Faith in oneself, faith in the inkwell, and faith in the ignorance of the readers who do not know the difference between Pontak, Bordeaux, Madeira, and Tokay, or narrative, portrait, sketch, novel, and so on.

I know writers who take on assignments by the line, by the page, by the newspaper page. They write literature for a ruble or for a gulden. And there are writers who write by the week and by the day and by the hour and even by the minute, and the literature they produce must meet a deadline, not one moment later and not one minute earlier. And it must not be one line more or one word less. How could they do that without sleight-of-hand? Especially, how could they write on topics about which they have so little to say?

And I had thought that it was all illusion. Long live Pinye Kuper! That simple Jew had revealed the secret that there is no illusion in the world. It is all faith! One must be able to believe! One must not have a moment of doubt that the one who drinks the wine or the one who reads the literature is an expert in what is wine and what is literature.

And I would say as Pinye Kuper said with a sigh: "If God would send me a bit of that faith in myself, in my inkwell, and in my readers, I could write for you with an easy spirit, like my friends the writers who can hear and think above all else in the world. From my inkwell I would draw novels, narratives, criticisms, and any kind of tract, in the same way that Reb Leybl drew Pontak, Bordeaux, madeira, and Tokay from his barrel."

But how do I get that faith?

The whole trick says Pinye Kuper—like my former rebbe—the whole trick lies in what one knows and the others do not know.

Akh, faith, faith!

ELEVEN

THE YIDDISH THEATRE

I

Yiddish theatre was born in a wine cellar in Odessa. It first stood up on its own two feet in a Romanian coffeehouse during the time of the Russo-Turkish War. When I saw it for the first time in Warsaw, it was still a young child just learning to speak.

You do not expect much from a small child. Whatever kind of faces a small child makes, it is charming. Whatever a small child tries to say, it is clever. Whenever you encounter a small child who loves to mimic and copy the adults around him, it is considered an accomplished child. Parents and relatives cannot praise the cleverness and smartness enough; even strangers may grant it a kiss now and then, or express their pleasure with a pinch on the cheek. Of course, if an adult did such childish things and said that he had copied it from someone else, people would say that he was acting crazy or, in fact, was crazy. But everything is fun from a small child; everything is clever.

Looking with such eyes at the early Yiddish theatre in general, and in Warsaw in particular, I cannot deny that I got more than a little pleasure from it. For a small child, *Ni be ni me ni kukeriku (Neither This, Nor That, nor Kukerikoo)* was cute; *Shmendrik* was a joke; *Kuni Lemls,* with all its brothers and friends, was an imitation of a life.

Real art and true-to-life qualities come with age, with further development, not only of the artist himself, but of the public who have to be educated to get intellectual use from the art. The public was itself rather childish regarding the newborn Yiddish theatre, playing with the theatre as with another child, and both getting childish pleasure from it. There was a kind of childish innocence and Jewish charm in the Yiddish theatre then. That charm and innocence can be felt in the artless Yiddish songs that began the plays and with which they usually ended.

I do not know whether the father of Yiddish theatre, Avrom Goldfaden, ornamented his newborn child with so many pretty ditties because he took his example from the older Yiddish presentations such as *Shprintse Haman* from the Purim plays, *Mekhires Yoysef, Melukhes Shoyl,* and other plays that were based on neat rhymes and songs. Goldfaden himself was hard put to present Yiddish theatre without rhymes or a treatment of a Jewish theme without singing, or had he just calculated it that way?

Feeling that both he and the Jewish public were little prepared for serious theatre presentations, and recognizing the weak side of his pieces, Goldfaden may have thought that the problem was with his songs, which in many cases he made stronger. Many of Goldfaden's songs were already familiar and loved by the public before he had even dreamed of the Yiddish theatre.

I am partly willing to believe that it was not the theatre that brought the songs to the world, but that the entire theatre was created for the songs. But it really does not matter which is so. I am certain that the entire interest in Yiddish theatre at that time, its entire charm for the masses and for the intellectual audience as well, was Goldfaden's songs, and so one can say that Goldfaden's Yiddish theatre songs can atone for all the childish mistakes and foolishness of his Yiddish theatre. Goldfaden's theatre songs from that time—not including the couplets—are still Jewish songs. The Jewish audience took them as their own, and in time, they became Jewish folksongs.

*   *   *   *   *

A Talner Chassid, an expert in melodies, told this story about one of Goldfaden's songs: "As is common knowledge, my Rebbe, Reb Dovidl Talner, may his merit sustain us, was, in a sense, King David of Israel returned, and although the world kept it a secret, it was possible to recognize it through his playing and singing. When he took the fiddle in his hands, even a Litvak would have to confess that this was no ordinary fiddle, but the harp of David, King of Israel. And what singing! Whoever did not hear his songs, especially those for Havdalah, did not know real singing.

"One time a Chassid from Odessa came to see Reb Dovidl. They called him Shepsl Odesser. During the day on Shabbes, when a group of Chassidim gathered at the Rebbe's house, Shepsl sang a new song that melted everyone's heart. Many of the young Chassidim recognized the melody and knew that it had come from a place where men and women sit together. But no one said a word, so no one would suspect that they went to places they should not have gone. As Shepsl sang, everyone sang with him, over and over, until Reb Dovidl heard the melody in his room and came out to the dining room from where the singing had reached him.

"Out of respect, everyone stopped singing. But he signaled that everyone should keep singing. He liked the song and they sang it again and again. When they finally stopped, the Rebbe said, 'A wonderful idea! The words are also nice; it's a good song. Will you sing that song again, Shepsl, when we sing *zmiros* after Havdalah?'

"Meanwhile, imagine what was going on in Shepsl's heart! If the Rebbe wanted to hear the song again and no one said a word, this material Chassid from Odessa should confess and say, 'Rebbe, this song came from an impure place. I heard it in Odessa in a Yiddish theatre hall!' and the Rebbe would excuse him. But now, since the Rebbe had specifically said, 'A wonderful idea! The words are also nice,' and had asked Shepsl to sing the song at *zmiros* after Havdalah, he did not have the nerve to say, 'No, Rebbe, this song is a coarse song because the father of the song is Avrom Goldfaden who does not even have a beard!' Everyone kept silent and it was agreed that they would sing the song right after Havdalah.

"Anyway, the song with the beautiful Jewish melody was indeed a pleasure to hear, but the whole activity was an embarrassment for the Chassidim, because what if the Rebbe knew who wrote the song? But the truth was that nobody really knew who had written the song, and it could be that no one would ever know.

"Everyone knows about Beni the Cantor. In our circles, even little children in cheder talk about Beni's voice. The bride and groom are led to and from the canopy to one of Beni's marches. His knowledge of melodies cannot really be compared to the Rebbe's knowledge of melodies—no one can stand against the Rebbe—but without comparing, it is truly rare to find such a fine voice.

"Back then, while this event was taking place, Beni was a fervent Chassid of the Talner Rebbe. Now he is in the Makarov sect. Do you know why he changed from Talner to Marakov? But that has nothing to do with our story.

"Once Beni wanted to write a new melody and give it as a gift to the Rebbe for a certain Shabbes. For Beni this was hardly any work; he just thought about it and out it came! So he came to Talner for Shabbes and brought along his merry new song.

"He was quiet all through Shabbes and did not speak a word about his new melody. But there are no secrets among the Chassidim. It became known and the Chassidim were talking the whole day about the new song that Beni would sing with the Rebbe's musicians right after Havdalah.

"The audience waited for the right moment for Beni's song. But there was a flaw. After Havdalah, the Rebbe gave the sign for Beni to introduce his new melody and Beni began to sing. But instead of appearing happy as usual, everyone noticed that a dark mood had descended over the Rebbe like a veil; and the longer Beni sang his song, the worse the Rebbe looked. The audience was worried that the Rebbe might fall into melancholy and perhaps the world might end.

Beni was signaled to stop singing, but he was stubborn and would not stop. He pretended not to see and kept right on singing. The audience was ready to throw him down and take him out of the Rebbe's house wrapped in sheets. When the Rebbe saw this, he himself said, 'Enough, Beni!'

"Nothing more was required. Beni's voice broke and he stood silent, his face stricken, and his teeth chattered in his mouth. The audience took this as a sign: Beni had stumbled into sin and the Rebbe had sniffed it out.

"It was clear that Beni was regretting what he had done. When his regret was evident, the Rebbe's face changed and he said, 'How did this song come to you, Beni?'

"'Rebbe, what is my error, what is my sin?' said Beni, encouraged a little by the Rebbe's smile.

"'This silly song; where did it come from?' asked the Rebbe, and perhaps meaning it differently, so that he would not shame him.

"'It is my own idea!' answered Beni. 'I am its author!'

"'Your own idea!' the Rebbe repeated Beni's boast. 'You yourself are the author? So are you surprised that I do not like your song?'

"Beni's eyes opened wide. He wondered why the Rebbe would not like his song just because it was his own creation, and he, Beni, was the author? The Rebbe understood what Beni's question was and answered in a very kind voice: "'A melody is obliged to be something that will please the whole community of Israel. It is not your own idea. One is not the author of such a melody. One does not sing such a melody. Such an idea falls from heaven into the heart of someone who knows music. There in his heart, the idea is clothed in the clothes of a melody, and when such a melody is torn from the heart, it is easy for it to penetrate the hearts of all Israel. You do not sing such a melody; the melody sings you. You may not even want to sing it; it sings itself even against your will. It sings itself and stirs your heart, so that you are possessed of the spirit of God, the source of melody and joyful song. Now do you understand, Beni, the difference between an idea and an inspiration, between a song and a joyful song?'

"Beni and the whole group of Chassidim heard the speech that went through all 248 limbs and all 365 veins of their bodies, but it was beyond their comprehension.

"'Such a melody, Beni,' the Rebbe continued, 'such a melody is the lovely song that can be sung every Shabbes evening after Havdalah. Do you know the song *God Spoke to Yankev?* Sing it, Beni!'

"When the Rebbe said, 'Sing!', one sang. Beni sang the melody with his voice, trying to appease the Rebbe for the earlier song. The Chassidim were excited simply because of its sweetness. But the Rebbe was not pleased.

"'Heart, Beni, heart!' said the Rebbe. 'You lack heart. A melody without heart has no vigor. The soul of such a melody is a cold, un-Chassidic soul!'

"So to demonstrate to the group and to Beni how to sing a song with heart, the Rebbe himself began to quietly sing the melody. Slowly the audience felt as though a kind of sweet fever had overtaken them. Soon the Rebbe's sweet voice began to get louder and deeper, clearer, purer, and stronger, and the audience had no strength to contain itself, they began to sing along with him. Their mouths seemed to open on their own as they sweetly sang along with the Rebbe. It seemed as though the melody had embraced each one, wrapping each in sweet voices. Everyone, even a Litvak, could feel this detachment from the corporeal. The body stayed there in the room with the Rebbe, but the soul was carried far off into other worlds by the heartfelt melody; worlds where nothing was desired but singing, singing, singing.

"After awhile it felt as though everything in the world was singing: heaven and earth, the stars and the planets, inanimate things, growing plants, animals in the wilderness. Everything sang, everything was carried up in song, up, far off into the high, deep blue air. If you looked up, it seemed as though the whole world was flooded and covered with a deep flood of song; and in the flood of pure, clear, and sweet voices, you could see how the souls of the holy and pure immersed themselves, bathing and splashing, dipping under and coming back up, swimming back and forth, on and on to the end of the world.

"Suddenly it seemed as though you could not see any individual souls. All the souls seemed to flow together into one great soul, and the one great soul poured on and became fused with the *Ayn Sof,* the One Without Beginning or End. Boundaries disappeared. There was no weight, no time. You yourself are an *ayn sof,* without beginning or end, and the *Ayn Sof* sings the great song that also has no beginning and no end. Now you know the secret of the end of creation: you are the song; the soul is the end of creation.

"How long this elevation of the soul went on is difficult to determine. It could have been for whole generations or just the blink of an eye. But suddenly it was torn apart, and the congregation was back to perceiving where they were and what they were. No more flood, no more song, but the voices carrying on like waves that pull you off to the great beyond.

"Soon the congregation fell silent, each person feeling a kind of exhaustion, the soul free, it seemed, and the eyes full of tears. Some wanted to cry; why and for what? No one knew.

"Suddenly another quiet song is heard and it captures the heart. The Rebbe sits lost in thought it seems, but everyone hears how his soul pours out in a sweet, touching prayer, a kind of longing and pulling towards heaven. It pulls like that, the quiet song pulls and you can see clearly how it flies up like a bird from Paradise, higher and higher, becomes quieter and quieter until it disappears, and the sharpest ear cannot hear it anymore.

"And do you think that the Rebbe sang a new song? No! It was exactly Shepsl Odesser's song, the one he had brought to the Rebbe from the Yiddish theatre. With that song the Rebbe had demonstrated that a holy, pure melody, even though a creation of Satan, can also come to the right people and be used to bring them back to the right path, and be brought back to the original inspiration for a Jewish heart to sing it.

"It seemed so simple that a Chassid could not conceive of it any other way; but that Beni was a hard-baked, stubborn fellow, and all this came hard for him. When bidding goodbye to the Sabbath, Reb Dovidl, may his merit preserve us, loved to have a sip of strong spirits and to drink a toast to each individual guest. Beni spoke up: 'Rebbe, how does this melody merit being raised to such a high level?'

"Reb Dovidl did not like being questioned about his methods. 'A Litvak asks questions!' he had once answered someone. 'First he asks questions of his father and mother; then of his Rebbe; later of the holy Torah; and later of the Holy One, may His Name be blessed! The beginning of all the questions is a lack of faith, and the end is heresy and atheism, may we all be spared!'

"And truly, who would need to ask about the Rebbe's methods? If the Rebbe sang the song, one must know that the Rebbe knew what he was doing, without questions, without wondering. But perhaps the Rebbe wanted the matter to be quite clear to everyone. So he answered Beni: 'If you do not like the song, do not sing it. You are not fit to like it!'

"'Rebbe, I like it very much!' answered Beni. 'But the composer, the composer of the song!'

"'Are you going to tell me that the composer of the song has a shaved face and lives for the material world? Never mind, I know even more!' said the Rebbe. 'But his soul, Beni? His precious Jewish soul?'

"Beni and the audience of Chassidim were shocked and disturbed, but the Rebbe was not finished and went on, 'You have only eyes, Beni, and so you do not see any more than his resemblance to Esau, his materialism, and his shaved beard. But if you also had just a little bit of ear, you would also hear in his song the voice of Jacob. The voice of a Jewish soul can split the heavens; the idea of a Jewish song knows no bounds. Whoever has an ear sings it and does not ask questions.'"

*   *   *   *   *

I do not know how true or how exaggerated this story is about Reb Dovidl and this song from the Yiddish theatre, as told by the Talner Chassid. Chassidim generally love to exaggerate things that they are enthusiastic about, especially in stories about their Rebbe and his teachings. But it could be that this actually happened with Reb Dovidl of Talner.

And every time I got angry at the Yiddish theatre as it was in those early days with its caricatures, awkward and false depictions of Jewish life, and other flaws, I would seem to see the wise Rebbe, Reb Dovidl of Talner, before me. He wags his finger at me and with a kind smile on his lips he says, "Just see how unfair you are, you modern young people! I, Rebbe Dovidl of Talner, am able to excuse him for his being materialistic, shaven, and everything else, may we be spared, because of his beautiful Yiddish songs. And you, modern youth, cannot excuse him because of his childish silliness and foolishness, although in truth you are still not sure whether you, in his place, would make it any better or more clever?"

II

The public does not wait for the critic to advise them what is good and what is bad. What is homey and familiar they take home with them. What is strange and not good they toss aside and forget about on their own. Nothing that the Jewish public looked at and listened to in that former Yiddish theatre made much of an impression for better or for worse. In *Shmendrik, Kuni Lemls, Brayndele Kozak (Breindele Cossack), Di Kishufmacherin (The Sorceress)*, and many other presentations in the Yiddish theatre, the public could find no trace of the familiar, so they soon forgot them once they left the theatre. In any case, no one considered comparing the plays to themselves, to their own lives, or to the lives of their neighbors. All that they took home with them were the Yiddish songs that they had heard there.

I do not know whether, when the new Yiddish theatre played in Warsaw, there was one Jewish household, one Jewish family, in which they did not sing Yiddish songs and delight in them. I am not speaking about those Jewish homes and Jewish families where no Yiddish word was spoken and where they were ashamed of their own Jewishness even in front of their own non-Jewish servants. Such embarrassed Jews, as I recall, were even afraid to go to the street where the Yiddish theatre was located, so that no one might think that they even entertained the thought, heaven forbid, of gracing the theatre with a visit. But I am talking about the Jewish homes and families where everything that is Jewish was precious and beloved. In such Jewish homes and families, the theatre songs were not only homey, they became their own dear possessions.

And who of those Jews did not sing the songs? Everyone sang them: Chassidim, Enlighteners, Polish Jews, Litvak Jews, heads of households and wealthy men, the Jewish slaughterer and the butcher, workers in the workshops, and clerks in the shops. Jewish mothers sang their children to sleep in their beds with these songs; little children, girls and boys, chirped the songs like little songbirds in all their games and jokes. They were sung on Shabbes and the holidays, at celebrations, weddings, and circumcisions. Musicians regaled the in-laws and the bride and groom with them, and Jewish paupers begged for donations with them at Jewish doors and windows.

And the songs have not been forgotten. Even now, eighteen years since there has been a Yiddish theatre in Warsaw, you can still hear the songs, and they have not aged or grown tedious. Would the Jewish public have embraced the theatre songs with such love and warmth if they had not recognized their own spirit, had not felt their own heart?

The Jewish public heard its own voice in the songs, the voice of Jacob, for which Reb Dovidl of Talner forgave the composer of that same song for his sins and shortcomings. And I forgive the creator of the Yiddish theatre for all his flaws and the failure of his theatre, because of the precious Yiddish songs that came out of it. And I hope that he, too, will forgive all those who seriously value the worth of his Yiddish songs on the Jewish masses in their time and in later times.

*　　*　　*　　*　　*

And since I am already talking about the value and influence of that Yiddish theatre song, I do not want to pass up the opportunity to bear witness myself to the influence that very same song had in homes and families where they did not want to hear or know of such songs.

At the time when the Yiddish theatre first began to play in Warsaw, I had, because of my business situation, become friends with one of the Warsaw Jewish families that not only did not know about the Yiddish theatre but, it seemed, did not even want to recognize Jews as people. That family liked me, as they had said openly many times, even though I never hid my Jewishness from them. The greatest flaw they found in me was not in my Jewishness, but in my Jewish language. I could not express myself well in Polish at that time as my friends did in their home, but knowing that they were Jews, even though they were ashamed of Jews, I had no alternative but to speak with them in the language which my father had spoken to my mother, and which both had spoken to me, figuring that my friends' parents had also spoken to them in Yiddish.

"We like you so much," the matriarch of the family said. "You should learn Polish so that it can be your support language, so I can introduce you to our other friends who will like you as much as we do."

Getting to know her friends and relatives was not something I longed for, and I continued to speak Yiddish with her and her husband as we had always done. There was an exception, however. Although we spoke Yiddish, I never discussed their own Jewishness with them. Reminding them, even with my language, that they were Jews, would be considered an insult to them in their own home.

In general, I looked on such enslaved Jewish souls as spiritually sick. In the worst case, I might despise them, but not insult them, and I knew I could not convince them of what I believed. How many Jewish souls has the Jewish Exile ruined? A few more or less will not make the people greater or lesser.

If I had been the complete believer at that time that I should have been, I would have believed that some ancestral merit would come in, that something would happen in their home that would awaken their hearts, so they would begin to long for a return to their Jewishness and be drawn back to their brothers and sisters from whom they had distanced themselves.

Once when I came into their house, I found a pretty young lady sitting at their piano playing a wonderful concert. Who this lady was, I still do not know, perhaps a daughter of one of the friends to whom Madame had promised to introduce me once I learned Polish. But whoever she was, I realized how much she was in her element, and how rare it was to hear such a young person play so well.

When she finished the prepared piece and graciously received all the praise from her listeners, she took out a new piece of music. She had just bought it, she explained, and asked if we could be patient for a moment for her to go over it, and then she would play it as it should be played.

In the first notes that she tapped out on the piano, I already heard the Jewish sorrow, the Jewish song, and I thought: now the player is going to destroy the impression she just made with her first beautifully performed piece. And it appeared that I was not wrong. Once my Jewish friends perceived that it smelled of Yiddish, the master of the house began to wrinkle his nose, and Madame drew her sweet lips into a sour sneer as though she had just licked a lemon.

Looking at the notes and grasping the melody, the young pianist did not notice the wrinkled nose of my friend and the sour expression of his wife, and she played on, at first slowly and with some effort, until she found the right style, and then played as only she could play.

It was a very familiar melody to me. I had heard it many times in the Yiddish theatre, but never so pure and whole as from the fingers of this unusually talented player. I gave myself over to the music, and for a moment forgot the house and the people I was with, and expressed my pleasure with many gestures. Then I noticed, as I shyly stole a glimpse at my friend, that his nose had straightened out as it usually was, but his normally happy expression was serious and deep in thought. And Madame's sour, drawn-up lips had become sweet again, and on her face lay a kind of pleasure and inner happiness. Only in her eyes stood a pair of tears, much more lovely and brilliant than the two big diamonds in her modern earrings.

Tears in eyes where I had never seen them are always evidence that the heart under them is not frozen and dried out completely; rather, tears that appear in eyes hearing glorious music or a touching melody, tell me much more: they show me that the heart feels, longs, melts with love for all that is dear and beloved anywhere.

I was very happy with my friend at that moment, and the young woman kept playing and playing. The touching melody poured from under her fingers as from a spring, pure and clear. The music stopped, but the effect did not leave us. No word interrupted the dreamy stillness that suffused the richly appointed salon. Each person remained sitting pensively in the same position they were in during the music. Even the pianist did not move from her place and stayed seated at the piano, her eyes resting on the notes that she had just played.

It seemed to me that each person had something to do for himself in that moment. He did not regard the others in the room. The mood was heavy. My friend seemed embarrassed in front of me. Why?

I recalled from the Torah: When it was too difficult for Joseph to play his role as a ruler over his own brothers, he asked all the other people to leave. Was he ashamed to let them know who his own brothers were? No! He was ashamed of the role that he was playing, the role of ruler over his brothers. It was not they who had once done him harm out of their jealously and anger and now stood guilty before him, but he, only he, the mighty and proud servant of the king, who stood guilty before them!

They had recognized their guilt long before and had regretted it. If they had only known where they could find Joseph, they would have gone to the ends of the earth to seek him out. He, however, knew where his brothers were. He could imagine how his old father wept and mourned for him, but he got lucky: he became rich, he became close to the king. He forgot all about them. And even when their hunger and persecution brought them to him, he still did not have the nerve to recognize them until their precarious situation and their just complaints finally awakened the denying brotherly heart within him. Yes, no other people could excuse his pride and estrangement of his own suffering brothers!

Something similar had happened during that moment in the hearts of my assimilated friends. They were embarrassed in front of me. Would it be better if I left them alone now and let them experience the heavy impression of the Yiddish song by themselves? I did so, and did not go back to their home for two weeks.

The next time I went back, they received me very simply but in a very homey fashion as before. The first words my friend spoke were about music and about Jewish musicians in particular. With special satisfaction, he rattled off a list of famous Jewish names, of those who had excelled in every age in every country as world-famous musicians.

"Fine harmonious sounds," he said, "can only come from fine harmonious souls. As it is self-evident that the Jewish people have, proportionally, more famous musicians than any other group, we have to admit, even unwillingly, that the Jewish people have proportionally more fine harmonious souls than other peoples as well. Still our enemies will not admit that we are no worse than they are. The Jewish people have given so many harmonious sounds to the educated world, and what has the educated world given back? Anti-Semitism, confinement, and pogroms! The ungraciousness of the educated world for the Jewish people cannot be comprehended in any normal sense," complained my friend, "and cannot be addressed with any honest language!"

I was surprised at this change in my friend's thinking. There are hearts that are not stirred by drums, but there are musical hearts for which it is enough to pluck one string and they awaken and begin to play all the songs that they have ever heard and loved. My friend certainly had such a heart, and I realized then that it was singing the old Jewish melodies like all Jewish hearts.

Speaking of purely Jewish music, my friend said, "But more than ever I want to know what the power of the Jewish melody is, how it presses so deeply into the heart, settles there as though growing, and one cannot forget it. It's been two weeks since those Yiddish notes were played here, and the melody follows me everywhere I go. Yesterday I was at a big theatre, a performance of Meyerbeer's *Prophet*, but it seemed to me that I could still hear that Yiddish melody that seemed to have no relationship to Meyerbeer's music.

"Today I was standing in the stock market thinking about something and caught myself quietly singing that song to myself. There is some power in the true Yiddish melody that penetrates deep into the heart. Singing, like music in general, is the language of the soul. Each folk-soul has its own soul-language, and it is no wonder that a Jewish soul understands the language of its folk-soul more deeply. The voice of one's father and mother, of one's sister and brother, one's near and dear, even if one distances oneself from them, can be easily heard in the folk-melodies! Their sighs, longings and sufferings as well as their hopes and aspirations ring in the melody. How can a child not hear the voice of its parents, how can a brother not hear the sighs and sufferings of his brothers and sisters?"

"Yes, yes," I answered my assimilated friend. "Blood is not water! And you cannot wash it away with water!" I lectured him.

That same evening, Madame also told me what she had dreamt that night when the Yiddish song was played in their parlor: "It seemed that I was still a little girl and was sitting on my pious mother's lap. She kissed me and petted me so warmly, hugged me so lovingly and comfortingly, and sang me some sweet song that made me want to cry and laugh at the same time. I felt so good, so comfortable, and so happy. I wanted to feel that way forever! And the song she was singing was the same song that I had heard played just an hour before. Then that song, because of my dream, became so dear to me that I cannot stop playing it whenever I sit at the piano!"

Perhaps she did not understand that the song was sweet to her even earlier, and that her dream was just the impression of its sweetness. Later I saw Madame and her husband at the Yiddish theatre a few times, and even later, I saw them often in the Jewish neighborhood visiting their poorer relatives.

There are various ways of awaking and reviving a weakened heart in an individual. There are even more ways to awaken and revive the abandoned and indifferent heart of a whole people. But one of the most effective venues that populists can employ is folksong, folk melody, and folk theatre. Today's activists know this, or else why is there so much talk now about the revival of the Jewish folk and its strengthened and revitalized consciousness?

III

A Jewish child's childhood is as short as a winter's day. Even shorter is the gay little song that it sings. As soon as the Jewish child perceives itself, it also perceives the Jewish Exile, and then it can only cry and sing no more. The still childish Yiddish theatre has not yet had time to reach its cheder years, to learn something and become what it can and should be. Now it has been confronted with the old Jewish Exile that has interrupted its song, driven it from the stage, and made an end to everything that was good and not so good within it.

Its friends and lovers are sorry. "How come?" they ask. "Did it do anyone any harm? Who could be angry with it?" And other such questions that receive no answers. People complain and are stuck with it.

But God does not abandon his people Israel. Soon after the Yiddish theatre closed, whenever people gathered for Jewish celebrations —engagement parties, weddings, circumcisions, and even when finishing a section of Torah study—a new kind of Jewish entertainer appeared who made the crowd happy by singing songs from the Yiddish theatre. "Actors from the former Yiddish theatre," they called themselves, and the audience was very much taken with them. That they were actually actors in the Yiddish theatre, I doubt very much. They had certainly been paupers and beggars, do-nothings, and coarse youths. They latched onto the fallen Yiddish theatre the way such beggars adopt a crippled child to take from door to door. Jews did not need to go to the theatre anymore. The Yiddish theatre had come to their homes.

"Do you see what has become of my heart's child?" Avrom Goldfaden, the father of the Yiddish theatre complained to me, on seeing a band of young good-for-nothings singing his songs at a Jewish wedding. "They've made it some kind of religious functionary. My child has become a beggar who goes from house to house whining for a groschen, and I have to look at him and not have my heart burst inside of me."

But what could he do except turn to the old Jewish remedies? So one fine day he called his better actors together, handed them the old Jewish wanderer's stick, and told them to find a new home.

"The sound of the old *ma yofes* song still resounds in the prince's ears," he said, "so he cannot bear to hear any other song from you. Go off to where your ancestors never had any princes over them and never had to sing *ma yofes!* Go off to where the Exile has already driven thousands of your brethren to find a new home. There, in the new home they have established, they sing my songs, and they will remember their brothers and sisters who long for them in the old home!"

They obeyed their Rebbe, took up the wanderer's stick, put the young Yiddish theatre on their shoulders, and went to America with him.

"Now I am calm," Goldfaden said. "Now I know that my child can develop freely and mature as he should!"

Unfortunately, he made a bitter mistake.

A smart Jew once said: "You know, when I go to say goodbye to a dear friend who has been driven to America by need, I am not overly sad. As the saying goes, 'Instead of seeing someone's trouble and woe up close, better to hear his bad news from afar.' But when I have to part with a small child whose Jewish luck has pushed him to America, my heart always weeps as though I had lost him forever. What does a little child know? What does a little child see? If I come to see him, he will not recognize me; if he grows up and comes back, I will not recognize him!"

That same smart Jew knew what he was talking about. The still young Yiddish theatre that went to America did not recognize its father just three or four years later, nor would it obey or come when called. In a letter to me during that time in America, Goldfaden wrote, "I do not have any complaints about the American Yiddish theatre not recognizing its father. For a people that is aging and whose children are forced to emigrate any number of times and often on different roads, it is not rare that children do not recognize their parents; or even that the parents cannot travel the road their children have gone. But I do have complaints, though I do not know to whom, that my dear Jewish child is growing up to be a coarse, un-Jewish, insolent boor, and I expect that some day I will be cursed for the very thing that I brought into the world. I do not deny that in the old Exile home my theatre had flaws, but it also had the merit of my own friends having control over it, and it was still allowed to grow. Here in America, however, where friends do not manage it, it has thrown all shame aside, and not only is it not learning anything, it has forgotten whatever good it used to know."

Since the day I received that letter, I did not hear anything more about the Yiddish theatre. Then three or four years ago, I heard that some Jewish merchant or manufacturer, probably with the sponsorship of some prince, had asked to be permitted to present Yiddish theatre performances that summer in Poland. For this, he had brought the Yiddish theatre from America and they were already playing in Warsaw.

Naturally, I was curious to go and have a look. So I went and I looked and looked, but I could in no way recognize it. In this American version, there was no trace of the Jewish charm and childish innocence that had once atoned for its flaws. I could not even recognize the former flaws because they had grown so much larger, coarser, and more arrogant than I could have imagined.

Yet a question bothered me: "Why is it still called 'Yiddish theatre?'" It was farther from Jews and Jewishness than America is from Warsaw. And I was not the only one who asked this question, but the entire public who saw the plays and paid well for them. So when one day the news came out that the theatre was going to leave, no one shed a single tear for the great misfortune that had befallen the people of Israel. "May no greater misfortune befall us!" everyone wished upon hearing that Warsaw would no longer have the pride of seeing and hearing the famous American actors in a Yiddish theatre.

Another few years went by and the remnants of the former Yiddish theatre that had stayed here all along began traveling around the country in various companies like vagabonds, never staying more than a day in the same place. Then the Yiddish newspapers informed us that one Mr. Fishzon, a director or leader of one of the vagabond companies, had fought his way up to the highest places and had pleaded that the curse and the excommunication order be rescinded from the innocent Yiddish theatre.

I did not know whether it was true or a fabrication that the Yiddish theatre in Russia was being praised. That it appeared at all, should be praise enough. Meanwhile, Yiddish theatre was being played in more and more cities. Even in St. Petersburg, the Yiddish theatre played a full season that year. Whether we should be happy with that news or not, we shall only answer when we are able to get acquainted with that theatre up close.

*   *   *   *   *

In Warsaw, there are now two Yiddish theatres in two different ends of the city. I went to one of them recently, and I will share what I saw there with the reader.

I do not mean to criticize it. To criticize the Yiddish theatre in its current standing would be work as welcome as searching for nicks in a saw blade. All that I saw, however, indicates that Yiddish theatre does not lack for actors who act well, but who lack a certain knowledge to understand what they are acting.

The question now seems to be not how one acts in Yiddish theatre, but what one acts. Posing the question this way, we have to confess that the Yiddish theatre acts like a little child, rides across the stage on a little wooden horse, makes a fool of itself, is childish and a little crazy; but there is no Yiddish theatre happening.

I have complaints about our Yiddish actors for riding out on the stage on a wooden horse instead of a live one. I have complaints against those who have so little sense, may they excuse me, as to think that the horse is really a live one. In that error lies the whole problem of Yiddish theatre because, first of all, it is the duty of someone who is interested in the Yiddish theatre and who understands what Yiddish theatre should be to explain to our directors and actors what a wooden horse is and what a live horse is.

If they have the sense to know the difference, they will see how silly it is, how unwise and how laughable it is, when a grown man rides into a scene on a wooden horse and shows it the same respect he would show a live one. The actors should know that it is a play, a drama or a comedy from life, but instead the play is silly, childish and mixed up, and the awkward dramas and comedies in which they are acting are embarrassing to themselves and to the audience.

But in order not to make empty words, I will try to describe the play that was presented that evening when I went to the new Yiddish theatre for the first time. *Ishe Roe* is what the first piece was named.

Knowing what a Jew understands from the words, *"ishe roe,"* I thought that the lead role would probably be a Jewish woman, stricken from God's graces, a kind of shrew with a fiery face, who is alternately cold and warm to her husband. There are such women in every race and tongue, especially among us Jews; children and grandchildren of old study house Jews, whose wives were the "women of valor." But what was presented was something else entirely.

Here it is: The first to appear on the scene is Peretz. With that name it would seem a Jew. But a glance at his clothing makes you think he is a Turk, a Tatar, or what you will, but not a Jew. He carries a drum. If you now think that he is one of the orchestra musicians, you have made another mistake, because then the mighty army comes in, comprised of five and a half soldiers, and he, Peretz with the drum, commands them around like a real field marshal.

Then a bedraggled young woman comes out and we can tell from their lovers' conversation, that he, the drummer, the field marshal, the Turk or Tatar, is actually a Jew, even saying the words, *" Yehudi b'loy,"* "careful of your words, a Gentile might hear you"; a slogan which he uses every minute. The bedraggled girl is a kosher Jewish daughter, born and reared in a synagogue courtyard, and using all the language of such a person. She works as a cook for the important and famous hero Avner, and he, Peretz, is actually Avner's attendant.

Then we find out that he is in love, completely smitten, with the girl, the cook, as she is with him. A pair, I tell you, that matches like a boot matches a psalm. But if they like it, good health to them! Love is blind they say, and since they love each other, they say it right out in front of God and everyone. They embrace, they kiss, they even slap. They sing a song that they will soon marry, that is, they will have children. He, Peretz, will carry them around and sing lullabies, and she, Malkele, will bake rolls for them. Can there be a more lovely or fitting rhyme than Malkele and *bilkele*, little roll?

This is how the first act ends and the curtain comes down a little lazily and embarrassed. The audience applauds enthusiastically. The sleepy curtain must be rolled up again and they sing the song about Malkele baking *bilkele* three more times.

The second act begins in the king's court, where the old Jewish King Hyrkanus, one of the Hasmoneans, sits on his throne. It is some kind of broken bench; it's a pity to have to look at it. He is wearing the king's crown on his head, and if it were not there, I would not know that he is a king, poor thing. It is not clear from his house or from his clothes or from his conduct. The bedraggled girl is going around in his house. How did she get here? Did she change jobs? Just like today's servants, every day it's a new cook, every day a different boss. Anyway, there is no end to the questions. One must be satisfied with what is presented.

But now the drum is heard. Peretz conducts a crowd of soldiers into the king's court—infantry, horse-mounted guards, Cossacks—he marches them out, halts them, tells a few jokes, and goes to welcome the hero Avner who is unequaled in his power and heroic deeds.

The great hero is carried in. Two "High Priests" with breastplates over their hearts and holy emblems on their foreheads, stand like two painted Swiss guards by the door, and you don't know if they are alive or dead. With a High Priest, and especially with two instead of just one, wouldn't it be appropriate for them to do something other than just stand there like two obedient valets at the door?

But once again this is like searching for nicks on a saw blade. Let's watch and get better acquainted with Avner.

Here he is, he falls to his knees before the king, tells him how he made a ruin of the Persian army. These are the prisoners. He tells him everything and lays everything at his king's feet, and he himself, too, as it should be for a true, noble hero.

These are his deeds, but if you look him over, how would you know he is a hero? His face, his movements, his soft-hearted voice, and everything you can see of him is more suitable for a nice scholar, for a person who knows only how to do good works, who has never held a sword in his hand, and never seen a drop of spilt blood.

Why Mr. Kaminski, who plays the role of Avner, is pleased with such a presence, showing such a soft-heartedness, and not allowing any signs of a real war-hero, only Mr. Kaminski knows for sure. The audience does not know, however, and asks: "This you call a war-hero? He speaks with this kind of tone and with these kinds of words?"

And while the onlooker is asking these questions, Avner's wife, Isabella, comes in. Whether Avner already knew that the Phoenician name, "Isabel," is Isabella, I have strong doubts, but let's suppose that Avner—who lived in the time of the Hasmoneans—already had a modern Jewish daughter who was ashamed of her Jewish name and decided to call herself Isabella. And Isabella, according to the playbill, is actually the *ishe roe*. And she, of course, will open her mouth and come out with a thousand complaints and ten thousand curses, as you would expect from such a character.

But nothing like that happens. The woman, Isabella, is presented with polish and civility, a proper Isabella from Madrid or Paris. Not one curse, not one angry word is heard from her. On the contrary, as one looks closely, one can notice that this is no bad character before us, but a deeply suffering and very unhappy woman who is torn ten times a day between faithful love for her husband and a bitter desire to avenge the spilt blood of her innocent only son.

At the time when we see her for the first time here, ostensibly in the king's palace, the shadow of her beloved child, who was her whole comfort and hope—as an only child is for every good mother—hovers before her. But the child was snatched from her breast and killed, and she does not even know where his bones were taken.

And it was not some enemy who robbed her of her child, not a wild beast from the forest who tore it away, but he, Avner, the faithful father of the child, her warmly-loved husband, who has done it. And not for his sins, heaven forbid, and not for the child's sins, heaven forbid, did he kill with his own hands, but because of a foolish dream that he once dreamed, that his own son would someday be a greater hero than he, and would triumph over him. What is still worse is that he, the murderous father, denies his guilt, has the nerve to deny it to his wife, and shows a face as though he mourns for the unfortunate child as she does.

Eighteen years have gone by and she cannot and will not forget her son, and now, in this moment when she knows who the murderer is, and sees the honor that people pay to him, the child's shadow hangs before her eyes. She sees how it beseeches her, she hears how from every wound that the murderer made in him, a voice screams out, "Revenge! Revenge! Revenge for my murder, revenge for my own father. A murderer, my father is a murderer!"

"Can one love such a man?" she asks herself. "Loving such a man, whose own child's spilt blood cries out for revenge? And yet, I do love him, I love him! But no, more than I love him, I love my child! It cries for revenge, and it does not know that with that revenge I would have to suffer, too. Yes, take revenge on myself, because I still love the murderer of my child!"

So she struggles with herself without stopping, until her thoughts turn very dark and she can no longer fight herself. In that difficult moment, an enemy of her husband enters, who presents himself as her loyal friend and tells her that he cannot rest as long as he has not taken revenge for her son's gratuitous death, and describes how he will carry out his plan. With her thoughts already muddy and dark, she says she will help him carry out his plan. She will bear false witness against her husband to the king.

But how much she suffers in the meantime! Eventually she returns to her clear vision and runs to the king, falls at his feet, confesses that she is a corrupt but unhappy woman, asks for any punishments for herself, just to wash her husband clean. But it is already too late. The king's anger has already poured out on her husband. They have blinded him and driven him from the country. When she hears this, she loses her mind and is insane forever.

There are a few more touching scenes as Avner's daughter, disguised as a young beggar, takes the blinded hero by the hand to lead him away as they go off begging. The actors play the scene so well, carry it off so well, but the whole scene is so false, so unnatural for a world-famous war-hero.

Those are the only two scenes that make a definite moralistic impression on the audience. But there is no way that the viewer can comprehend why such an unfortunate mother is called *Ishe Roe*. The viewer hardly knows whose misfortune and loneliness is greater: the man's or the woman's? Only our actors understand it better.

The original piece is called *Belisarius,* before it was Germanized and ruined, but they did not like the name so they called it *Ishe Roe*. *Ishe Roe* is the whole center of gravity of the tragedy. They want to show the world what a woman is and what she can do. They understand this in the entire handling of the tragedy.

I asked one of the actors, "Why do you call it *Ishe Roe?*"

He looked at me like a simpleton. "What's that?" he answered.

"Doesn't the author know what an *ishe roe* is?"

And they do not know that authors, especially "re-write authors," can know even less than they themselves. We should not be ashamed to admit that only coarse, ignorant people, and dishonest ones, too, have written most of the material in the Yiddish theatre. People without talent, without a crumb of information about the Jewish life they are walking around in. They do not write their big shows about present life, because they are afraid that the falsities and lies will be caught at the first step. So they only "work" on historical pieces.

True, you can write a thousand falsehoods into a historical novel or historical drama, but even to write the lies you have to know history and have some sense about the hero and the personalities that you bring out onto the stage. Our authors of the supposedly historic dramas, however, have never looked at history, or if they have, they have looked at it only with the eye for an innocent victim among mortals.

It is no wonder that this author clothed the Byzantine hero Belisarius in a Jewish cloak and named him Avner, and gave the East Roman emperor Justinianus the name Hyrkanus, despite the fact that a period of almost seven hundred years separates the two figures.

What is going on with this Jewish author? It does not seem to bother him much that in the entire play, except for the words, *"Yehudi b'loy,"* there is no sign of Jewishness, and the entire story is so strange and far from Jewish historical life. But does he even know what is meant by the term "historical novel" or "historical drama"?

He took a historical Christian hero, Belisarius, gave him the name Avner, and whipped up a historical tragedy, a real Jewish one, and kept going with it. Even, it seems, given how little love the Jewish people have always had for converting other nations to Judaism, even those who beg for it, "Teach us your Torah, we want to be Jews!" And in Jewish literature, in the new literature especially, we see the opposite— you grab a German or a French work and give Jewish names to the characters—from Fritz to Peretz, from Lucina to Leah or Yakhne-Shoshe, and you have an original Jewish novel, pure and wholly Jewish.

What, for example, would the supposed author of *Ishe Roe* have lost if he had just simply taken von Schenk's tragedy, *Belisarius,* and translated it word for word, leaving the play to remain a play? A bad translation is still not as bad as a bad re-write.

Is a French author ashamed to translate a German, English, or even a Russian drama? No, our Jewish authors cannot bear to be simple translators. Our authors have to convert the Gentiles; they have to "improve" and corrupt until no doctor can help.

A large part of our new literature in Hebrew and in Yiddish is full of such self-injuring cargo, God help it. What have we not "Judasized," not made over, not over-used, and not turned on its head with its feet in the air?

I once encountered a Jewish version of *A Thousand and One Nights*. Instead of a vizier or pasha, a pious Jew—a tax collector or some rich person—played the role. *Robinson Crusoe* is called "Alter Leb" in our Jewish literature, and Alter Leb prays—poor thing—without a prayer shawl, but he blesses the New Moon, lights Chanukah lights, blows the shofar, and curses Haman; all on his deserted little island!

The ignorance of that kind of author is so huge, the shamelessness so broad, that even poor Shakespeare could not make it through. Thank God, we have books with titles like *King Lear* by William Shakespeare, that have been improved, corrected, and reworked by Duber Tursh, and so on. This licentiousness is in our general literature and even more wanton in the literature that is especially created for the Yiddish theatre.

I am not speaking about moral crime, as those authors have little to do with moral obligations, but about the moral shame that they bring to our literature with such work, and to the Jewish reader and the Jewish theatregoer. There should be some authority established over such authors that could show them their place.

Now there is a desire to drive those re-worked dramas and ungainly plays from the Yiddish stage. We should not be content with giving them a look, a spit, and letting them rest. The Jewish actors must advise them of the great falsity and coarse ignorance that has crept into such supposedly "Judasized" theatre work.

Meanwhile, the Jewish actors should learn not how to act, but *what* to act. Time and their own feeling and their own talent will teach them how to act. Some of them already play their roles well. May the roles only become roles!

After this we must demand much more of them, to understand that the roles that they are now playing with such passion and sincerity are really not roles at all. When they realize that, they will no longer allow themselves to ride out onto the stage on a rocking horse. They will know how forlorn and foolish they appear to their audience, how laughable they make themselves in the eyes of the expert.

Once they can do that, they can begin to search for proper, true theatre pieces from today's Jewish reality. And if you search, you find!

ACKNOWLEDGMENTS

Many people must be thanked for their contributions to this volume: Kathleen Southern for discovering that Jacob Dinezon wrote a collection of autobiographical short stories, the staff of the National Yiddish Book Center for finding a copy on their shelves, and Tina Lunson for her masterful English translation from the Yiddish.

Thanks also to Rabbi Raachel Jurovics, Curt Leviant, and Miriam Koral for their assistance with the manuscript, Lynn Padgett for her proofreading and graphic design help, and Sylvia Holtzman, Maxine Carr, Bill Nichols and Thomas Rain Crowe for their friendship and ongoing encouragement.

And finally, my heartfelt appreciation and love to my sister, Robin Evans, and to my sweet companion, Carolyn Toben, for their unending support and loving kindness through the long process of bringing this book to completion.

Scott Hilton Davis
July 2014

GLOSSARY

Algebrenik. The "Algebra-man." The word is pronounced with a hard "g" as in good, and not with the "j" sound used in English.

aliyah. The honor of being called up to read from the Torah or to recite a blessing before the reading of Torah.

Apikoyres. Heretic.

asher yotser. The blessing recited after going to the bathroom.

Ayn Sof. Without end. In Kabbalah, the Infinite Divine.

Baal Shem. A faith healer or miracle worker.

bar mitzvah. The confirmation ceremony for Jewish boys when they turn thirteen.

Bava Metsie. A volume of the Talmud.

bechor. A firstborn male.

bilkele. A small bread roll.

bimah. The speaker's platform in a synagogue.

bobe. Grandmother.

Borekh. Blessed.

borscht. A cabbage or beet soup.

bris. The ceremony of circumcision performed on a Jewish boy when he is eight days old.

chametz. Leavening which is forbidden in foods during Passover.

challah. A braided bread eaten on the Sabbath and holidays.

Chanukah. The Festival of Lights; a holiday celebrating the liberation of the Temple in Jerusalem by Judas Maccabee and his followers in the second century B.C.E.

Chassid. A follower of the Chassidic movement.

Chassidim. The followers of Chassidism, a mystical Jewish religious movement founded in the eighteenth century in Eastern Europe.

cheder. Traditional religious elementary school.

chuppah. The canopy under which the bride and groom stand during the wedding ceremony.

der kahalisher bok. The community goat.

dreidel. A wooden or lead top used to play a gambling game during Chanukah.

Erets Yisroel. Land of Israel.

eruv. A community area with marked boundaries, inside which one may walk and carry things during the hours of the Sabbath. Normal observance of the Sabbath would not permit long walks or carrying things if one were not within the *eruv.*

esrim. The number twenty.

etrog. Citron used as part of the Sukkot holiday.

Esterhazy. French officer, Major Marie Charles Ferdinand Walsin Esterhazy, who falsely accused Captain Alfred Dreyfus of treason and later admitted his own guilt.

eylim. Rams. A single ram is an *ayil.*

gemalim meynikot uvneyhem. Camels suckling their young.

gehenna. Hell.

Germanized Jews. "German" or "Berliner" Jews were those who had broken away from, or appeared to have broken away from, the traditional orthodoxy of Eastern Europe and followed some or all of the precepts of the Reform Movement, which had begun in Berlin.

golem. A clay figure in the form of a man, into which life has been breathed by supernatural means. Also means a dummy or clumsy person.

goy. A Gentile; a non-Jew.

grogger. A noisemaker used during Purim.

Haggadah. A book or booklet containing the home seder service used during Passover.

hamantasch. A three-cornered Purim pastry.

Havdalah. The ceremony used to end the Sabbath or holidays.

Ishe roe. A complaining, shrewish, evil woman.

izim. Goats.

Kabbalah. Jewish mysticism.

Kaddish. The mourner's prayer for the dead.

kapote. The traditional long black coat worn by observant Jewish men.

Khumesh with Rashi. A study book, which contains the five books of the Torah with commentary by "Rashi," the acronym for Rabbi Shlomo Yitskhaki (1040-1105 CE).

kliatshe. Mare or nag.

komedia. A small stage set up for performances.

komediant. An entertainer.

Koyrekh or Korah. The biblical figure who challenged Moses and Aaron's authority and was buried alive by God for his rebellion. Many stories are told of Korah's wealth.

l'chaim. "To life." Often used as a toast.

Lag b'Omer. A joyous minor holiday that celebrates the end of a plague during the Bar Kokhba revolt against the Romans in the second century.

lamed-vovniks. So called after the Hebrew letters "lamed" and "vov," which have the numerical value of thirty-six which is the number of saintly people who hold up the world. These are never obvious people, and usually are the last person anyone would guess, and their identity is almost never known. Only God knows them, and sustains the world because of them.

latkes. Fried pancakes, especially those made with grated potato during Chanukah.

Litvak. A Jew from Lithuania; also refers to a Jew who is intellectual, pedantic, skeptical, and opposed to Chassidism.

ma yofes. Originally Sabbath table songs. During the eighteenth century, the Polish gentry used to coerce Jews into singing these songs as a form of humiliation and by the nineteenth century, some Jewish performers were presenting these songs before Gentile audiences in a kind of Jewish "Uncle Tom" fashion.

matayim. The number two hundred.

matzo. Unleavened bread eaten during Passover.

mazl tov. Congratulations.

Megillah. The scroll containing the Book of Esther, which relates the story of Purim; a long,convoluted story.

mentsh. A moral and ethical person of worth and dignity.

Meshiekh. The Messiah.

mezuzah. A small parchment scroll inscribed with religious texts and attached in a case to the doorpost of a Jewish home.

mikvah. A ritual bath.

minyan. Ten men needed to hold a public Jewish prayer service.

mishegas. Craziness.

mitzvah. A commandment or good deed.

Moykher sforim. A book peddler.

Montefiore. Sir Moses Montefiore (1784-1885). Born in England, he became a wealthy Jewish merchant, stockbroker, and philanthropist.

moyhel. A man who performs circumcisions.

narishkayt. Foolishness.

parsha Vayishlach. One of the weekly readings of the Torah in which Jacob prepares to meet his brother Esau.

peyes. Side curls or earlocks.

Pesach. Passover.

Purim. The Feast of Lots. A joyful holiday celebrating the events in the Book of Esther and the victory of the Jews over Haman and their oppressors.

quicksilver. Mercury.

ransom. A gift or payment of money for assistance; often required by a rebbe for his help in resolving a personal, family, or business matter.

rebbe. Teacher. "Rebbe" may also be the title of a Chassidic rabbi. By contrast, the term "Reb" is simply "Mister," and a term of respect for any adult male.

rebbetzin. The rebbe's wife.

Rosh Chodesh. The New Moon.

Rothschild. A family of European bankers, merchants, financiers, and philanthropists. Baron Edmond de Rothschild (1845-1934) was born in Paris. Instead of entering the family banking empire, he devoted himself to art, culture, and underwriting Jewish settlements in *Erets Yisroel.*

samovar. An urn of metal, usually silver or copper, used to heat water for tea.

Shabbes. The Sabbath.

shatnez. The mixing of wool and linen threads, which is forbidden in Jewish religious law.

Sheol. The lowest level of hell.

sheymos. Pages from holy and secular books that have God's name printed on them. In order not to desecrate God's name, these pages are collected and provided a sacred burial.

shiker. Drunkard.

shiva. The formal mourning period of seven days during which friends visit the home of the deceased to comfort the bereaved.

shloshim. The number thirty.

shmone esrey. The eighteen blessings recited in the daily prayers.

shofar. The ram's horn blown during High Holy Days.

shtibl. A very small Chassidic house of study and prayer, often just a single room in a house or other building.

shtetl. A small Jewish town or village in Eastern Europe.

shul. A synagogue or house of prayer.

Simchas Torah. A celebration that marks the end of the Torah's yearly reading cycle.

skhakh. The foliage that covers the roof of a sukkah.

spies. "Spies carrying a huge cluster of grapes." This refers to an account in the Torah, that while the Jews were returning to their land from Egypt, "spies" or advance men were sent to inspect the land, and they returned with a bunch of grapes so huge that it had to be carried by two men.

sukkah. A temporary hut or booth erected during the holiday of Succoth.

Sukkot. The Feast of Tabernacles or Booths, which takes place in the fall.

tallis. Prayer shawl.

Talmud-Torah. The traditional, tuition-free elementary school maintained by the community for the poorest students.

Targum. The Aramaic translation of the Bible.

Tartar. A native Muslim inhabitant of Tartary or Tartaria; a person of Mongolic or Turkic origin.

tefillin. Phylacteries; the leather boxes containing scriptures which an Orthodox Jewish man from the age of thirteen, binds with leather straps onto his left arm and forehead during the morning prayers.

tikkun olam. The repair or healing of the world.

Tishah b'Av. A fast day on the ninth day of Av to commemorate the destruction of the first and second Temples in Jerusalem.

treyf. Not kosher.

yas. Liquor is called *yas* or *yash*.

yayn soref. Liquor or spirits.

yehudi b'loy. A warning to watch one's words when a Gentile is present.

yeshiva. Jewish institute of higher Talmudic learning.

yetzer hore. The evil inclination.

yetzer tov. The good inclination.

Yiddishkayt. Jewishness; Jewish culture.

Yom Kippur. The Day of Atonement.

yahrzeit. The anniversary of a death.

zmiros. Devotional songs or hymns sung around the Sabbath table.

Zola. Emile Zola defended Alfred Dreyfus, accusing several high-ranking French Army officers of fabricating evidence. Zola was tried for libel and forced to leave France to avoid emprisonment.

Zohar. "The Book of Light"; an important text of Jewish Kabbalah.